ORIGINALS

n.p. figgis

the fourth mode

PENGUIN BOOKS

PENGUIN BOOKS

Published by the Penguin Group
27 Wrights Lane, London W8 5TZ, England
Viking Penguin Inc., 40 West 23rd Street, New York, New York 10010, USA
Penguin Books Australia Ltd, Ringwood, Victoria, Australia
Penguin Books Canada Ltd, 2801 John Street, Markham, Ontario, Canada L3R 1B4
Penguin Books (NZ) Ltd, 182–190 Wairau Road, Auckland 10, New Zealand

Penguin Books Ltd, Registered Offices: Harmondsworth, Middlesex, England

First published 1989
10 9 8 7 6 5 4 3 2 1

Made and printed in Great Britain by
Richard Clay Ltd, Bungay, Suffolk
Typeset in 10/12 pt Lasercomp Bembo

THE FIRST MODE

MOONLIGHT HESITATED, brushing the ceiling, uncertain. Ice scaled and scratched across the windowpane, blinding the glass with Byzantine complexities. Within, the room was small and clenched and bitter; a listening room, its books open, its posters crinkling forward from the walls, pages of lined paper unwritten on and stiff in the nervous light. The small alarm clock wheezed among its tickings, some small metal coil contracting deep in its secret knowledge, although the clock did not really know what time it was. Winding it had not been enough. Five years ago, in Uttoxeter, a nineteen-year-old girl had idled over the machine that had tightened the clock's last screw and caused it to become a measurer of time. She was called Sharon, like many of her generation, and had been ignorant, finalizing many clocks in her three years in the factory. Now they stood beside beds all over the country, telling the time. She was not responsible for the time. It had been given to the clock, by Sharon's machine, to tell the time. It was not entirely in its gift to come to Now, or not to come to Now. There had been so many variables and conditionals, but it was unable to stop itself.

The room was trembling. The whole house, of which it was the nucleus, was trembling. It did not falter or sway, just shivered, vertically, from the foundations; ripples of terror running upwards from the soil through the stones and plaster and into the roof. In all its two hundred years of existence it had not been so afraid, nor had its parent foundation, remembering back further and deeper into the ground. One of the joists gave a sudden, high-pitched little crack. A flake of smoked yellow emulsion sifted down from the ceiling and settled on Stephen Ridley's forehead, waking him.

He believed in the sound and the trembling before he recognized them. He did not react fast, there was no need to. The rumbling was still quite far off and he opened his eyes slowly, acknowledging the icy sweat on his shoulders and the sickness in his stomach before his mind rose up out of belief into inquiry. It could not be happening. That was instantly obvious. The cold air beyond the blankets hurt his lungs and his diaphragm could not cope. There was iron in his neck under the wet skin. The hand that had been curled against his face was shaking already.

It was closer now. Still only the evasive moon made shadows of light. He had moved his bed into this small room (where one Willie Davies had died of diphtheria during Lord Palmerston's government) because the portable gas fire defrosted it more quickly than it did the proper bedroom next door. This room was little more than a cupboard, with the bed directly under the window; cold, but very pure. He did not take women into his bed and the austerity suited him, as long as he could dress and undress over the fire. He pulled himself half out of the jumble of blankets and leaned his elbows on the window-sill, peering through the frost-havoc on the little panes. He could see nothing but the dim silhouette of the ash tree at the bottom of the garden. He picked rapidly at the frost, tiny lines of white sticking under his finger-nails. His breath puffed irregularly in front of him. The glass was too cold to quiver in the old putty, but he did not want to rub it hard in case it fell out in an entire block. He unlatched the window and pushed it slowly open.

The whole garden there; white-pathed; wildly cold. Space

defined by glittering privet and sparkling lawn-spikes. Stars in the throughways between clouds; ash and damson furnished with hoar-frost.

There was little light in the road where it came down over Dybart Hill between the hedges. Only a long ribbon of dimmed lemon-coloured shade washing the trunks of the trees and glancing laterally through gaps and gateways on to still furrows or iron-hard tussocks in the fields. The glow of the citrus beam slithered down to the bridge and crept up again, coming now almost directly towards him, its length still trailing up the far side of the hill. Very long. The rumbling became so deep that the metal grille on the gas fire began to tinkle. A cigarette, extinguished half-smoked, rolled off the rim of the ashtray.

To his right, further along down the road at Crosby Spring Farm, the Medways' dogs began to bark, but the rumbling, and the high-pitched purr which Stephen could not hear over it, drowned out the dogs after a few seconds.

The first pair of motorbikes cruised gently round the bend and moved along the far side of the privet hedge at the bottom of Stephen's garden. They were driving with yellow fog-lights only, dipped down on to the glazed road. As they passed his gate he saw the riders, shapeless in wind and bullet-proofing. The starlight tricked around on their black helmets.

Some childish instinct provoked him to count them . . . two, four, five. And another two, four, five. An unfamiliarly shaped car with its own escort and two pairs of lights and a fifth in the centre of the front bumper, all dipped; frost on its roof like myriad eyes. More flakes of old paint settled on his pillow and the dregs of tea in the bottom of his mug spun eerily round in obedience to established physical laws. The great, truck-like carriers in the middle of the convoy passed neatly under the ash tree now that he had cut off the two lower branches that used to overhang the road.

The Area Planning Officer had been insistent that it had been done before the end of last summer. At the time Stephen had been innocent enough to be aggrieved.

Once he had seen the carriers he did not really look at the following trail of bikes and jeep-like lorries, or at the white saloon car in their midst. He clambered backwards off the bed and ran clumsily to the bathroom where he kneeled on the cold edge of the bath, opened that window too, and watched the subtle yellow line draw itself softly round the dangerous bend past the Medways' farm and tip uphill again towards Croke's Wood, three miles away.

There was a greenish sheen on Croke's Wood, faint, as the moonlight had been, but clouds covered the moon now and the delicate shimmer came from the heart of the press of spruce, green-dim as if a million glow-worms were dying. As it came within the wood's aura, the yellow light-line shortened until it was swallowed up altogether by the green when the end of the convoy turned into the plantation.

After a while the rumbling was suddenly not there. The Medways' Dalmatians fell silent. The washer on the bath tap was old and slow. Half-gelled drips slithered down the side of the pendant icicle they were themselves forming.

'No light to guide . . .' Cliché from times before electricity. Still, no light. There must be only darkness in the few houses along the missiles' route. How did he know that? Why was light suddenly unsafe for him? He had gone to sleep with his socks on and their wool was slippery on the bare boards of the landing. Hands out, feeling, he passed under the little window on the stairs and down into the sitting-room. The air was warmer here and odorous with last night's woodsmoke. In the grate, goblins' eyes and hares' eyes winked redly in the embers.

★

The dog fox stood utterly still beside the brushwood pile just inside the old Forestry Commission fence around Croke's Wood. He held one pad slightly raised, and the thick brown ruff on his neck and his tufted cheeks prickled outwards with tension. He was sharp with hunger. The stink of diesel, normally cold and patchy by this time of night, was warm and thick. It had lain across the road and on all the fields on either side of it, the frost keeping it just above the ground so that it smothered all other scents. The traffic that had caused it had roused the Medways' dogs just as the fox had been arriving at the mesh wire of the hen-runs and he had headed away, down to the Dipyard where Stephen Ridley had crashed and lumbered in his dark upstairs. So the fox had abandoned the rubbish bins there and had come back to his hole under the brushwood before starting out again on another of his familiar circuits. He was suffering a great urge to slip down into the den where his vixen lay already pregnant, to rub and lick and sniff a little, before starting out again. The last few nights she had hunted reluctantly and unsuccessfully, preferring to sit grooming herself in the dark until her pregnancy settled.

The heap of brushwood was shimmering. Not lit from above by the sky's light but shot through at ground level by greenish-white darts which reached out between the spruce trunks, striking silver and pitch and aquamarine in minute cycles of prism along the frost-thralled sticks. The wood was singing too, a thin little song so high that he could hardly hear it. In the heart of the wood, where he could no longer go, the usual noises of men were multiplied and the taut ground vibrated with movements. The wire-link fence that kept him out, kept the men in, and he had paid them little regard before. But tonight their numbers distressed him, and all the shadows were in strange places, cast at alien angles by the low, new light. He failed to slip under the brushwood to the hole of the den, but turned away towards the kale-field, leaving the vixen, if she were still there.

Barbara running. Barbara running and running. Once a little girl with a tangling skirt and strap shoes not made for running away; and later running still, through pelting sweat and ice-cracks on lips, from desperate terrors of boys with beer on their breaths and lewd gestures in their hands, and also from the biology book spoiled before school; and now with a pain in her heart like fire. She could run no further.

Flame ate into her heart and a hundred miles into her gut, particles lacerating her gullet. In the film of Joan of Arc, she was, or in the field below Montsegur where the women had burned and burned and burned. Only Barbara was alone in an empty road and a still sky where stars burned out when time finished with them, if time was at all. The cold laid touch to her thighs and throat and fingers and the silence waited outside the chaos of her lungs. The pain in her heart and the pain in her mind crashed together and rocked her to and fro, lacking the breath to cry, but crying all the same with raucous hiccoughs and retching and spinning, streaming head prolapsed down into her breast where blood-breakers broke and roared through empty cavities. 'Methought what pain it was to drown' in my own blood-barrel of ribs.

When the fire in her heart eased, she sat clumsily in the grass at the edge of the road. Frozen stalks seared the backs of her knees. She put her head in her hands, clutching a fistful of hair, a nailful of skin and sweat and dirt. The empty road and silence waiting to feed on her. She looked along the road one way. The other way. No creature. Not a colour in the star-dusk. Not a sound between her and the great curve of space except that of her own arteries shouting, 'No, No, No, No, No'; the extreme word, the great word, the word everything said at its own personal end. 'No, No, No.'

Then even this stopped. Silence took a threatening step forward and she, Barbara, screamed at it, 'No, no' – slapping, kicking, slut-

screeching it back into the future which had not come yet because
it was still unrealized in the green glow in Croke's Wood
plantation. Joan Ruddock had not known the wood's name, nor
had St John the Divine or Nostradamus or probably even Margaret
Thatcher, much less the hawks on the back-benches whose monies
and jobs and auras had been scraped together and laid, luminous,
over the spruce needles which Barbara, from where she had
collapsed by the road, could see shining in the frosty night.

But Barbara had known Croke's Wood all her life – from the
time when it had been a stand of half-dead elms and bramble cover
in the middle of meagre sheep-fields, and the terrors it housed had
pissed her infancy; witches and flying saucers and cavemen and
Hitler's ghost (with its brains spilled on its lapels). She knew it
right through the Forestry Commission's purchase and subsequent
ploughing, trotting after the uncle they had nick-named 'Ptolemy',
searching for flints, coins, bones or bits of pottery that the great
machines exhumed in files, and which looked exactly the same as
the patterned globs of mud thrown up off Uncle Ptolemy's
brogues. The first generation of Forestry spruce had half-grown
when the dog had climbed on to her bed and set its wet, huge
bottom on the biology book so that all the ink had run and all the
miserable work been destroyed. The spruce grew quite adolescent,
gawkily green in spring, before the chain-saws screamed into them
and for each oozing stump a spindle-shanked infant had been
popped in its place, reared and broken-in in the nursery institutions
for baby trees. Foxes moved in and ousted Hitler, and badgers
bustled the witches out of the shadows. Vipers coiled on the
boulders the JCBs had foisted on the symmetrical brakes.

Barbara Curtis had been in the crowd that had waved home-
made banners when the Ministry of Defence had taken over the
plantation, and when, a few days after the demonstration, they had
gone back to daub slogans on the gateway and had found a new

chain-link fence around it and a prefab sentry-box at the entrance. Croke's Wood might have done a Birnam for all the contact they ever had with it again. 'Martinminster Reserve, North' the MOD called it now, saying that Dutch elm disease had felled 'Croke's Wood' for ever and so it did not exist any more. Some zoologists intimated that insects survived everything – sick, really, to Barbara, if the little scolytid beetle were to be the sole survivor of the consequence of having killed the last elm in Croke's Wood.

The moonlight showed Barbara to the dog fox, who had heard her screaming from right across the kale-field. His elliptical pupils focused on her far-off figure, her hand to her face as if she were eating. Humans were killers, too, and he gave her and her unseen prey a wide berth, leaving two thick holly and hazel hedges between them, as well as the sheep-wire, before he turned into the stiff blue leaves and close cover of the kale, heading up a furrow towards the headland where the rabbits came out.

The moonlight showed the fox to Stephen Ridley, by then in his kitchen. He was staring out of the window, across the kale-field and up towards Croke's Wood, when the small dark shape slipped out of the hedge shadow and showed for an instant on the bare, frosted edge of the field. Stephen was enormously glad to have seen it. The three or four wild screams that had cleft the night must have been a fox or an owl, for he knew of no other wild animal that cried out with such desolation in the moonlight. Often, on wild nights, he had heard men screaming in the rack, or against the electrodes, the gallows, the spear, the caterpillar-track; heard women, too, in labour or burning, and sprites, glaciers twisting in Pleistocene torment, angels leaping from Paradise, and the screaming had ended in a curt bark or an alto hoot and he had sworn at his fantastical terrors. But these screams had had no such familiar end. Only the silence of the cold land and the cold sky and his terror had lasted. The more because he knew he was alone this time.

He felt that it was no longer unsafe to have light and clicked on the table-lamp, but not before he had drawn the curtain over the window. The house cuddled itself into the kitchen, grateful and expressing it in little tickings and creaks. Stephen opened the gas cooker and lit the line of blue flames at the back of the oven, leaving its door open to give warmth. Tinker crept out from under the table and stood against Stephen's legs, shivering. Stupidly he said, 'You're cold, little one,' and rubbed her paws vaguely as if she were a Victorian outcast and not a little white terrier. 'You should have stayed in the sitting-room by the fire.'

He filled the kettle because he did not know what else to do and because it was what people might be expected to do when the end of the world came. He did not think of this Now, this present tense, as being the end of the world, although he knew that it was. He thought about how he was feeling a bit sick and how glad he was that he slept in his socks because all he had to do now was to put on his thermal foot-warmers and pull his gumboots over his pyjama trousers to keep his feet warm. He put a cardboard box of cleaning stuffs in front of the oven and sat the dog on it to raise her to the level of the heat. He fetched her bowl and his mug, put a tea-bag in each and a spoonful of sugar in hers. She liked sweet things. The steam from the kettle and the warmth from the oven crept around the room and the walls drew in a little further, seeking something in his activity. By the time tea was ready, he had put on his gardening cardigan and wrapped his muffler around Tinker and the anorak on the back door had lost its stiff look and relaxed softly on its peg.

At the same time, he was alone in the house. Tinker was the only other creature that he had any contact with (he could not tell one spider from another, or one mouse's footsteps from another's) and she was certainly frightened – may even have understood that the last of days had come; but she would accept that without context, not being human. Being human, he had context and told the other things that lived there that he – being human – could not bear it. He knew his words were meaningless; the flaccid retrospect of the killer. Humans, after all, were killers.

Why did he not go into his still-warm living-room? It was comfortable in there, and the hares' eyes and St Bridget's eyes that glittered in the grate could be turned into live heat by throwing sticks on them and then a log. It was comfortable, lined with books and pictures and minor *objets d'art*, artifacts for the expression of humanness. It would say, 'You made me. Now redeem me,' and he could not, even though he was the only man in all Britain who might have prevented the end of the world. He was crying into his tea-mug by the time he thought of Lucy, in No. 3, The Dipyard, the mirror-image cottage adjoining his, and he hurried to the garden window to see if her lights were on, shining out in artificial yellow on the other side of the low, dividing wall. Ridiculously they were. Equally, it was ridiculous that she should open her door to his flurry of knocks wearing a blue dressing-gown, properly fastened, and fluffy bedroom slippers on her feet.

'Lucy, it's only me, Stephen. I – I have some tea made. I thought' – he floundered – 'I thought, under the circumstances . . . Would you like to come over and have some?'

She said, 'Thank you, Mr Ridley, no,' pushing quickly at the door. Her grey hair was rough and six decades had settled on to her features. He wondered if she slept in her NHS glasses and NHS teeth as he slept in his socks. Ready.

'Lucy, please come –'

'Is there something wrong, Mr Ridley? Are you ill?'

'Wrong?' He stood on her step in his gumboots and cardigan and navy flannelette pyjamas, in the very severe frost in the cottage garden, at 4.27 a.m. inviting the retired chemist's assistant to tea in her fluffy bedroom slippers. He thought, There must have been emergencies, endings, surely, in Glasgow in the Forties when she was growing up. Could she have forgotten them? Or was this the way her mother, aunts and the air-raid wardens had taught her to meet them: 'Is there anything wrong' – with the Luftwaffe hurling Dolly's and Grandpa's limbs into the street, or hammering a roof-tile into baby Duncan's new Moses-basket and into baby Duncan? No, nothing wrong. Just what was expected. What was due. Was that how Lucy met this present Now?

Lucy's framed, blue eyes stared coldly at Stephen. 'Taken a bit too much drink have we?' in an Alka-Seltzer-sales-as-soon-as-the-doors-open-on-Saturday voice.

Very carefully, he said, 'Did the convoy wake you?' He could see past her into her sitting-room, photo-studded, pink-lit and embossed with veneers and velveteen and dark reproductions of cart-horses looking inscrutable in fords.

'It did. And I am returning to my bed with cocoa. I advise you to do the same, Mr Ridley.'

'It wasn't manoeuvres, Lucy,' he said gently. 'It was deployment.'

'And this is very unseemly. I'll thank you to stand back so I can close my door.'

'Lucy, it's the end of –' The silence that surrounded Lucy was different in quality to the silence out in the garden. It was tangible, like cotton, and impenetrable. Bandages, Stephen saw, wound around and around her; mummy-eyes, behind glass, beamed no heart, no viscera, no brain; a cadaver, prepared to wait until the end, upright in a dim room. 'Lucy, there's going to be a war. It's going to happen. There's war –'

'Is there, now? Well, I'll read all about it in the morning, thank you.' And she closed the door with a snap. He heard her slide the chain into place and after a minute the pink light went out behind the curtains and another pink light went on behind another curtain upstairs.

There was nothing he could do but go back to his own kitchen, so he went back and put his hands right into the oven to warm them.

Polly Anderson pulled the duvet so far up around her neck and ears that her toes were bared at the other end of the bed, and her coils of luscious black hair almost hidden. It was a double duvet, and Danny Gregson had involved himself in more than his fair share of it. They had been to the sort of party which Danny called 'brilliant', where there had been a great deal of drink which everyone had said coyly that they might as well sink since it looked as if the balloon might well go up. There had been a few self-conscious cracks about the PM switching on the Deep Fryer, or the Microwave, and no one had specifically mentioned the collapse of Austria or the fact that normally they would be wishing each other a happy new year. Everyone had dressed brilliantly and been brilliant, and Polly was bloody exhausted. Fortunately Danny had been too tight to do anything about sex beyond giggling lasciviously when he flopped on to the bed. He had begun to put on weight lately, as she had, and she could no longer manage him unless he was voluntarily careful of her comfort, and comfort was becoming important to her.

Because Danny had exhibited strong feelings about using up the whisky, Polly had driven them home. Having once suffered the humiliation of puffing into a little plastic bag in a dark lay-by while joy-riders and holier-than-thou bridge fiends had swished merrily past, she had lately learned to stagger her drinking-times so that they did not necessarily include end-of-party hours. Merely a lot of hours. Danny still preferred the traditional timetable.

The drive had jolted her more awake than she wanted to be. She would have liked to have been asleep, not aware of anything, particularly the things people were not talking about in voices that had a brittle snap in them, like the cracking of dead twigs on the frozen ground. Any word, phrase, which called up the time, the Now, that they had arrived at, had taken on that dry rustling which might have been Death walking slowly through a dead wood. Or through the frost-stiffened litter of the streets in Martinminster. The police station had been blazing with lights when she drove past it; a score of motorbikes, some white and some black, a couple of Land Rovers and an oddly shaped white saloon car filled the forecourt. Polly guessed that there must have been a derailment or a coach crash in the neighbourhood, for the infirmary was brightly lit and even the hill where the fire station stood glowed yellow into the bitter night sky. She had switched on the local all-night radio station, but there had been no news, only nostalgic songs and people talking about people and remembering lost people. She had shut it off in a fury of irritation that they did not understand that all people were lost, in some way. Not physically, like run-away children or vagrant grandfathers, but like she was and Danny was.

She tucked her arms around herself under the soft duvet, and her hands moved, uninformed, as if they were seeking caresses which her own body did not answer. She smiled at them lovingly as they sought out Frankie in her. Frankie was so far off now, just on the other side of falling asleep, too far for emerging in dreams, too close for remembering. Remembering was something that owned a past, but Frankie was not in the past; there was always more of Frankie in her than ever out there in the processes of time. She had never really left Frankie, only in a superficial, physical way, once. She never would be able to leave him, for he slept there with her on the frontier of sleep, night after night after night, no matter

what other man she lay with her back to. It was one of her
conditions of sharing her bed, that she should sleep with her back
turned, no matter what had passed. Even on the rare occasions
when, alone on a summer evening after work, she might fall into a
doze, there was Frankie. After so much time; so many men! So
why should she be expected to grieve for him? Frankie was still
there. It was the others she turned her back on.

Oh Polly Anderson, he was saying now, did you really fuck it
up? Oh Polly Anderson, it's so forever in your arms/my arms, in
the down of the eider-duvet, the only home we ever made
together, built of warm air and sin and the plumage of dreams.
Sweet Polly Anderson, how beautifully clever you have been . . .
and his marvellously dark eyes swam like lake waters on which her
sleep floated in a silver barque of passage.

　　　　Stephen, Barbara running, the dog fox in the kale, sweet
Polly Anderson and Frankie and Danny, Lucy in No. 3, The
Dipyard, Tinker the dog – these were all the names of Croke's Wood
tonight. Names holding their arms up in the night which the angels
had left empty because Christmas was over and all the expectancies
and alleluias had dropped out of the dark, leaving it so cold, so bare.

Croke's Wood itself was dead. The earth-movers and JCBs had
torn it, screaming, from the hillside and burned it, crushed it,
scattered its blackened fragments in disparate furrows and council
playing-fields. One stone, which had been caught in the roots of a
skeletal elm, had even ended up, fragmented, in the concrete
bulwarks of the council bunker under the Martinminster Job
Centre in Gate Street. Had it a voice, it would have cried, or
maybe laughed, or maybe said, 'So?' But it had no voice. It was
only a splinter of shale, and could name no names. Not even the
names that held up their arms like the dead boughs of stricken trees
into the very cold night. Dead woods tell no tales.

The dog fox saw Barbara before she saw him. In the end he had taken, not a rabbit, but a hen pheasant that had gone to roost late, far out on a snow-burdened hazel branch. The intense frost had stiffened both the young wood and the sleeping bird, and the fox had taken her with a single, extreme leap, knocking the pheasant from her exposed perch and rounding in a whirling gyre of teeth and black claws, thrashing brush and agate eyes, and now, carrying her in his long silky mouth to his vixen, he would not drop her for Barbara. He could not in any way love the vixen, but he held her inside him, wore her on the inside of his skin, as it were, rather as Polly Anderson wore Frankie inside her skin, except that it was the reality of the vixen that consumed the fox, whereas it was the knowing of Frankie that moved Polly. The fox had mated before. He knew what winter was, what spring would demand; the pressure of incessant hunting, the bitterness of cold; the extremity of being himself hunted. The needs of the vixen, and later those of her cubs, would drive him from within against the hectic hail and the cold that drove against him from outside; they would lock him into a perpetual hunt, a perpetual trail back to the den, dragging prey; his thick fur would wear, his supple skin stiffen as the powers outside and the powers of his habit tore at his pelt. The fraying, the scarring, were within the compass of his memory. There were no 'ifs' in the fox's world, no conditionals; only imperatives and death. And on the perimeter of life, the presence of that other great killer, man.

So he stood just below the lip of the ditch, the hen pheasant heavy in his jaws, watching Barbara as she struggled to her feet, up through the thick smell of diesel that was slowly chilling and dying in the cold. Her enormous height lurched grotesquely upwards, taller than a fence-post, taller than most cattle, thin and unbalanced and disorderly, with chaotic, tangled mane and swathed in clinging drapes and hugely muffled feet. The sour stink of her, hot and

tanged with vegetable matter and salt and acrid sweat, drifted over
the ditch as she loomed horribly in the high, frosty air where only
owls and stars belonged. She clenched her fists and shook them
towards Croke's Wood, towards his den, his vixen, his imperatives;
gestures of anger and unconsummated threat. Yet there was no
other creature around to threaten, and she had not seen him, a few
yards across the road from her. Who, then, was her enemy? As still
as the stones in the ditch, he watched her stare around, up the road,
down the road; finally, at him.

At first she did not see him. A shape among dark shapes in the
ditch, he was grass, twigs, lumpy tussocks of last year's growth. It
was the pheasant's bright blood-drop, catching a gleam of nervous
moonlight, that revealed him. She gazed at him and he watched
her still, sly. Lit tears ran down her cheeks like silver springs in
summer rain. The fox did not know tears; to him it was that her
round eyes were wounded by something he did not understand,
which had turned her blood to water. In such a case, she was
disabled; possibly blind. He turned into the ditch bottom and was
gone.

Barbara's heart clenched. She took a step forward into the road,
her hands went stiffly out in front of her. 'Come back,' she was
whispering. 'Come back.' But the dog fox was gone.

She knew, with extreme pain, that she might never see another
fox. She guessed that he was bringing home his kill, that he had a
mate, that there should be cubs in the course of events. But events
had come to an end. For a few more nights there would be
hunting, killing, feeding, but there would never be another
February for the cubs to be born into.

She had attempted, often, to imagine her own dying; her own
agonies, her own terror, set in film terms, in scenes lifted from
films, hearsay out of Hiroshima, leaflets and holocaust novels. She
had called it spiritual preparation. There had been nothing to

prepare her for the last fox in the world, crossing the road from Martinminster to Croke's Wood. A coldness was born in the darkest part of her mind from which she knew she would never become warm again.

When she began to walk along the road towards Martinminster, her knees were unsteady, there was no rhythm in her gait and the movement of her head was jerky. Although the iced road was as smooth as glass, she stumbled as if over stones. The frost glazed the saliva and tears on her face and from time to time the muscles of her stomach rippled in small spasms. The fox, a man, or any other carnivore, would have recognized the symptoms. Death would not be long.

Death would follow. So the fox, glancing at her over his shoulder, allowed her to see him – if she was seeing – as he went diagonally away from her along the headland of the west ten-acre on his way to Croke's Wood.

The Dipyard had once had three cottages, tied for the use of the sheep men who used to work the hill flocks. The westernmost had fallen vacant. Damp, crows, mould and toadstools had taken possession and eventually it had been taken down by the generation that had never 'had it so good'. Its relic heaps of brick and hardcore nourished nettles and brambles, field-mice and coal-tits. The combine harvester, muckspreader and silage tower eventually released the labourer who lived in No. 2, and he left the land to drive buses in Martinminster. The cottage was put up for sale and Stephen Ridley had found it just within his means, moving in with nothing left in the bank for any modernization. Instead he had struggled for eleven years with the wayward plumbing and insecure lime plaster; he had dug patiently and hoed in the vegetable patch and grown an eccentric collection of plants in coveys in the front garden, finding it all beautiful.

The cottages faced south, their brick faces sun-browned and melliferous with honeysuckle and climbing roses. Nos. 2 and 3 were conjoined reverse replicas of each other, having in common a chimney stack and the main bedroom and sitting-room walls, a circumstance which had caused Stephen some anxiety. When Lucy McDowell had moved into No. 3, the nails she hammered so sharply into her side of the wall had knocked down one Persian plate, a framed daguerreotype of the Brighton Belle at Victoria and an extremely heavy seventeenth-century sword which had dented its hilt in the fall. As a result, most of Stephen's possessions were now huddled furtively at the kitchen end of the cottage, and the wall backing Lucy's assaults was lined with heavy Victorian bookcases, standing an inch and a half clear of the plaster. Half-way up the stairs a nail of inordinate dimensions had come right through and Stephen had stuck a champagne cork on to its vicious point, thus creating a peg on which he hung a yak's tail fly-whisk which his brother had brought him from Gilgat. He never discussed the matter with Lucy.

Before Lucy, No. 3 had been inhabited by a young couple with a dismaying number of children. The parents were called Joe and Mary, a coincidence which delighted Stephen but seemed to pass unnoticed by everyone else except his friend Christopher, who was a priest and inclined to be churlish about Stephen's amusement. Stephen thought it was a shame that the children, who should have been called John and Martha and Thomas and Barney, were instead Tracies and Chucks and Buddies and Michelles. None the less, he loved them when he was not hating them, but he never learned which was which. They kept cats, budgies and a tortoise in the front room, goldfish in an old bath in the garden, herds of white rabbits and orange guinea-pigs in crates and wired up cupboards and a few paranoid hens who used Stephen's garden as an extension of their own habitat when resources were low, which was often.

All the children called him 'Hey, mister,' and offered him greying Polos, pieces of birthday cake, coloured pebbles from the river, dead rubber balls for his dog and once, a rare Iron-Age coin which they found while digging a stuck Chuck or Buddie out of a badger hole on one of the banks that ran around the crown of Dybart Hill.

'It's old, see,' they had explained, 'like all them funny things you have. Shops won't take it.'

Agreeing portentously that the coin was indeed out of current circulation, Stephen had carried it inside with trembling hands. Though awed by the historical significance of an iron-age man whose image had been imprinted on a gold coin, Stephen had yielded without a fight to the temptation of not telling the county museum anything about it. He had cleaned it as well as he could, mounted it in an old velvet-lined medal case and stood it on his windowsill. From there the proud profile of Antethos of the Dobunni stared eastwards to where the sun rose mercilessly over the ruins of his influence.

Stephen had missed the family when they left. Lucy's neat flower-beds, grim with Hanseatic tulips and bellicose with trooped dahlias, were colourless after the broken tennis-rackets, flying wash-lines, Arabian palaces of defunct car-bodies and Amazons of split hose-pipe. He missed the jumbled bodies in their assorted garments: wellies and an apron; bobble hat, gloves, plastic sandals and a bare bottom. He never gave his spare damsons to Lucy as he had to Mary; never had to field her cat as he had the rabbits when they made a dash across the wall to his Cos lettuces; never learned what the DJs were saying or the DHSS perpetrating. Lucy listened to Radio 4 and had a professional pension. Joe used to be able to make Stephen's car go in winter, and Mary, although she was fifteen years younger than he, had taught him how to fight the Council for an Improvement Grant and thereby win himself an indoor lavatory. But even Mary, he thought, would not have been able to keep the boughs on the ash tree which might have impeded the great carriers in the night. So Joe and Mary and the Marlenes and Chucks and Stewarts and Tracies had been rehoused on a council estate where there was a playground with a broken swing and dog-shit in the sand-pit; Lucy had moved into No. 3, restored its exhausted functions and marshalled the ruined garden into disciplined profusion.

Lucy must once have been married, for she was styled 'Mrs' McDowell, but Stephen had never discovered what had happened to Mr McDowell. Presumably he had met an unnatural end, for Lucy never referred to him and there was no photograph or memento that could conceivably represent a husband among the tempest of ornaments and portraits on the pink sitting-room walls. Stephen had not, of course, ever seen the rest of No. 3. But who did Lucy love? Everything was about to end – how could he know what that meant to Lucy if he did not know whom she loved? He believed that she must love something, if not somebody; it was endemic to humanity.

His hands held his head; palms pressed to the skull as if the skull was precious. His mind told him that it was no longer precious – that he could go and ride a Vespa with no helmet on, as if he were in one of the beautiful Italian films, all black and white, of his youth. He could run amok, his head told him, for his brain-pan was worthless.

He would stand up and pace, but it was too cold. Minus 12 or 13, bitterest before dawn. A time for love.

The notion of love came winging out of nowhere, madly. 'If you only have love, Then Jerusalem stands,' and Croke's Wood, with its weird, fluorescent glow that seeped out around the roots of the spruce, was forced away by the printed daisies on his kitchen curtains, refuted, vaporized by the strength of human skin. Stephen was in love with no one. There was no human skin between him and his death. He pressed his skull tighter in his hands. Disorientated, shocked, incomplete, facing Croke's Wood on the other side of the printed cotton curtain.

It would be easy to drop down into the flesh, into that procreative dumb urging which was dark and hot and seething with animality. The other plane, where Croke's Wood glowed, was too elevated. He suffered sharp divisions of seconds in which the ending of the world was almost comprehensible, but they were intolerable and his body closed over them and swallowed them up, lest they destroyed him before it was time. It was almost funny – so much talk about tension and irresponsibility, anarchy and terror and flight and hysteria – and no one had warned him that when the time came, what he would need was to mate. Yet it was obvious really. Just as there had been so many little brain cells that had understood overcrowding and pressure and had promoted so many bachelors like himself and so many women who felt no need to breed, now there must be a frenzy in the little cells which did not understand nuclear physics, but which did recognize threat, and were answering. Generate. Go on. Perhaps in the morning, when Martinminster woke up and understood what had happened in the night, it would turn into Arcadia with shepherds and nymphs dallying beside every kitchen stove, swains and paramours entangled in each other's thighs on the rear seat of every Datsun and Ford Escort, satyrs awash with pleasure on every bed in the neon-lit furniture store.

He was crying. The little old dog was asleep on the cardboard box in front of the oven. It was nearly morning. Three hours to daylight.

Knock knock knock knock. Wake Duncan, Bush, Gorbachev, with thy knocking. I wish to God thou could'st.

'Wait, I'm coming.' Running at eyes and nose, running through the dim sitting-room, dead hares' eyes and goblins' eyes cold now, to the door where there was knocking, knocking like his heart in his throat and ankles in case a luminary with pinions were standing in his garden, knowing his name.

But it was a girl. She was shaking. She wore a great many woollen clothes surmounted by a striped grey and brown woollen hat pulled tight over her hair. Beneath it her pointed face was terrible. She opened and shut her mouth but said nothing, as he did in dreams. She was him, dreaming, and he must shut her out before – but she put out her hand against the door with horrible strength.

'Let me in.'

Her voice gurgled, like a foreigner's. Perhaps there was blood in her throat. Her wild hair was framed by the filigree of the ash tree at the bottom of the garden. A black and white photograph of a splintered halo. She said she was the angel Gabriel, but Christmas was over and he knew she was lying.

'Let me in,' she said again. 'Please.' Then, 'For Christ's sake, let me in –' and he saw that she was going to fall inwards, right into his sitting-room. He reached out and pulled at her coats, kicking the door shut behind them and drawing her into the kitchen.

'I'm sorry,' she was saying, over and over again, 'so terribly sorry . . .'

Tinker woke up and barked dutifully. Stephen filled the kettle again and when he set it on the flame it spat like viperous daemons as if a witch were near by. For a moment he watched it, then he turned to the girl sitting in his chair.

'Well?'

It came out austerely. Interrogation rather than interrogative. It frightened her and her fingers scrabbled on the wooden arms. He was acutely sorry. She was so important, being human, being in his kitchen. It was imperative not to hurt her. Her eyes were morning-glory blue; not just the irises, but even the skin around them, as if something which she had seen had overflowed sight and stained the flesh around the faculty. He knew what she had seen, why it had stained her eyelids as approaching death stains the hands of the old.

He said, 'Are you lost?'

Surprisingly she said, 'No, I'm not lost. Not in one sense.' Her speech was clearer now, still husky but no longer sounding foreign.

'And in the other?'

Again she surprised him. 'Oh, damned, yes, but not lost.' There was a high note in her voice.

Slowly he said, 'Isn't there a difference between being damned and being condemned?'

She looked at him, a large bright look, as if he had said something wonderful. 'Is there?'

If there had been such a thing as hope, he would have attributed it to her.

'Maybe only in English,' he said sullenly. Her little laugh was gorse stems clattering in an east wind.

There seemed to be no boundaries between them, although strangers. When he put a mug of tea into her hand, he touched her. He stood close to her in his pyjamas, cardigan and wellingtons, close enough to smell the frost in her hair and to see how her hands had been grazed in a fall. After a silence, he said, 'I'm Stephen.'

'And I'm Barbara.' She said the name firmly, as if laying claim to something.

It had to be spoken about; why she was there; why he was in his kitchen, awake and half-dressed. Why they were together. In the end it was Barbara who said, 'I couldn't find anybody. There is no one who seems to know . . .' Her voice ran out on her and she went on with difficulty. 'You know, don't you?'

'The convoy woke me,' he said. 'The house shaking, you know?'

She nodded, her hands clenched around the now irrelevant Save

Wildlife mug which he had given her. 'It shook the fields on either side of the road. I was running after it – behind hedges, under the bridge – you could hear the icicles hitting the water. There are no other houses on this road – nobody to be woken.'

'That's why they came this way.'

'Oh yes, of course.' She wanted to ask the final question, the one she knew she had the answer to but did not have the courage to bear the knowledge of on her own. And she would be alone with it as long as it was unexpressed in words. She was unable to make the words, because they were too terrible, and because she was not even sure if there were words for her knowledge. The strange, slight man with the greying hair who was staring at her, pulling another chair out from the table with his boney, ink-stained hands and setting it opposite her across the open oven, he would make the words. The responsibility for her knowing what she knew, could be his. She had been unable to find anyone else. She looked back at Stephen as if she had set him there on purpose to do something for her. If she had not set him there, by wilfully coming in, then who else? Let him speak. Her face was blank as she waited.

Stephen stared at her, willing her to talk about what she had seen, but she sat impassively, her scraped hands cuddling the mug as if it were a live pet. She would only have run after the convoy if she knew what it was. She presumed that he knew, too. And although she was now still, at rest in his house, she was still running away from what she had seen. Perhaps she wanted him to deny it? To say that it was a defensive manoeuvre that had brought the great missiles to cower in Croke's Wood. To believe that, to pander to that hope, seemed to Stephen a dishonesty of such magnitude that it was beyond his capacity to even understand it. Without the knowledge, where was the freedom? He thought, perhaps ridiculously, I want to understand the end of the world; want everyone around me to understand; want quintessential humanity as in a great girdle, hand in hand, to embrace the earth as they kill it together. None more guilty, none less, than the neighbour whose fingers entwine with his.

If he was, therefore, to hold Barbara's hand, it could only be on those terms. Otherwise, she must go. Christopher would understand that, he thought, being the priest of a religion nucleated in death. And Ian, being a doctor. Familiars of freedom, both of them. Ian might be anywhere on a night like this; the aged died and infants were born in the land's transitions. Ian would be with them, maybe even holding their hands. He could have met the convoy in the narrow roads that were presumed to be empty; could have seen the low-pitched seepage of light over the hill-curves and questioned its reality. Would he know if they were real or unreal? Would Christopher? A spasm of loneliness shook him, who had never been lonely before. Its strangeness clutched at his ribs, stiffening his shoulders into ropes, eeking out in drops of sweat on his temples and upper lip. But still the girl said nothing, just stared at the legend on the mug, her face hollow with an impossible hunger.

'He was the last fox in the world . . .'

Oh, the fox. Yes, he had seen it too. Skulking up on the side of the hedge, knowing everything that had ever been important. But dumb. Stephen leaned forward, muttering. 'Why, why was he the last fox? There are millions of foxes. They're on the increase – why's he the "last"?'

'I thought you knew.'

Now he had damaged her. She pressed back in the chair as if he had offered her violence. Suddenly he felt violent. He would impale her on her freedom.

'Why – why, Barbara? Damn you.'

But she cried instead of answering him. The useless, heavy sobs of the betrayed. It went on for a long time, noisily. Fear came up in his veins from some cold thing in or under the house.

Something that lay beneath the damp flagstones, very deep down.
It crept into Stephen's body from beneath, inching upwards
through the blue veins until it came to his heart where it pained
like frostbite. He could not put his hand out and touch her again,
could not be with her again until she freed herself. Could not stop
being alone . . . That was what death was, of course, going into it
absolutely alone. That was why it was frightening. That was why
Christopher had to be there, or Ian, because for so very far along
the way you can pretend, and they in mercy pretend, that they
have some special understanding. Priest and doctor can go just that
bit further with you than anyone else.

And this was only the beginning. You were supposed to have
five days of conventional war before the day you died. On which
day did they move the missiles out from the bases?

'What do I know, Barbara?'

Old men try to catch elves. Disenchanted by the unending
mysteries of the earth, they look for elves and gods against whom
there used to be magicks and spells. Seeking Barbara was seeking
elfdom. She even looked elfin. Pale and pointed and weirdly
clothed; not put together like the women of Martinminster, but
translated out of frost and night and terror. She smelled of the soil
and there was dead grass on her clothes. She smelled appallingly of
outdoors, cold and unhouselled. It came to him that perhaps she
herself were unreal – not Barbara, but an idea expressing itself in its
extremity. Whether related to himself, or emerging from some arcane
necessity of the Land's for which there was no longer a vocabulary
– did it matter greatly? If he were to touch her, she would be cold.
The unwordly are always cold.

Stephen moved abruptly. He rose and went over to the window
where the radio was perched on the sill. He moved as if Barbara
were indeed not there. He might have swung around so that, had
she been unreal, his carnal limbs would have passed right through

her unreality; or if she were corporeal, he would have stumbled. But he just missed doing so. His animal senses knew that he did not have the courage to make that test. But because he moved so independently of her existence, he seemed to Barbara to be denying her; to be thrusting her aside as if she were incompletely realized. At any moment, she thought, he would open the door and usher her out into the end of the night. Always darkest before dawn. The moon would have set by now and the warm lamplight of the kitchen would have obliterated the stars. This was the only person alive, then, and he shared the knowledge with her; she could tell that by the cords of raw nerve rippling under his skin, but for some reason the fact that she, too, knew, repelled him. She saw herself as an omen to him – a precursor of events which were too a-human to be acknowledged. For an instant she could see that he might kill her as if she were a messenger of pestilence or famine in other times. To shield the community from her knowledge . . .

He was fiddling with the radio in the window. There would be a voice in the radio, and behind the voice, a mind which might or might not know what she and Stephen knew. If the voice were to escape and make words and sentences out of the knowledge, then it would not be she who would be responsible for realizing the unreal . . . but a disembodied Ariel who could not be brought to account.

She was becoming frenzied. They had always said, in the Peace Movement, that illogicality would be the first behaviour breakdown to show – but so soon? Her hair was hanging over her broken face like Hibernian ivy; her clothes were trailing and dishevelled. She brushed hesitantly at her face – disguising the gesture as one of impatience. The radio was pipping.

'They won't make it public, yet,' she said harshly, hurrying, running to catch up on herself, to overtake the moments of panic. Running again, always running, Barbara.

'Make what public?' His eyes blazed. They were grey and set far back as if the spirit inside him had to beam through long tunnels before it could be seen. He took a step towards her but the radio came alive –

'That the missiles are loaded. That it's for real,' she cried out – a howl of victory.

'You said it – you said it –'

They were both shouting now, both on their feet. Both in their own ways, and for once, victorious.

'– *the shipping forecast issued by the Meteorological Office* . . .' Ariel said. By the time he had reached West Finisterre, they were gripping each other like lovers or enemies in a lock. From the box-top the little dog watched them and saw doom and her damnation in their embrace. She whined softly and her tail was tucked guiltily under her hindquarters. Stephen was the only man who would save her, and he had turned away to his own kind. Tinker turned her face to the wall.

At the end of the shipping forecast there was no change in the tone of Ariel's voice as he said: '*Here is a special announcement. The Government requests that all shipping not on Government occasions return to their port of registration immediately. I repeat, all shipping to return to their port of registration immediately. Incoming vessels due to dock in the next twenty-four hours may proceed to their destination. Further detailed announcements will be made on this channel, on Short Wave and VHF FM frequencies, at the normal times for shipping information.*'

It was two minutes to six. Snow was coming from the north-east. There were travel problems. Due to internal difficulties and unforeseen weather conditions, there would be no flights to Iceland, the Irish Republic or the Isle of Man.

Stephen's hand moved up into Barbara's hair.

In his den under the brushwood, the dog fox turned his face sleepily to his vixen and she began rhythmically licking his fur.

It was eleven minutes past six. Most of Martinminster and the country around was still sleeping, and it was darker here, two hundred miles west of London, more relentlessly night-time than the place which Ariel spoke from. Only the dairy farmers and the post and milk men and women were already at work, and some of the old folk in homes like Woodview, just outside the town, stared eastwards, hoping for day.

'. . . *an unverified report from Vienna states that the Austrian Minister for Defence committed suicide in the early hours of this morning. Soviet military officials, currently in control in Vienna, have not been available for comment.*'

The house knew about suicide. It had embraced it once. It knew the moods that shifted into the act; the sudden comprehension that the act was not impossible but potentially consequent; finally, inevitable. The Austrian Minister for Defence had shot himself on the hahn-danced snows of the forest floor above a little village called Rauris where he had been held in house arrest. His guards had watched him do it. They were from around Krasnoyarsk and had stood very still in the snow. None of this came over Stephen's radio but the house felt it as if it had. It felt it in the old mortar and gravel in the interstices between its stones, where it was cold and eternally dark; felt it as an ague of doom deep in its structure which weakened it and made it less able to warm its tenants. Little beads of cold humidity broke out on the plaster by the stairs and in the larder cupboard. Outside, the temperature fell to −14, and beside the path that ran round the house, a split opened between the house wall and the paving. It was only a hair crack, minutely thin, but intolerably deep.

It was an insidious dawn, crawling among the fence-posts and drain-pipes in the yard, reluctant to develop into day, deserted by the secrecies of night. It brought no sunrise and no warmth, revealing, as it did, the piles of frozen snow shovelled into corners, the overhanging bulks of ice clogging the gutters, the stains of yesterday's movements sealed in this morning's frost. In the big iron barn the horses' breath was thick and pungent, but even so it was not warm enough to melt the layer of ice on the water-trough in the corner. Polly Anderson stood on one leg and pushed her wellington boot through it, dreading the moment when she would have to pick up the sheets of ice in her fingers and throw them out into the yard. She had been doing it every morning for a week now, as soon as Danny had been pushed off in the almost-dark to open his shop. She knew better than to keep her gloves on and suffer the freezing wool numbing her fingers when she broke open the hay bales afterwards. Behind her, Hopkins, her own personal horse, shoved roughly at her shoulder, waiting to drink. She plunged her hands into the water and dragged out the ice. He put his nose down and blew into the trough. It was just one of the things she did for him, for all of them.

There were eleven horses in the barn, all shapes and sizes and colours and ages. Her riding-stable catered for all comers – that was her only legitimate reason for pride in it; that and the pleasure on her clients' faces, whether they were five years old or fifty. Polly was a bad teacher. She cared too much about delight. Recently she had been granted a new pleasure – Danny had taken to coming out in the evenings and hanging over the fence with the littlest ones, putting his carefully kept hands into their shaggy manes, patting their dusty, plump backs, a little shy with them like a child with an unknown doll.

She did not love them all, but she cared about them, was responsible and concerned for them. She often thought that; saw herself as an essential commodity in their lives, without which Hopkins would one day be fed to the hounds; and Derry and Tammy, now old, would be long gone to the knackers' reeking shed, sprawled across the far side of Dybart Hill, and several of the others would have suffered the indignities and neglects of any superseded luxury. She found it a fair exchange that she should be a commodity for them, since they worked for her. They were bound together, making their living together, failing and surviving together – she and they. That she was one sort of animal, with different attributes to theirs, equalized their interdependence. That was all there was to it; that profound, spine-to-spine belonging, each to each. Except for Hopkins. There was love there; possibly even mutual love. She put her arm on his back while he drank. What he gave her was greater than any physical service she might perform for him. It was constancy. She did not weep for constancy, or ever demand it of her lovers or friends – certainly never expected it. It was one of the charities that life had not offered Polly Anderson. But Hopkins, dumb thing that he was, with his over-big bones, his ewe-neck and his scraggy mane, Hopkins was constant. One hand on his plain brown back, she put the other under his long neck and felt the water flowing down it. Where there was water, there was life.

Only now? Now they said there was going to be war – the war that they also said could not be. Nobody believed it – she knew that. Not even Stephen, however passionately he might proselytize CND. She had wandered into his bookshop once, not long ago, looking for a leaflet on how to protect farm animals from fall-out. He had laughed at her. She had never been able to rid her mind of the picture of Stephen offering her a mug of coffee in the back of his shop, laughing at her innocence.

'Angel Polly,' he had said. 'They withdrew that ridiculous thing all the fuss was about, some years back, do you remember? *Protect and Survive* it was called. I wrote to Wiltshire County Council – someone told me they were very on the ball – and it has actually been updated, but there's still no mention of pets in it at all. I don't think you're going to find a leaflet telling you how to shield your horses or dogs. You'll just have to use your common sense – apply what you know about people getting radiation sickness.'

'Stephen,' she had said, 'what would you do?'

'I'd put them first,' was all he would say.

In the book she had bought from him that day she had read about the vomiting and the slow deaths. She had put it in the stove to burn up, for some reason not wanting Danny to find it; but that had not obliterated it from her mind. She knew she did not have to think about it, because it would never happen, but thinking, and the brief sensations in the mind which the words had left, were different. Now, with her hand under the strong throat-pipe of the drinking horse, she felt the hand's liability. Horses could not vomit. Her caring had to encompass that – the agony and the concept of constancy. The horse finished drinking and raised his head, dribbling water on her shoulder. It was one of the things he did. Feeling strangely hard, love-strong, bound, she moved away from him, but only in space. In some other dimension she remained at his shoulder, unmindful of the fact that he was only an old horse.

Morag Medway came out of the Co-op nearly in tears. The silly, dribbly sort of tears that made Andrew, her husband, despise her, and now, too, her daughter Tansy. The boys, Sam and Malcolm, being younger, did not bother to notice.

'It's ridiculous,' she was saying, 'no one has fresh food after Christmas. Nothing but Spanish veg. and Danish bacon, and we can't eat that three times a day for ever. What's Daddy going to say? And Malkie won't eat any of that, anyway. It's ridiculous. Now it's snowing again. Oh God, how can I be expected to manage?'

'We could have Spanish omelettes. I know how to make them,' Tansy offered, but looking away.

'Don't be silly. Daddy won't eat eggs for a main meal. He needs good red meat.'

'Mummy, no one needs meat – they just like it. I've told you that.'

'– headful of ridiculous notions.'

'It's a fact, Mummy.'

'It's not a fact. Excuse me for knowing something! It's a way-out notion stemming from God-knows what lefty fringe . . .'

But Tansy had stopped listening. She had shrugged her narrow shoulders and stopped to stare at herself in the window of the boutique, Smarties, sidling around on the pavement so that the white stetson swinging on its tinsel chain fitted her reflection as if she were wearing it. She still almost wanted a Mohican hairstyle, but there was no way it would go under a stetson and it was pretty old-fashioned now anyway. Anyway, she was no longer sure that she could be bothered with the row that so radical an enhancement of her image would provoke at home. It might be better to go for a Thirties shingle, which in any case she could have done free by her friend Rachael's new sister-in-law who worked in a salon. Her mother was crying again, dismal, very small little tears that were always to do with food. Tansy knew, quite certainly, that if her father were out, Morag would see nothing threateningly Trotskyite about herself and the boys having eggs for supper. She also knew that her father liked eggs and that Morag's insistence on meat was more to do with Morag than with her father's diet. The problem was compounded by the fact that Malkie would eat nothing else unless it came out of a tin and tasted of preserved tomato and monosodium glutamate, and for weeks now all the baked beans, alphabet spaghetti and canned hot-dogs had been virtually unobtainable. Sam was delighted and begged endlessly for chips and even though he was beginning to have spots round his nose, he usually had his way. Tansy would not eat the chips because of the spots; Morag would not eat the chips because you couldn't take up sport again in middle-age if you were fat, and so, since the turkey and plum pudding, she had eaten very little indeed. Andrew was tired of the chips and last night Malkie had thrown a whole plateful of them on the floor and trodden in them.

Today there had been no tinned fruit either and, although it was still early, no batteries, sanitary pads or powdered milk. At the far end of the shop the Medways had passed a girl, little older than Tansy, encumbered with a fat and howling baby, staring desperately at the empty shelves where the little mini-tins of baby food usually stood. There was only one left: prunes and custard. The delivery lorries, they said, had been held up in the heavy snow; coming straight after Christmas, what could they do, they said.

The sky was a wicked dun colour, sucking up the lights from the shop windows and feeding them into the whirls of tiny, bitter flakes that were whistling up the Buttermarket. They made the artificial snow, so carefully Gothic across the shop-fronts, look cloddish and dusty. But the Christmas trees, regularly swung out at an angle over the frontage of each shop in an organized line of illuminated flambeaux, turned back into real, growing trees, forest trees invading the houses. Their needles held the snow in great clumps; their branches rustled in the wind and dropped white showers on the pavement. Suddenly Tansy saw them as entire trees, thrusting arms and torsos into the artifactual world through the facades of buildings; from behind each upstairs window where ruined rooms were full of holly and ivy re-quickened; firewood regenerated and throwing out pale suckers and moist roots; furniture shedding its dreadful veneers and gulping air, gasping for water. Fox-furs, snake-skins, leathers sprouting coarse hairs; from the cold storage of the butcher's shop a dim bellowing . . .

Tansy felt queer. She put out her hand to steady herself against the window of Smarties and the glass swung inwards, dragging her after it, the wind suddenly crashing into her back and pitching her on to her face. The floor writhed, quaking like a marsh-surface as she fell towards it, a huge, fleshy cheese-plant reaching out and laying its chilling cut-out leaves across her neck. She cascaded, liquid, into the morass, knowing that her mother, because she was crying, would not know where to look for her; knowing for a particle of a moment that she was lost. Dying. The same as dead.

The knowing about being the same as dead stayed with Tansy. She was a sharp-shouldered child with a narrow chest and a pointed face not unlike her mother's, and surrounded by the same lank brown hair. She worked too hard at school, felt too much at home and dreamed too much for her light bones to hold it all together. For some months now she had been dragged around in a vortex of personal dismays which were drawing her down into the tight little channels her father told her were the rewards of growing up and doing well. She felt herself, and all her generation, to be set up for the marketing of other people's professions – excuses for their lives, caged into their reasoning like battery hens. She knew that battery hens ultimately turned cannibal upon their own kind.

When the black politics of Warsaw and Washington, Prague, Vienna, London, Moscow, Paris, had begun to tighten in on Advent and detach Christmas from reality, Tansy had watched it happen more with awe than fear. She had not believed that people of her parents' generation had enough power to destroy the world; she had thought power belonged to the young, the vigorous, the still unrevealed. But the first poison-gas cylinders had been moved eastwards before the young knew it; the action was exposed, vilified and decried; then copied. No one asked the young about the deployment of troops that followed, were railed against, and copied. Fear moved an unreachable generation; fear of each other, fear of their own power, fear of their own people. Fear of their young? There was no need. Their young were powerless. The same as dead.

Understanding had come to Tansy Medway ludicrously. She had woken up one morning thinking about the ridiculous amount of her youth she spent doing maths, in which she was not interested and which she would scrupulously avoid from the day the State allowed her to stop going to school. Then she had thought, If there's war, I won't have to do maths. I'll either be dying or actually dead. Even parents would concede that that was of greater personal significance than Venn diagrams. Like a mole creating hollow cavities under the sure ground, the idea had been in her mind for a long time. Now it showed on the surface and she could not look at it. It had to be unthought. There was no way of unthinking a thought.

It had come again, upside down, when she had looked at the white stetson in the window of Smarties. It there is war, I will never wear it.

Tansy did the only thing possible without knowing it. She removed herself from the thought by fainting against the plate-glass door of Danny's shop in Buttermarket Street, Martinminster, on the fifth day of Christmas, so that for some seconds at least, she did not have to be alive in a world that would not outlive the twelve days of Christmas to celebrate Epiphany.

Christopher was having his postponed breakfast by the window of the rectory kitchen. His hands and feet were so cold that they were almost tingling, and there was a blue tinge under the stubble on his cheeks, but the steeply enclosed garden outside was so rigidly white and ferric that even the mist of his own breath on the glass seemed like evidence of indulgence. The robin was gone; the palm tree black and brown; the bricks of the surrounding wall whitely cracked and drained of colour. Inside, the overhead light impoverished the shadows among his features; the texture of his coat. He crouched over his coffee, reduced and deactivated by his tiredness and nature's withdrawal. As if integral to the same process, old Luke Lyons had died just before dawn, and Christopher had spent the early part of the morning with Freda, so suddenly altered from wife to widow. They had prayed and then Christopher had tried to be efficient on her behalf, for her children were unreachable; Celia, being an hostess with Qantas Airlines, was two days away, and Jimmy, the son, a bartender and handyman at a hotel in Kirkwall, was probably even further. Eventually Christopher had left Walford Scott, mortician and undertaker, in charge, dropped in on Alice King to ask her to go in to Freda an hour earlier than her daily visit would normally have brought her, and scuttled home in the frightening gloom to take control of his morning chores. Since the church had been opened for him, he made straight for the coffee-pot, knowing that he would be no use to anyone in this void and grey state. The coffee did not help much; Xanthe had made it at 8.30 and it had stood thickening and acidizing on the Aga ever since. Xanthe herself had gone, leaving a clothes-brush, a circular about distressed donkeys and a note which said, 'Rumours of fish for lunch. Kiss kiss, Xanthe.' Most unrectory-wifely. Everything about Xanthe was unsuited to rectory-wifeliness. She could not cook, would not sew, was intimidated by the parishioners and distanced by their problems, unstable in her faith and quite undoctrinally enamoured of Christopher, horses and the Ecology Party. Christopher thought that if she loved him less, she might listen to him more and so become more certain in her faith and less often absent, on sit-ins on ridgeways and gull-rescues in Norfolk. Moreover, she was quite extraordinarily beautiful in a North American Indian sort of way and had inherited a substantial package of stocks and shares from her father who had been in plastics. And Christopher thought he loved her uncritically; bewildered and blessed.

None the less, he was glad she was out now. Her riding-hat had vanished, which meant that she had gone over to see Polly Anderson at the riding-stable. He hoped, fervently, that she was gossiping in the cosy harness-room which had so unnerved him on the only two occasions when he had been allowed in there, and was not astride some capricious creature driven beserk by the cold and the harsh little snowflakes which were just now starting to smudge the window. He wondered if some boiling water might improve the coffee and why death and the Three Wise Men seemed so often to approach together. So many poetic alliances between myrrh and morbidity, King Death and the Kings, were to hand as a theme for Luke Lyons's funeral that Christopher automatically distrusted them, as he did anything that came easily. Funerals, he felt, should be hard-won or they were not worthy of the most terrible of occasions, despite the fact that he knew exactly what Freda wanted, probably needed, to hear him say. He was not in a position to evaluate the relief of his own conscience against the deserts of Freda Lyons's pain. Like slum-children with no shame, images begged, importuned, haggled at the skirts of his mind, obscuring Luke's thinned-out body and Freda's certainty of the resurrection – from a grave it would be impossible to dig in this iron weather. Scottie would know what to do; you didn't have to bury people straight away in these days of embalming fluids and fridges – not like the cow-sledge biers of his January childhood.

'Christopher?' Ian's voice ricocheted off the icy plaster of the passage walls.

'In the kitchen. I'm in the middle of a death and hating it. Come on in. Old Luke Lyons – used to keep the newsagents on the corner before the building society took it, remember?'

'Timely,' the doctor remarked, but Christopher misunderstood him. He watched Ian slide his gauntness on to a kitchen stool.

'Not really, he wasn't ill, or even senile. Just a bit old and cold.

His doctor had nothing to add to or, if it comes to that, take away from Freda's pain.'

'Which is what you're hating, isn't it? Not the death; the pain.'

Christopher shrugged. 'Don't know me so well, blast you.'

'I know you well enough to give you this: how about a good substantial pain of your own? Have you still got a bicycle?'

'A what?'

'A wheel, man. Pedals. Ting-a-ling and failing little light among the pot-holes in a head-on rainstorm. Remember the things?'

'Too well.'

'Good. Un-earth it then. You're going to need it.'

'What on earth are you talking about, Ian? Have some coffee – it's appalling, like mud.'

'Pass it over, then. It has to be nectar in this weather, even if Xanthe made it. Petrol's off.'

'Off?'

'Off. Like jam, or semolina pudding, or anything else you fancy. Off the menu without notice. As from today. Is that going to hurt you enough to square your conscience?'

'The hearse,' Christopher said obsessively.

'Maybe Scottie's got a throw-back handcart, or Polly's black horse –'

'Ian!'

Such impenetrable eyes, Ian's. Blue, certainly, but without clarity. Like a mist when it obscures what it is most necessary to see. Narrow eyes, with ginger lashes and ginger brows that added nothing, and horizontal lines which sloped neither down from sorrow, nor up with merriment, but strained out, away from the restrained eyes; lines of scrutiny and none of conclusion. Scrutinizing Christopher now.

'Well?' Ian said.

★

Stephen had brought Tinker into the shop, a thing he had not done for years. She was lying in a wooden seed-box from the Fruit Salad grocery shop next door. They often gave him boxes to use in his stock-room for incoming parcels of new books and immobile blocks of second-hand ones. Barbara was in his stock-room too, sitting at the littered table he used as a desk, gazing gently at his invoices. Some years ago he made himself a number of bill-prongs. Carefully choosing wood which held some meaning for him, he had sectioned them diagonally, sanded them down, chiselled out a slot in the undersides and drilled a hole through which he passed a barbeque skewer, the ringed end sitting politely in the slot. He kept postal requests on the silver birch from Dybart Hill; shop requests on the pear branch which had blown down in Joe's and Mary's garden; bills on the Christmas tree he had bought for the year when his mother came to stay for the festival, and invoices on the laburnum from the vicarage. They were all polished and worn silky with handling. He loved them all; their hearts and grains and elliptical growth rings. On some he had even worked out which rings had been formed in years that were memorable to him, and he would occasionally sit, staring at these 'when-marks' as if he could read his life's headings in the life-process of the trees. He had a maudlin fancy to have himself buried in a coffin the planks of which showed all the ring-marks laid down during his life, but he did not know how to organize it and let the idea lie unrealized, just to amuse himself. It would be just, he thought, for a bookish man to be interred within the physicality of a book, as so often the insubstantial essence of a man lived after him on the pages for which trees had given their lives. A little Jacobean, but very pleasing, he thought, and it might soothe the books. His shop was mad with words; millions and millions of words pressed between covers, willy-nilly, silent, screaming in their shelves, impotent, dumb because unheard, but none the less screaming. Sometimes he thought he could just hear them, when it was raining hard against the shop window, or as he turned away from the locked door on a dark night.

Now Barbara and Tinker were there and the books were silent. He wondered what it meant, their being there. On the face of it, Barbara was there because he had not thought of her being anywhere else; and she had simply climbed into the car beside him when he left the Dipyard in the morning, as if there were not another place to be. He had not had it in him to leave Tinker behind on such a day, and so he had put her in the car too. They had been together for seven hours, he and the girl and the old dog. Had Barbara nowhere else to go to? No home, no job? He had not thought to inquire. Now it was too late for such questions. If she had somewhere else to be, she would be there. It was not where people were not that counted, but where they were. Her coming had had a strange feel to it, as if it were ordained, predestined. He had lived all his adult life alone, by choice; a threat and a warning to less solitary souls and, he thought, to the received ideology of his generation who found offence in his constant solitude. He had few friends and very few acquaintances outside his shop, but he numbered Christopher among his friends and had often meant to ask him what medieval anchorites and Celtic saints had replied when accused of failing in humanity, or, in the modern phrase, inadequate social response. He had thought to carve an epigram to that effect on the beam over his front door. But he had let Barbara in through his front door as if it were not for service against intruders; or as if she were not intruding. He remembered his action clearly. She had pushed and he had let the door flow open as if it were part of a river course along which he, she and Time were being born. In the same way, she had come to rest now, for a little, against his table, her fingertips smoothing the laburnum wood under the invoices.

What had brought her fingers to rest particularly on that wood, of all woods? To Stephen the laburnum was the Machiavelli of trees. Coming from an alien land, its bright flowers vulgarly called 'golden chains', he saw at all seasons its will to ripen poisonous pods. Saw how it expanded its brilliance in suburban roads where the ignorant welcomed it in spring, fancied that it was nothing more than beautiful, bright Nature in fancy dress. And all the time, while the poison pods ripened, the laburnum kept them happy so that they saw their little private prisons as gardens, saw the golden chains as flowers and did not wish to leave. And in secret the pods ripened; in secret the quiet men who rested in the quiet gardens ripened into power and these killers who had learned that might was right, sat behind the bow-windows in the quiet streets where the pods fell from the laburnums and broke open upon the public footpath. Maybe he, Stephen, should have joined in this boycott or that march or such and such a protest outside an arms factory, but he never had and now it was too late. Now Barbara was there and Barbara's fingers rested on the bright, secretive wood. Why?

Suddenly, burning all over with hope, he called out to Barbara, 'Suppose –?' and nothing more. The words stopped there. To cover his mistake, he said, '– we have a cup of coffee?'

Barbara said, 'I don't want to stay awake. Have you any tea?'

She was very direct. He liked that. It was almost as if she had stopped running and was looking around at the thing pursuing her. Or maybe she had run into a high wire fence and could go no further. Her hair curled into little wriggles right down its length, minute, delicate runnels of ringlet, such as Jane Austen might have admired, or Hepplewhite. He must touch them. He said, 'You'll find tea in the bottom drawer, in an old Colman's mustard tin. We forgot to bring any milk.' We? I?

'I'll go across to the Co-op. Biscuits?'

'Doughnuts?'

She looked better standing up, even in the stock-room. Not so sick and abused. She draped a woolly bag on her shoulder and searched her pockets for mittens.

'Where did you get the bag?'

'Herakleion. You can pick lemons off trees there.'

'Buy lemons,' he said, handing her money for her purchases and the hope of Hyacinthus and lemon-scented midnight and the bull-dance as a cleaner way of dying while the Geiger counters whirled like Aston Villa rattles. His body knew, he thought, dreaming of sharp lemons in his saliva darts. Would it suffer illusion? Would it let him fondle its fears away as lotus-eating might? He knew it would not. None the less, he wanted the lemons.

Barbara had gone. Tinker was asleep. There were two policemen patrolling idly outside the supermarket with a blue glitter in their eyes. The books were silent. The salt off the street and pavement had frayed into a fine, buff dust like loess, eddying and sifting in the wind. Lemons came from geographies where olives ripened and asses and oleanders and the stink of Africa roamed the roads; much of it belonged to NATO, which Stephen had always visualized as a heap of lumpy grey waves with sleet slashing their crests, or as tanks in dark fir forests where minds clicked like electronic machines and all the birds had left. There were no glades in such forests for howling mammas with infants gluttonous at the breast, or for old age with its fumy pipes and garlic-laden donkey meat to rest beneath a lemon tree. NATO covered him and the lemon groves like a horde of pests leaving the trees stark. He shook his head against the thought and heard the dead branches rattle. Barbara would not come back. That was the sort of thing he expected of life, celibate that he was, touching the warm vulva of Europa in an empty bookshop while Barbara walked past the Co-op and on down the street and on out of Martinminster, almost as if she were real and it was not.

Morag Medway was neither the same as dead, nor troubled by degrees of reality. She was enormously alive, but dying and abundantly aware of it, although as yet she had told no one. She was dying of slow strangulation and although she wanted to fight desperately and dirtily against it, she did not know how. The process was discolouring and deforming her who had seldom served a double fault and had been almost exceptional at the net. She had been a lovely dancer, too, not confident enough for the tango or the *paso doble*, but a biddable partner with grace and energy in a quickstep or waltz. She used to own sunglasses, a real gramophone, a pair of Murano glass candlesticks and a Russel Flint print; things like that, most of which she no longer bothered to remember. Sometimes she used to tell Tansy about the dances, the knock-out tournaments, the dresses and boys and Fenwick's cottons and Triumph Heralds, but Tansy liked jeans and camouflage jackets and metal chains and thought that Morag's world must have been dirty to have so infected her own with corruption and necrophilia and AIDS. Morag gradually stopped talking to her and lost touch with her sunglasses, screwing up her eyes against sunshine and gathering lines about her face with disremembering. Her sons were into science-fiction models and lavatorial jokes and fighting, and Malkie would not eat. Whatever emotional umbilical cord Morag still wanted to believe in was hacked at mercilessly by Sam and Malkie each mealtime and whenever the television was on. Their rudeness frightened her. She was not particularly worried that Tansy was moody because she thought that fifteen was too young to be happy and therefore, by extension, too young to be unhappy. So Tansy was only moody. Until this morning, when the child had fainted through the swing glass door of Smarties. Even then Morag had put it down to a combination of Christmas fare and period pains. She had to. Anything else implied emotion and that, Morag knew, was a killer. Oh Andrew. Anything but Andrew.

Another CND leaflet thrust its way into her laden hand and flickered down to the lumps of salted ice on the pavement as she steered Tansy towards the carpark. The girl would not talk. Sam wanted to hurry home for the matinée movie. What was she going to give Andrew for lunch?

'Mad – mad. Everyone's got hysterical with all the broadcasting and panic – the media's got no sense of responsibility,' she muttered. 'No one's going to bomb anyone, no one ever has.'

'The Americans did,' Tansy said whitely.

'That was in the war; that was quite different. Darling, you aren't worrying about all this, are you?' But Tansy had nothing to say. No one had said anything to Morag for years. 'You can talk to me, you know,' she said, lying.

('Do you really go around in wellies and keep lambs in the oven?' Prue had asked, one girlish school reunion lunchtime in Fortnum's soon after Morag had married Andrew. 'God, I can't imagine it! All growing rhubarb and manure on the back doorstep. Whatever are you going to do?' She had done nothing).

Tansy leaned on the bonnet of the car. She looked insufficient, Morag thought; unequal to whatever it was that being alive meant – battle, struggle, defeat certainly. Tansy was green and fainting, opting out before life came within screaming distance of her. At least she, Morag, had got further than that. Was not Sam there to prove it? Standing there in the cold, not green, not running away, just being there in his curiously flesh-and-blood way so that she could snap at him, 'Sammy, open the door for Tansy.'

'Why? She can open it for herself.'

'Sam, please, she's not well.'

'I know. She's got spots on her back. Concealed spots: beware! Has she got the pox? That's awfully dangerous now, you know. A boy at school's baby died of it. I mean, it wasn't his baby – it was his parents' and it got chicken-pox –'

'Door.'

'Say please, then.'

The thing that was strangling Morag shifted its hold on her throat, thrusting what must be its thumbs against her epiglottis. It made her eyes water. She fumbled the key in the lock – so tiny, and her watering eyes were a little short-sighted now, anyway. 'You shouldn't have to lock everything in this paranoid way,' she shouted.

'What's paranoid? Like paranormal?'

'Sam, get in the back and hold this. Tansy, the rug. Malkie –'

('Darling, I couldn't care less what the bloody pill does to me when I'm sixty. I'm going to have fun like my mamma never knew about!' Prue had said, laughing, in Fortnum's long ago.) What had happened to Prue? Andrew wouldn't have the *Guardian* in the house, which was where any notice of Prue's affairs would appear. Had she taken the pill? Had she had fun? Had she, Morag, had fun? It was too late now to be bitter about that. But she did have something, she thought, even if it hurt more than fun did – she had Sam. She gripped his arm to push him into the back seat, only she was not pushing, she was holding him. Holding on to him.

Malkie said loudly, 'Ugh – I don't want to sit with all these fucking dog-sausages.' So it was Malkie she pushed into the car, beside the pink, plastic-coated offal, and Sam whose arm filled her hand, was in her hand like a piece of equipment for living. Certainly, she loved Sam.

Why was there so much pet food in the Co-op? It had even spread into the paper-crockery department, there was so much. Reduced, too. She had bought dozens of tins. Why had she bought all these plastic-sealed sausages of heart and liver and rabbit? The school, of course, he learned to say these things at school. And from Andrew. Morag thought that the name of the thing that was killing her might be 'Andrew'. Its given name. She gave it the name 'Andrew' and started the car, laden with livers and hearts, dead and dying.

The oil was too cold to drip out of the nozzle of the can into the little hole in the hub of the back wheel. It globbed, and sat heavily across the hole without going in. Christopher felt silly and flustered, kneeling in the garden shed among geraniums shrouded in frozen grey mould. His hands, in canary-yellow, fingerless mitts, were shaking. Ian watched him, chain-smoking because there were no patients to see him at it.

'I take it you have a bike yourself?' Christopher said, furiously.

'Yeah.'

'But you'll get petrol, being a doctor.'

Ian said nothing. Christopher did not notice, working the back brake out of its arthritic rigour. 'You're certain this is necessary? I've a lot to do.'

'Man, the pumps are locked. Locked. The police put seals on them at six this morning. Phil Ritchie told me that they did his as soon as the tankers had filled up. They were actually there, with the tankers. Got Phil out of bed to do it.'

'What tankers?'

'Didn't know. He said there was a collection of them. One of them was Andrew Medway's slurry tanker – he recognized it – and a lot of them looked as if they'd come off farms.'

'What was in them?' Christopher turned round and stared at Ian.

'Empty,' the doctor said, flicking a cigarette away so that he did not have to look at Christopher, who was not at all a stupid man. Then he said, gently, 'They filled up the frozen-food lorries at the Riverside Garage, I heard.'

'Who did?'

'The police.'

'Frozen foods? The police? Why on earth?'

Ian watched the clergyman, but there was nothing new to see in Christopher's face. Just the usual driven look that started far away inside the man, and the frustration stamped on the surface by the secular world and by the archaic bicycle.

'They were empty too.'

Christopher went on staring, hopeful that Ian would explain, but the doctor only lit another cigarette. Then he said, 'Dear Christopher,' and left. His footmarks were very clear and heavy in the crusted snow.

Christopher watched him go. Heard his car start. Felt his absence in the dormant plants which might be dead; in the heavy silence in the garden; in the fact that there was no living thing anywhere about. Snow had that effect, he thought, rationalizing. Earth hard as iron – you could not drive an axe into the lawn. Three nights ago – on St Stephen's night – Nellie Garlock had died in her caravan, Sunnybank, because the Calor gas had frozen. She had been chapel, not church, but Christopher had known her because they shared a secret passion for butter, and used to meet at the dairy stall in the market. Ian had told him about her death, and others. And now there was Freda Lyons and that death, and whatever significance Ian was reading into the fuelling of frozen-food tankers. Why did no one want a christening or a wedding, suddenly? The great furnace in the church crypt would keep even a baby warm, as long as its name was not Emmanuel.

He wished Xanthe would come home, even if she brought an element of fetlocks and forelocks with her – he wanted her worldliness between him and the world. She attracted the world, like a concave mirror; encapsulated it; framed it; controlled its wild aspects, leaving him free to stare into other spaces. He wanted Xanthe because, in fact, he wanted God. He wanted God very badly just now – a little like the night before the first Christmas, he thought loosely; before the apparition of God. It had been cold then too, traditionally.

He did not know that one of the bier fatigue, carrying the body of the Austrian Minister for Defence down the mountain above Rauris, had slipped, and that the corpse was now rolling stiffly on the snow, bumping grotesquely against the fir-trunks at the edge of the forest. Somewhere, someone was laughing, awkwardly. Christopher could almost hear it, but not quite.

'You know,' Polly said, pouring some Glenfiddich into the two plastic mugs from the top of Xanthe's vacuum flask, 'I don't trust Andrew when he gives presents. I can't think what he might want in return. He (and Morag) gave Danny (and me) this as a Christmas present. It can only be my bottom he's after. He doesn't wear Danny's sort of clothes.'

Xanthe stared at her over the rim of the cup. Polly was so extreme – her great coils of sumptuous hair, her deep eyes the colour of old mahogany, even the double chin forming under her vigorous, mobile face, were all so full of life, so extraordinarily generous, that Xanthe found it difficult to imagine anyone wanting anything from Polly which was not already given. 'I'm not going to ask,' she said, in case Polly intended to tell her, but Polly had already gone on without waiting.

'The leg, of course, he gets anyway. He always manages a pinch when he tries to give me a leg up, and he doesn't even know how to do it and I always land on my tummy with my knickers showing through my jodhpurs. He loves it. I'm going to kick him, one day, when Morag's watching.'

'Polly! Poor Morag.'

'My eye! She hates him. She'd love to kick him herself, but I suppose if you don't ride you don't get these God-sent opportunities.'

'Morag hates Andrew? Don't be daft, Polly, she slavers over him.'

'Watch her eyes, ducky, watch her eyes. And she doesn't love Tansy, either, or Malkie. Sam, yes. That's in her eyes as well. Ever noticed how she holds on to his arm? No? As if it were something she could defend herself with? Against Andrew, maybe, and Tansy and Malkie; or herself; or life even. He's the only one of the whole lot of them that she loves, including herself. Who she'll kill first, herself or them, is anyone's guess. But it won't be Sam.'

Xanthe slammed her flask top on the greasy table. 'That's a dreadful thing to say, Polly Anderson. I know Andrew treats Morag badly, but she'd do anything for him – to the point of degrading herself. And for her kids. She just doesn't have much ability to be demonstrative, that's all. Some of us haven't you know.'

Polly glanced at her quickly in case there was anything defensive to be seen in her face which was not in her voice, but Xanthe had always accepted her own reticence without question. It had never troubled her that in her marriage it was Christopher who was overtly affectionate, Christopher who used the endearments. The way she leaned on him, needed him for her very identity, required no expression. To her that was just the way it was between them. For Polly it was different. Polly had to love; so Polly always did the loving. Sometimes Xanthe found it wonderful to watch, but never enviable.

Now Polly was saying, a little wistfully for her, 'Wouldn't it be better if we did all show our love more? I mean, you can't show love and build weapons at the same time, can you? And look at us now – it has to work the same way between people as between nations and governments and so on. If Andrew showed Morag a bit more love instead of wiping his boots on her mind and then hauling her into the breeding-pen he calls a bed, she might not be so cold and absent. She's so wispy inside, Morag. Nobody's ever taught her about love – only about being used.'

Her hair in a scarlet bandanna – all black curls and coils around her neck and ears. Warm, decorative, animal. She had gaps between her teeth, just like the Wife of Bath (according to Stephen), denoting lust and humour and opportunism, and she was recently beginning to put on weight. Since Danny had moved in she had been drinking more, and liking it. She could tell a horse's temperament just by standing by its shoulder and leaning on it, and she was invariably right. Maybe she had leaned against Morag in some way that was impossible for Xanthe.

'I hate it when you say that sort of thing. I can't forget it and then I have to go home and face Christopher with these horriblenesses in my mind.'

'You and your saintly Christopher ought to start reading the *News of the World* and hanging around street corners – just ten minutes a day to start with –'

'Christopher on a street corner! Anyway, shut up. He isn't a bit saintly. It's just that he has nice manners and that confuses people damnably these days.'

Polly's eyebrows wobbled dangerously. 'He even has nice manners to me,' she said.

'And why not?'

'Well, he can't think much of me – men and so on.'

'And what makes you think you're so special that he'd treat you differently from the rest of humanity?'

Polly laughed. 'What a put-down! They should have made you a bishop's wife, not a saint's.'

'Bishops' wives aren't allowed to swig whisky in the middle of the morning in other people's harness-rooms, gossiping about the congregation. And I'd miss that. I'd never know anything about anybody. I don't mean gossip things, I mean what they're like. I'm no good at people, Polly. I can't see what they're about under their nylon blouses and lousy ties. I never could. I just crash about people's lives, bumping into the outside bark of them as if they were trees, and not even knowing what sort of trees. Other people, like Stephen, look at a tree and can tell you how old it was when they bombed Hiroshima, or how tall it was when Harold Wilson came in – like you with people.' She stopped, staring at her fingers; fingers that did not do anything humane and only ever reached for Christopher's. 'It's good the way you are, and not good the way I am.'

'You're not telling the truth, Xanthe.' Polly put out a hand. The nails were short and a bit grubby and the fingers were cold, but it was an irrelevant sort of cold.

'I am. I damn well am. Suppose you're right about Morag? I turn my back when I see her because she's a bore and a drip. She asks me what I give Christopher for lunch and whether too much reading could give you astigmatism and I run away because I'm bored. Now you say this about her, and here I am being bored by someone in an inconceivable sort of trouble. I mean, fancy not being able to love your own children and feeling raped by your husband, because that's what you've said. There's no way that assuming the right to be bored by that can be anything but bad.'

'And now you'll tell Christopher and go on a search for the real Morag under the housewife. He's a good egg, your man.'

'Maybe he knows already.'

'Nobody knows. Including Morag.'

'How can you tell, Polly? How can you be so positive about other people? How do you get there, inside them?'

Polly laughed. 'By cuddling them, ducky,' she said lightly. 'They're all the same: mares, men, Labradors, kids who want to kiss ponies' noses, killers and geldings – you know that. You actually know it, with all your wildlife and studies and Greenpeace. They're always the same, except one.'

'Which one?'

'Who knows? There's always one, for everybody. You have Christopher – everyone has a Christopher of some sort. You're just lucky – he'd call it blessed, I expect – to have found yours and not to have to leave. The Morags are the ones who haven't found theirs when everyone around them thinks they have.'

'And the Pollys?'

'Oh, the Pollys are funny animals. They have big eyes for looking and very very long legs for running away with.' She laughed again. 'Go home, Xanthe, and open a tin of carrots or something for the poor man. It's too cold to stay here; there won't be anyone wanting to ride today. I'm going to sit by the fire and do my accounts in the kitchen.'

'How are the accounts?'

'A dry well, ducks. Hay's an immoral price. I can tell you that Mary and Joseph would need one hell of an overdraft to get a stable this Christmas. It'd be cheaper to put them in the bridal suite.'

'I'll tell Christopher!'

Xanthe knew she was being sent away. Probably Danny was coming home early. She wanted to leave in a hurry in case she saw him. He was fun, but it embarrassed her that it was so obvious what he and Polly had for each other. She knew life was not as simple as that, but some part of her knew that perhaps it was. She left rapidly, the car skidding on the ice in the yard and the heater taking too long to warm up. It was the same sort of simplicity as Morag hating Andrew – if she did. She could see why, but not how. How could the man you loved and went and married, turn into the man you hated? How could they be the same man? There was only one of Christopher – that she knew. She had never loved any other man, not even in a teenage magazine. Just Christopher, suddenly, one day at a church social where there were trestle tables

covered by flapping sheets and jam sandwiches, a dog that wagged
a pile of plates off a chair with his tail, and the new curate called
Christopher, picking daisies for a little girl but quite unable to
make a chain of them because his nails had been bitten so far down.
So Xanthe made the chain, blossomed in what had to have been
sunlight, and married the curate without in the least understanding
him, without ever really thinking about him; simply perceiving
him with total clarity as the form her living was going to take.

She could imagine neither love nor marriage in any other way.
Had Polly ever felt like that? Who was Polly's 'Christopher'? She
had never spoken like that before, not even to Xanthe. To her,
Polly's life was a mess. She seemed to lose men and money all over
the place. The riding-stable was mortgaged up to the tilting
chimney-pots despite grants from the Sports and Leisure Trusts, the
Local Facilities Committee and Riding for the Disabled; everyone
had a stake in Polly's place. One stack of bills was so high that
Polly used it as a coffee table, and the man lurking in the
rhododendrons last year had turned out to be spying for the VAT
offices. There had been a jewellery designer called Paul and a
computer buff who ended up on a cannabis charge, followed by a
fleet of Airedale bitches who never seemed to come in season to be
mated and produce the money-spinning puppies. Then there came
a gentle herbalist who grew comfrey for the horses and wore
orange shirts, but he left to practise homoeopathy in County
Kerry. Now there was Danny who ran the fashion boutique in
Martinminster and should have grown out of it. Xanthe knew his
hair was dyed because she had seen the roots one afternoon when
he had obviously just crawled out of bed. He was lascivious and
ageing and completely unserious and he spent his time selling
unisex garments to pubescent girls and worrying Polly into bed
like an immature sheep-dog. Xanthe could see nothing else to him,
but Polly told her that he worried about cancer and ate wholemeal

bread and lettuce when no one was looking. Mysterious why Polly should allow him to yap and nip her upstairs after the computer buff and Paul and the herbalist and whoever had gone before. The herbalist had left in tears with his aura dented and a lot of IOUs which he left on Polly's windowsill; Paul had done something emotionally untidy with a broken vodka bottle. Each time Polly had wept and sworn and declared for chastity and Xanthe had believed her because it was so obviously preferable to the recurring messes. Christopher would come and mend the broken chair, windowpane, door-hinge, whatever; Stephen would come with a bottle of wine and an improbable tale about his plumbing or his neighbours; Morag would bring a vegetable marrow or eggs in a shoe box and there would be a giggly, weepy evening; and shortly afterwards someone would have a party and Polly would start all over again, heading for the next mess. Wretched and exuberant, full of crying and turmoil and troves of bodily joy. To Xanthe, it was an inconceivable way of living. And Morag's more so, if Polly were right.

'Christopher,' she said abrasively, when she reached him, 'what would it be like to hate your own child?'

He turned from the lame bicycle. 'Look inside any car in any traffic jam on a hot bank holiday,' he said lightly, thinking about brake-blocks.

'Christopher.'

'I'm sorry, love. The worst, I imagine, of any family hate. A killer, perhaps. Why?'

'Have I ever met it – without knowing?'

'Are you asking me about someone in particular?'

'Yes.'

'Then perhaps I shouldn't tell you.'

Suddenly aware, she said, 'You look tired – what on earth are you doing with that old thing? Has the old dear broken down again?'

'No, bless her, she's fine. Xanthe, my love, is there any petrol in your car?'

'Not a lot. I meant to put some in, but I forgot. Why?'

'Ian was here. There seems to be a petrol crisis. You can't get it today.'

'Why ever not?'

He had not expected her to understand immediately. He had not done so himself. He said, slowly, 'I imagine it has all been withdrawn for use by the army, or officialdom in some form. The police are in control of the garages.'

She went so white that her eyelids looked dirty. He felt such pity for her, so much desire to hold her and turn her face away that he dropped the bicycle on the frozen ground and put his arms tightly around her.

'Do I have to know?' she whispered.

'I'm afraid so.'

'It can't be in our time – it can't be us . . .' It was the definitive cry, the one they would all make. He could not answer. There was silence all around the rectory.

She had come back with a bag full of lemons, some tins of dog food for Tinker and a torn carton of frozen chicken legs.

'Found these under the freezer,' she said casually, dropping the woolly bag from Herakleion on the floor. 'It's weird out there. Half the shops are shut, and the ones that are open are selling mad things – bathing caps and embroidery thread and milking machines – at half-price. You can't get anything sensible.'

He wanted to cry out. It was careering and gurgling in his throat; that she had come back after all; that now she would never go away until the end of time and that she had juicy lemons in a coloured bag; that there was madness outside. Soon there would be singing and bright hot blood spilled in the snow. His or hers or someone else's, it would be all the same. And there would be singing, he was certain of that. And there was something else; when he was going to shout, his voice came out stiffly and crookedly as if divorced from this degree of experience. The freedom was within him, in some terrible, brilliant part of him which was quite separate from his physical voice and had to do with the power of singing and the power of blood and the relationship between them. He drew his breath in raggedly as the sense of both swept up in him and at the stretch of his lungs, at the point of capacity before the muscles reversed direction, he heard the books. Heard them with his physical ears. They were humming.

The freedom and the humming were the same thing. They were part of a glory, a violence, a collapse of restraint, an explosion of energies not confined to single individuals. Stephen wanted to cry out, to make a pure great sound that would carry out of the shop and into the wild frost outside, into the wind and the winter, proclaiming tremendous action, summoning times and legions and Antethos the warrior and the essential part from under the foundations of his house. His spirit grew enormous, a crested mountain roaring out of the dark towards the tentative shore where his consciousness began. At last his breath came freely and he pressed his head back because there was no room in his frame for his vast heart. When he looked down again he was smiling, bursting into laughter. It was his first experience of ecstasy and he had no name for it. Barbara was watching him along the aisle of humming books.

He said, 'I have wings on my sandals and my arms are made of iron. Why?'

She shook her head, and he thought he understood what frightened her.

'Can't you feel it?' he said urgently, moving towards her so that his rapture might touch her too. 'Can't you feel hope dying away, falling off like an old shell? Setting you free? Taking you further on and higher than anyone has ever been before? Because we know where we are?' She was still shaking her head, taking little steps backwards away from him, her Rossetti hair aureoled in the strip lighting.

'Knowledge, don't you see? We have the purest knowledge of all . . . we're set free of hope and need.'

'I loved my hopes,' she whispered, turning away.

He heard her weeping softly as she took the lemons out of the bag and set them among the wooden bill-spikes on his table. He could not see her, but the sound of her filled the shop. Crying would be as good as laughing, he thought, but not this muted weeping. Howling, wolf-baying in the empty steppe that had once been called Martinminster by men, when men were alive. That policeman strolling down the pavement, Danny muffled in his military swagger-coat, heading for the carpark; they were not alive. Not as men had once lived, with livers and red blood cells and pearly brains to look backwards and forwards with. These things in the street were mere shapes of ones he had known as men – of a Danny who drank Glenfiddich whisky and held his women around the shoulders so that his hand could slip around their breasts and brush their nipples. The policeman was no more than a photograph of what might be a brother, lover, husband, perhaps once a scrum-half, made for others and now lying face down in the waste desert where a Martinminster had once stood. Stephen wondered how different they were from the skeletons of lemurs and australopithicenes over which dust had also blown.

It was a peculiar moment, this. Stephen, who had his hands in his pockets and was staring out of his shop window, was wearing the same clothes as he had worn yesterday, and had letters addressed to him still in the post, was the same as dead. 'Where there is life there is hope.'

Now, as long as men were alive, there was no hope. The live men had put a stop to the dead men's hope.

'I loved my hopes,' Barbara had said. But Barbara was the same as dead too.

In one of the terraced houses in Station Road, an unemployed plumber burst into flames in his kitchen. When the neighbours and the police reached the burned-out cadaver, it was assumed that there had been a gas leak, but the haulier from next door said it was a case of spontaneous human combustion. SHC he called it, familiarly, pointing out the unburned lower legs and shoes. Stephen and Barbara heard the sirens at the far side of the church. It was a peculiar time, this time of absolute doom. It was slightly comic, Stephen thought, that the woman in the woolly bobble hat and duffle coat outside the Co-op was still handing out CND leaflets. He watched, curious to see what the same-as-dead would do with them. Some of them dropped them straight away and they floated down on to the dusty snow where the faceless primates and anonymous photographs already stained the pavement.

Morag stood right in the middle of the room. Neither Andrew nor any of the children could pass her easily, carrying the shopping from the car to the dresser at the far side of the room. Tansy pushed at her.

'Don't touch me,' Morag screamed.

In the absolute stillness which followed, the only sound was that of a Christmas card flapping on its drawing-pin above the rising heat from the Aga. It depicted a robin with a flowing white beard pulling a sledge full of brightly wrapped, square parcels. Listlessly, Morag thought, Why not?

'If there is a war, Andrew, could robins grow beards? You know, afterwards, when everything goes funny?'

He said, 'Bloody hell, Morag.'

'Don't be cross. I want to know.' She sounded petulant, babyish almost.

'There's not going to be any fucking war.'

'War!' Malkie yelled, making sten-gun noises at the cat, the crockery, the window, Morag. 'Gotcher – pow!'

Sam was staring at him. Then he shouted suddenly, 'Shut up, you silly little sod.'

Morag's eyes filled with tears. From inside her they looked yellow, thick like pus. From outside they seemed thin and watery.

Tansy said, 'I'm feeling sick,' and threw up on the vinyl tiles. Morag burst into laughter; burst like an enormous boil in an embarrassing place. There was a great deal of sudden movement and banging doors and shoving and sharp, nostalgic smells from the time when Morag had had children that she loved and, long before that, Mummy. She stood thinking about Mummy and the Displaced Person who had cooked and sewn and the noise of Malkie's sten-gun rattling away behind the calf pens, and eventually she sat down by the Aga where she would be out of the way. Andrew was so good at clearing up disgraces. She was quite able to recognize that, having been good at things herself – lacrosse as well as tennis, but she didn't play games any more.

'Why are you doing that?' she asked Andrew.

'I'm not going to spend the rest of my life wading through puddles of puke,' he said furiously.

'Oh yes you will. That's exactly what it's going to be like.' Tansy was shivering.

'Tansy, go to bed, for God's sake. And take a basin with you.'

'My bedroom's cold.'

'I'll bring you up a hot-water bottle,' he shouted. 'Go.'

'Not very sympathetic, are you, Daddy? Are you going to shout at all of us when we're spewing up all over the cellar, dying? Like next week?' She was gulping at her crying; gulping and dribbling a little. 'People like you who've done nothing to stop it, who've made it happen by telling us it won't, all shouting at us because you've made us sick ourselves to death? That's why we sick up. You'll find out by the weekend.' Then she ran away towards the stairs, making fiendish little moaning noises that drove him into a frenzy.

'Hysterical bitches!' he yelled after her. 'Just like your bloody mother, both wailing and pissing yourselves the minute things look rough.'

But that was not true. Morag had never flinched, not even when her opponent had come straight for her face, stinking of girl-sweat and vaselined leather – she had never dropped the ball, never fouled it up. She had been a brilliant catcher and cradler, and fast. But an inaccurate shooter. Why? Because she would not be inaccurate now. There was an astonishing fact. Now, she could feel it in her eye and her arms, now she would shoot straight. Why? How did she know? What had happened in the twenty years since the wind-grey lacrosse pitch above the Forth, to turn Morag Colquhoun into Morag Medway, a deadly shot?

It was too viscous, too clayed and clogging down here in England. She was provoked by the memory in her lungs of the sharp north-eastern air, the thinness and salt sweetness of its purity. She struggled to her feet, upwards towards the cleanness. Andrew was still shouting. She had forgotten him for minutes, up there in the north. She found herself close to his face. It was large and square and foul-mouthed and had been coming fast at her for years and years. It had nearly reached her. It did not know how good she had been at lacrosse and tennis – how strong.

'. . . going to pieces,' Andrew was shouting. 'Letting the kids get sick with fright because you're too stupid to see that nothing can happen. Don't you understand, you stupid cow – it can't happen.

It's mass hysteria that will do it all for them. They won't need any bloody bombs.

'Morag, Morag, listen, for Christ's sake. Nobody's going to drop nuclear bombs, ever. They're going to frighten us into submission, not bomb us. Can't you see it?' He clutched her arms as if she were a burglar or a whore; hurting her. 'It's all the fools like you that they're relying on. They're panicking you into doing it all for them.'

'I must get lunch.' She was not quite ready yet. Not north enough.

'Jesus Christ!' He dropped his hands and stared at her. 'Are you mad?'

'I'm terribly sorry, it's only omelettes. There wasn't anything in the shops. You've no idea what the shops were like, Andrew.'

'Is this craziness or your idea of the Battle-of-Britain spirit? What are you up to, Morag?'

'I'm doing the only thing I know how to, just yet,' she said softly. Her eyes were narrow as if she were searching for something against the light.

'What? Cooking? You're a lousy cook.'

'Not cooking. Apologizing to you.' It was like crossing the stone bridge on the way home to Ardcollie; you could walk from there, it was so nearly home.

Andrew turned away, grabbing the heavy kettle on the Aga. There was pale damp on his temples. He was wearing a bulky, oiled sweater against the cold and his face was sweaty. Morag smiled.

'What about the boys? Are you going to feed them, too? On junk out of a tin or a polythene pack? What about Tansy, for God's sake? You're her mother, you ought to be up there with her –'

'No I shouldn't.'

'Why not?'

'I don't like her.'

He let the kettle fall back on the ring with a crash. When he turned round his big face was pale and rough, like a blanket. 'My God, Morag, what are you saying? What are you doing?'

She made no answer, just shaking her head, smiling, thinking about the stone gateposts shrouded in straggling rhododendron at the entrance to Ardcollie. When Andrew stepped closer she did not back away. He did not look so big from Ardcollie.

He said, 'Morag, please. Don't go to pieces. It's all right, it's going to be all right – it can't happen. You'll see. Please? Go to Tansy, she needs comforting – here, make her a hot-water bottle. The kettle's hot –'

'Did you really not know, Andrew? We hate each other, Tansy and I.'

Outside, in the dreadful cold, Malkie was taking his clothes off, one by one. He knew it would put his mother in a bate and she might strike him. Then Daddy would take him out after the fox to make it up to him. Daddy had been after that fox all winter.

The afternoon was darkening when Danny came back. Polly saw the car lights curling around the kitchen as he turned in, before she heard the engine. The radio was on loudly, playing rather silly Golden Oldies, more suitable to a Sunday evening than a weekday afternoon. But it was comforting and rather sweet and she would rather have gone on cleaning bridles lethargically and listening to it, than react to Danny's coming in. The room was heady with heat and the thick sweet odour of saddle-soap and horses, and Polly was sitting at the end of the wooden table with her back to the big stove, staring at the rows of photographs and rosettes that covered the opposite wall. Her eyes meandered nostalgically over the faded satins high up near the smoke-dimmed

ceiling. They were nearly all violets and whites and pinks up there
– not the triumphant reds and blues and tricolours with swallow-
tailed streamers of lower down. Those old, just visible ones were
her own – very private and special and hard-won, and each had
oceans of tears and sweat and love and terror lapping around its
frayed edges. They were the dried button-holes, the immortelles, of
her great loves who drifted in and out of her sight, their thick coats
curly with sweat, their great, lacustrine eyes drowning her in past
adorations; Twinkle, Silver Arrow, Fred, the Witch. The agony of
growing when love demanded stasis had racked her childhood with
the phrases, 'Getting a bit long in the leg for old Arrow now . . .'
and, 'Polly Anderson, you're too big for that pony now . . .' She
had warped and twisted under those partings. She had learned too
much from them; about her own strength and about loss. She
knew it but no one else ever had because, they said reasonably,
they were only ponies after all and girls grow out of these things.
But Polly Anderson had never grown out of knowing that for her
at least, love and loss were only one thing and that she would not
live without it. So she had gone on loving without fear, believing
that she could bear it, and appropriating to herself only its hard
sequel.

She did not often think of the child she had conceived with
Frankie, but she could feel its aborted bones in the bundle of
leather in her lap, its unmade mewing in the whine of the wind
behind the scullery door. If Danny's car lights had not come to
rest, glaring, on the draining board, she might almost have seen
who it might have grown into. Almost, for there were tears
between her and the child.

'And how's my little sex-cat this evening?' he said, letting the
back door crash on its hinges. 'Give us a hand, Poll, there's going
to be a war, and Danny's brought in supplies to see us out – come
and look.' He smelt of brandy and cars and expensive cloth and his

thinning hair was fluffed out drily behind his ears. He was the summation of Polly Anderson's experience. The killed child faded out of her senses as her mind came to terms with his actuality. Whatever he thought, and she had never asked him, it was she who had taken him, not he her. Hers was the requisition; hers the authority.

'Not crying are we?' he said anxiously, peering at her across the unlit room. He was as big as ever, as broad and desirable and warm and weak. Her choice after all the pain. He was to know nothing about her. No one was ever to know anything about Polly Anderson except Frankie and the child who had been scraped from her womb to live on in her bone marrow. She was their secret, not her own.

'Danny, love me.'

Because he did love her, he knew that she did not mean it sexually, and held out his stout arms, clumsy in affection for one who was so deft in lust. He privately rather liked the small, untidy ponies she kept in her riding-school for the younger children, and he patted her now as he would do them on a summer evening when he wandered out to the yard after the shop was shut – endeared by their little strengths and the unexpected softness of their summer hair. They were very good for those who found adulthood hard. 'Poll, it's going to be hell, this,' he mumbled into her curls.

Curiously, she answered, 'It puts a stop to this business of growing up,' and he could not tell if she were talking to herself or to him, or who. None the less he went on, hurriedly, not giving himself time to think because thinking had never worked out for him and, in any case, it was too late now for thinking.

'You wouldn't ever marry me, Poll, would you?'

'No time like the present,' she said. Sweet Polly Anderson, for whom griefs and memories were closing up like summer flowers in the evening.

'We can use the booze for the reception,' she said, unevenly, 'if we get time for one.'

He started to cry a bit, or laugh. 'Life was a bit of a fart, anyway,' he said.

It was very cold outside and very moonlit. Iced pampas, plumed dingy and brittle, as irrelevant as trilobites in an arctic showcase. Looking into the case through the still, impervious glass, imagining the impossible cold and the lifeless light at the beginning of the end of the world when the dead people were still alive, pressing lip to lip, touching, giving birth, stroking each other's hair, defecating, lying, praying. Some even dying before the dying began. Odd, that.

'When?' Danny said. 'How?'

Polly said, 'Christopher,' and Danny nodded. It did not seem ridiculous that they should go to Christopher.

The dog fox was out again. Again, Croke's Wood was shot through at ground level with humming green light which had no eye, no focus, no beam. The undersides of the spruce fronds were heavy with light, the tips heavy with snow. Stars and satellites blue and blinking. The moon passed in silence over the dreams deep in her planet's essence, her light revealing nothing but the back of the sleeping pigeon, the icicle on the blackthorn. There was no cloud, no wind, no weather. The fox's desultory munching of the kale leaves was automatic. Tonight, so cold, wrens would fall. Already he had eaten a blue tit which he had found breast-up under a hedge, no heavier than the weight of its own bones and feathers. The ice had locked up all the water. For himself, the fox used the bawn cattle-troughs and yard drains after dark; his mate sufficed herself by eating snow crystals and licking icicles, but the birds died of thirst. Pellets of hard snow had congealed on the underside of his brush, making a tiny, vibrant thrumming as he moved. He sat between the high stalks, agitated, licking them into thaw. Beneath his hips and ribs the earth was ungiving. Hardness and cold without memory or anticipation – hunger without past or future; endurance was all there was for him until the sparrows fell, marked out by him and by Christopher on his knees in St Martin's Church, his heartbeats tapping like the little thuds of those little, little corpses.

A new God, this. A God Christopher had always been slightly afraid might be there – behind, as it were; unrevealed, except to the unlucky. Psychology, he had been afraid, anthropology, 'historicity', the sciences of psychosomatic determinism, modern translations, had all done a lot to obscure this God, not new, no, but very old; these things had helped to keep Him (or older than 'Him') hidden away, lost out of sight of this generation. But He was there now, like the sun at desert dawn. Unstoppable. Unspeakable. Unquestionable about the fall of sparrows. This, they said, was His world; now He rode high over it in absolute disinterest while it prepared to die.

So Christopher could not pray. Only watch what he had to name 'the Riding Out of God'.

When he came back into the rectory, because he was only a man and could not endure Godhead, there was blood on his lip where he had bitten it and shudders ran through him like an ancient ague or even the fading out of frenzy. He panted like a man who had run for his life. There was icy sweat around his neck and forehead. He bumped into furniture like a stranger in the dark although his kitchen was brightly lit. When Xanthe asked him, in ordinary words, 'What is it?' he answered with complete truth.

'I don't know.'

From the electric wire that ran from the Medways' back door to the outside light over the pigsty door, a starling fell (Andrew Medway had been after the fox all winter).

Stephen had been afraid before. When he was little he had been terrorized by the corgi next door to the newsagents; once by a herd of cows in a lane that was too narrow; by a woman selling polythene buckets door-to-door, who had only three fingers on one hand; several times in motor cars. But these had been lurid knife-cuts across his sense of fear, scarifying but not dangerous in the long term. He had never been afraid for any length of time. He noticed now that he was beginning to split into two parts. Stephen-mind was filled with a tough, furious logic. All that was happening was something long forecast. Something they had all known for years was going to happen. Something they could have stopped, only they had never quite got round to it. Dinner, or visiting mother in the old people's home, or the weather – things that had seemed to prevent them all from marching enough, protesting enough. Once, a girl on the train from London, opposite him in the carriage, had been wearing the badge on her denim jacket. He could have said something, made unity, but he had not. He had returned to an article in the *Bookseller*. It was not lack of responsibility; they had all known that they were responsible. It was just failure. Sensibly, if men were able to bring the world to an end, then men were able not to bring it to an end. There was no 'act of God' involved, no 'extra-terrestrial threat', no 'circumstance beyond control' even. Just people who had failed. Which was why he was the only man in the world who could have stopped it. Everyone was that man. It did not make him any less culpable that he was one of millions. The logic in his head was steady – heavy and dense like molten metal in a wax mould.

Stephen-body, though, was not able to think. It was cold and sick and sometimes had a lump in its throat and sometimes a loud laugh. Its hands trembled and its bowels grew loose. It did not want to flame up like a piece of chip-paper on Guy Fawkes night, or flash its bones briefly like a negative still in a pop video, or canker away, fungoid and fetid in a howling dark Ice Age. Death was abhorrent to it. It had no reaction to death. Only to fear of death. Sweat swerved out through its pores and bile scalded its throat, regardless of what its mate, Stephen-mind, was doing – feeding the dog, or watching Barbara-running brush her thick, curled hair. Stephen-mind had told Stephen-body over and over again that the chip-paper suffered less than the cancerous organism, but to Stephen-body, death could not be preferred to anything. They had been out of the way of pain for a long time in Europe; bodies knew little about it. Death was, and life was, and no mere artifacts like words or thoughts could link the two. Stephen-body wanted chocolate.

He pushed aggressively out of his sitting-room and into the kitchen. 'I want some chocolate,' he said, standing there in the door with his hands in his pockets.

'Can I have your car?' Barbara-running – preparing to run again?

'To go where?' he said.

'Around. See it all. You know?'

He did not know. He had no curiosity about people unknown to him. 'See what?'

'Where they're all at. Whether they believe it, I suppose. Let's go to a pub.'

'A pub?' he yelled.

The lights dimmed suddenly. He heard Barbara's breath scrape inside her. The fridge made a silly noise. He looked at Barbara's eyes, but they were as if they had black contact lenses over them – solid ones. She was not seeing out of them. His eyes saw everything – the flowered curtains, submarines, Bruce Kent dead over by the pantry door, the stricken trickle of power in the cowboy wiring, last summer, the Ice Age, Barbara's arteries going black.

'It'll come back,' he said breathlessly. It did not come back.

Tinker twisted round from her emptied dinner-bowl to scratch. Stephen watched the gas fire greedily.

'Jesus, I hope it lasts out,' he said, scrabbling in his pocket.

'I want to go out. Coming?'

'I've just lit the fire –'

'There'll be a fire in the pub.'

And chocolate. He was craving for that chocolate. Strange, chemical knowledge in his villae that the chocolate would give his muscles the energy to stay or to flee. There would be slot-machines.

'Have we enough cigarettes?' he said, suddenly frantic. There would be a slot-machine for those, too.

'How many is "enough"?' Her voice sounded high, as if she were calling across a bad party.

He calculated quickly. 'Four hundred.' He had two hundred in an unopened carton in his bedroom. He would not tell her they were there.

'Can you get, you know, a smoke, in your pub?'

He said, 'I don't think they sell them by the hundred,' not understanding.

She laughed like crackling tinder. 'I don't suppose they do, no.' She began combing her hair again, using the dark outside the uncurtained window as a mirror. He thought she was brave and stupid to use the dark as a mirror. How did she know what – who – she would see out there, looking in at her through her own eyes, transubstantiated eyes which might look directly into the quick heart, the gaudy innards? Was she not afraid to know who she might be? He was afraid. He turned his back on the window; he did not want to see who the 'he' was outside, the 'he' inside him.

'What do you want to do in the pub?' he asked her softly.

She shrugged. Her narrow shoulders lifted her clothes so that they made new shapes down her body. Her eyes were seeing again, herself mainly, in the dark. 'I suppose I want to see the people,' she mumbled, 'all the people who believe it, or don't. Sort of, find out if it's true – not for me, though.'

'For who?'

'Who cares? Them, you maybe. The dog.'

He wanted more. He moved towards her as if by coming closer he might force his articulate habit upon her. He knew about words – thought and merchandized in words. 'What sort of true? You know it – you saw the convoy – you can look out of my windows and see the light in Croke's Wood. And the light cutting out here in the very room you're standing in. Isn't that truth?'

'It's true for you. You look like it's true for you.'

'Say again?'

But she did not want to. She made a boxing movement at the window, a sort of feint that Antethos of the Dobunni or the dog fox or Polly Anderson would have read as Stephen read words. She would not, the gesture said, fight. She would not, because she did not believe she would. She was small and vicious and would scrap meanly, but in the end she would need the pack behind her, or she would turn and run. Antethos had seen it all before, seen the certainty of defeat become a killer. It had killed him. He felt it as a sorrow like a cold lode in his heart and belly. This time his death would be absolute. Antethos, like all his pig-eating, horse-loving, blue-beautiful race, would only live in the Afterworld as long as there were men alive to hold it in place with their memories. Now the men were dead and Antethos was dying of their death. Just outside the black punch-bag window of Stephen's kitchen, two of Antethos' tribe had died at the hands of eleven men of the II Legion. Antethos did not know exactly where; it was all very long ago. Barbara did not know, even Uncle Ptolemy had had no idea of it. Nobody now alive had. But it had happened. Those men, unlike Antethos, were already absolutely dead, because no one any longer knew that their souls had ever been. For this reason the window remained absolutely blank, reflecting only Barbara's movement and returning it to the kitchen unenhanced even by death.

She dropped her fists.

THE SECOND MODE

SO AGAIN it was night. It was night for fourteen hours out of twenty-four at this time of year. The corpse of the Austrian Minister for Defence was shut up in a coffin in a special coach in a siding just outside St Polten. Two of the guards from Krasnoyarsk stood below it on the snow-covered track and two more dozed on cheap plastic-covered chairs inside the coach. One of them was seventeen that day. It had been his birthday all the time it had taken to bring the corpse from Rauris to St Polten. The corpse was in the siding because no one could imagine what to do with it or where to bury it or how. Or even if. It was quite possible that it could soon be forgotten altogether, now that there were many pieces of paper which could be left in drawers. As the hours sifted by on the snow, the birthday-boy from Krasnoyarsk became indistinguishable from his own birth-certificate – became just one of two bits of paper in drawers with a coincidence of dates upon them. As neither bore a photograph he became a sequence of Cyrillic shapes – very pretty and evenly spaced along the line. It was the first time he was killed and he was not aware of it yet, but his mother had bad dreams that night.

In all sorts of peculiar places in the world people were having bad dreams. For those for whom it was still yesterday, or those who were already awake in tomorrow, it was mostly a question of goose-pimples and something like morning-sickness. For the sleepers it was much worse. They had no switches or computers or bows and arrows or bright coins to push around and their muscles leaped and jerked, or quivered in chattering ripples, as their minds spun down the back-race of all the secrets of Europe and Africa and Asia, with gods inside them and three faces on their antlered heads. Power, power, power, they dreamed, but they were only dreams. There was no power left, not as an akond or an earl or a pharaoh would have understood it; only momentum. It was an eerie night. Very silent. There was no news on the television, only sex-scandals and a child missing in Cumberland and a flock of sheep missing in Powys and a curious item about a medical squad who had asked the queues still waiting outside such Oxford Street department stores as advertised sales to disperse, as the temperatures forecast for the small hours were so low that they would be dangerous to those inexperienced in sub-zero conditions.

Ian Hoskins was the first to notice it. He was watching the news on Christopher's television, leaning against the Aga, a glass of mulled blackberry wine in his hand.

'Who the hell are they?' he said, leaning forward to look more carefully at the set, but the frame had changed. The newscaster wore cheerful cherry-red. 'They weren't St John's or Red Cross or police or anything that I've ever seen. Christopher, did you notice those grey uniforms?'

'What? Notice what?'

'Oh you! Xanthe, were you looking?'

'Sorry. This duck, Ian – how would I know when it's cooked?'

'When its legs fall off. Didn't you see the telly?'

'No, I was looking in the oven. Are you sure about its legs?'

'I'm sure that hope is a poor substitute for accurate assessment. Hold it up here and I'll give it a prod.' He poked the duck and its legs fell off. 'There,' he said, 'dinner.'

Xanthe balanced the roasting-pan on the Aga rail. Together they stared at the duck.

'He was called Mr McAdam,' Ian said.

'Oh,' Xanthe's voice fell a little, 'was he?'

'They said he won't need a sauce, he's full of apples. They've been feeding him the mushy ones since September, to save trouble I suppose. Their sheep all eat a lot of mint too, I've noticed.'

'What was this particularly grateful patient suffering from? Sadism or terminal Heath-Robinsonitis?'

'I don't discuss my patients. But I can tell you that I've known Mr McAdam for a long time. I first met him under a bed, and then I sat beside him on a sofa every week.'

'Poor McAdam.'

'Mr to you, Xanthe, and don't weaken. Shall I look for plates? We'll need them, won't we? Will we?'

'Try the draining-board; I have an unpleasant memory of a recent tangle with a washing-up mop. God, you both look so ill with blue chins and purple lips –'

'Like the poor frozen stiffs in the John Lewis queue,' Ian said, harking back. 'You didn't notice that; I wonder who did?'

'What's bothering you about it? Oh Lord, this wine is ghastly. Can't we have something that's at least heard of a grape? I can't stand it – it's Christmas, after all. D'you know, I hate your self-sufficiency patients, Ian, I really hate them. Why don't they get a different doctor who has a wife and a brood of adolescents who all adore rosehip and nettle Benedictine, and leave us free to pay for some self-respecting plonk in the Co-op without feeling guilty about it?' Xanthe sat firmly at the table. 'Christopher, will you come and carve Mr McAdam, please?'

'Will I do what? It doesn't look all that dangerous on the weather map, does it? It was -13 last night and they said nothing.'

'So glad you can still hear,' Ian said drily. 'Tear yourself away from the cheerful glooms of John Kettley, man, and apportion the feast.'

But Ian was watching the television himself, out of the corner of his eye. Christopher came slowly to the table. 'Gracious, Xanthe – duck? We can't afford duck.'

'Darling, it's not a bought duck. One of Ian's alternative-type patients exchanged it for a tonsil or something.'

'I wish you weren't so detailed, my love. Is it cooked? Or burnt?'

'Ian supervised the falling off of its legs. It's perfect.'

'For what we are about to receive . . .'

'Mr McAdam,' Xanthe and Ian said softly.

Christopher looked cross. When he had finished Grace, he said, 'Who are these McAdams, anyway? Do I know them? Are they that family living in a sort of wigwam behind the Medways' lane?'

'Oh Christopher.'

'Didn't you notice?' Ian said. 'No racing, no football.'

'They can't. The ground's frozen.'

'Xanthe, it can't get too cold for ice-skating, but they've cancelled the ice carnival those youngsters were going to hold tomorrow. I heard it on the radio. Uncertain weather conditions, they said. So it's too cold in London, and thawing in Peterborough? Theatres are out – cinemas are shut, carefully preserving electricity, they say. Now they've even dispersed a little queue in London. Don't you make anything of it?'

'They're all such different sorts of things. What do you expect in a crisis, for heaven's sake? "Expo Great Britain" at Wembley Stadium?'

'But they aren't different. They are all about one thing.'

'What? Fun?'

'No, fun's OK. Crowds are the thing.'

Christopher put pieces of Mr McAdam on their plates. He did not seem to be listening. Rather, he seemed to be listening to something else.

'They're keeping us all at home tonight,' Ian said. His voice suddenly had an unpleasant, abrasive quality. 'No petrol, no trains, no excuse or reason for any gathering. Not forbidden, mind you, nothing overt. Just, no opportunity. Everyone snug under their own little roof, with a cosmetic television between them and the reality of what is going to happen to their skin. Telly cuts down on the talking too, doesn't it? That way rumours don't spread – panic doesn't show. That's why the domestic supply of electricity has been cut down for us rather than cut off; we haven't been asked to sit in the dark and think, have we? We can watch James Bond and *Star Wars* and see Superman overcome all categories of evil, and forget whatever else may be going on out there, because there's no one out there any more – just a series of computers clicking away along a programme laid down when "If" was still in the vocabulary. Listen. You can't even hear it – you can't hear anything out there. Nothing's happening. Just a flock of sheep lost in Wales and an unknown grey uniform clearing the streets of the capital. Is it unknown, do you think or is it that we are not normally shown it? Not abroad in the high streets, as it were. There's been such a recruiting drive over the last few years and it wasn't just a bad answer to the unemployment problem. I wonder what sort of uniforms our noble army really wears these days. Anyone know? Do they have the gas masks sewn in, or are they optional zip-on extras? Do they all wear radiation protection or only a select corps, do you suppose? Who do you think tells them when to put it on? Who do you think knows all the answers? All of them?'

'I don't want to think,' Xanthe shouted.

She looked at Ian, hard; refusing him access to her mind. She was very beautiful, dressed in dark green, the colour of holly leaves. The diminished light brushed her hair with a soft, delusory glow, like candle-light. Her voice had been taut, forcing an idea into words which did not complement it. Her knuckles were pale, so tight was her grip on her knife and fork. To Ian, it looked as if she were clinging to them, as if they were lifelines attached to some form of reality she was being sucked away from. He wanted to put his hand over hers, but he knew that it would be to loosen her grip, and he had neither the courage nor the anger to do that, yet. Instead, bitterly, he said, 'What are you going to do, Christopher?'

'I am going to eat this delicious duck, and then I am going to sin quite extravagantly.'

'Jesus, what an answer,' Ian said. 'I'm talking about your wife, man.'

But Christopher did not answer him. He was eating voraciously, purposefully, as if he were doing more than feeding. His eyes, which had always been large and gentle, were, now that they had both turned to look closely at him, hard and out-looking. It might be that the profound brown of the irises had turned to sharp agate, some inner self showing, which had always been hidden before.

Xanthe said, 'Don't go away,' her voice rising and very thin.

'I was thinking, in church –'

'You weren't thinking,' she shouted suddenly at him. 'Something happened to you. Was done to you. You didn't do anything, even thinking. I saw you when you came in.' She stared at him, then at Ian. They had left her behind. They were believing in something, accepting something she could not understand, only fear. They seemed less afraid than she was; she loved them; they were in her life, the texture of her existence, her habitat. She could not live in and about them if they altered. If they changed she would have no home for her spirit. And they were changing, as word followed word into the evening.

The duck nauseated her. It had been a joke, almost. Now the joke was sick; black. Yet Christopher was eating it as if it fed him something – what had Mr McAdam to give him that was other than food? She pushed her plate away; there was nothing on it for her. Ian's thin, examining eyes stared back at her from wherever he had gone on to; long-sighted, like a ghillie's or a game-keeper's who could turn away and go elsewhere when dark came and the only creatures left in the habitat were those without responsibility. Take your chance – the only forest law that still stood. Every forest had its losers. She began to run, stumbling a little, never much of a runner. Trunks or trees at angles, at queer intervals; crabbed boulders hidden; sudden saplings. No moonlight, so where is the moon? What other runners in the wood? Who? Why? Running from whom? Their footsteps all around, fast, uneven, some quite close. Running in which direction, for God's sake? A branch snapped, far out to the left. Spruce needles stroked her arm, soft as dead hair.

'Xanthe?'

'Xanthe, my love –' Christopher's hand closed over hers and she screamed. He jumped up and grabbed at her, pulled her from her chair, out of – was it Croke's Wood? – into his arms, wrapping his muscles and his flesh around her, visible, warm. He pressed her face against his cheek, caught her hair in one hand, her back, her ribs in the other.

'Christopher, don't go.'

'Xanthe, Xanthe –' he kissed her. She was as stone instantly. Had not Judas kissed, also in a wood, also at night? She suffered his rough handling. It was meaningless. In the end she found his eyes. Like Ian, he was looking back at her from further on.

She said, very softly, 'You'll kill me. You, Christopher.'

He set her back in her chair and kneeled beside her. The weakened electricity made madness of their shadows; huge grotesques, fondling in too few dimensions. He said desperately, 'I would have died for you.'

'Exactly.' Her voice was weak and flat. 'That's the key to a murder, isn't it? If you can tell why and how, you can tell who.'

'Ian,' Christopher shouted, 'help me.'

But Ian did not move.

Xanthe went on, 'Ian, too. Both of you. You will kill us all because you know we have to die.'

'We didn't always have to,' Ian said softly. 'There was a time when we wouldn't have had to. Forty years – a whole generation that could have opted for not having to. If. You know the If.'

Christopher was saying, 'Xanthe, my love, my beloved, I'd never leave you, never go from you –'

'No.' She pushed him away, out of physical touch. Her arms were extremely strong. 'It's too late for lies. And all those Ifs were lies. That's what came to you in the church, wasn't it? The time it is now.'

He was crying, but the tears only made his eyes brighter. 'Perhaps,' he said.

'Dear Christopher.' She used the words Ian had said in the morning.

'No,' he said, answering her directly. 'Not now. Not any more.'

'I know. That's the how of it.' After a while she added, 'I'm staying here. Where I know myself. Where my am-ness is,' and reached for his hand. 'God go with you, my love . . .'

And he repeated himself, 'No. Not any more.'

Ian made a sick sound in his throat and Christopher's bright, pure eyes turned to him. 'Oh no. God's there. It's not as simple as that, Ian.'

'Don't explain. I don't want to hear.'

'Why not? We're dying, aren't we?' Xanthe cried out. 'Bloody doctor – we're dying. Save one soul, Doctor.' She watched him light a cigarette.

'Doctor?' hoarsely.

'You're not dying yet, my dear. Just living. That's all we're doing right now. Living.' Then, viciously, 'Ask your priest.'

'Christopher?'

Christopher was kneeling on the floor. The home-made wine had blackened his lips and his face was white. His fingertips touched the floor, like a runner's at the block. In the dimmed light his pupils were huge so that his eyes were now black gems set in silver. For a while he said nothing at all, and then, 'Why should you think that living and dying are different? They are the same thing, aren't they? Words – just words. Like "saving" is a word. There is no saving. There never has been. He failed, you see – Jesus. It wasn't enough for Salvation, what we did to Him. He was only the Son, after all. The nearest we could get, but still not enough. You can't kill God, and there isn't any other way.'

It was very quiet in the kitchen when Christopher had said that, but a quiet without thought. There was no room, no time for thinking. A woman in a crowded wood, running; a theocidal priest with a painted face; a medicine-man turning away the dying. Not even Christopher and Xanthe were touching each other in any way. They were all separated from each other by the bulk of their own consciousnesses, each taking up vast areas of space, so vital had their feeling for themselves become and so different from each other's. The room had become uneven, its walls tilting in, its ceiling sloped, all its angles acute. In it, their breathing was large and warm, almost excretal. They gave out odours and moisture from their skins and clothes; even their food steamed and released greases and compound atoms that knocked, cluttered and repelled each other in the overladen atmosphere (and outside, the air was as still as the heart of a feldspar).

Ian said, 'Dear Christ, what are you going to ask of me?'

Xanthe said, 'Christopher, Christopher, I love you,' beating her hands on her thighs, her face and hair awry, her neck sinews like a high-wire on which her frenzy pranced. It was a moment of panic, of screeching for help.

Christopher said, '. . . and that the world pass away . . .' as if that
was all that was known of the sentence. There were still tears
running from his eyes but he did not sob.

Ian said, 'Hello? Hello. No, it's Ian Hoskins. Can you hang on a
moment and I'll see.' He was talking into the telephone. It must
have been ringing. He covered the mouthpiece with his hand.
'Christopher? Can you? It's Polly. Are you in?'

'No, he's not in, you fool. He's not in.' Xanthe had never been
heard to speak like that; so violent.

'Why not?'

'Can you hold on a moment, Polly? He's just coming.' Ian held
the telephone against his palm, turning his back on Christopher. He
did not want to see him dry his tears or push himself up. He did
not want to see Christopher in need of help. When he felt him
beside him, he turned round. Christopher had made no attempt to
dry his face; he held himself very upright as if he wore his crying
like a medal or a mark made as Cain's was, and for that reason.
And he was without shame.

'Polly?' he said, taking the telephone. 'Are you all right, dear?'

The telephone gabbled, hollow, emotional in its robot way.
Christopher said, 'There are rules, you know,' and, 'I'll deal with
all that,' and, 'Can you give me your full names, dates and places
of birth, so on? Parents' full names?' When he put the receiver
down, he said to them, 'Polly and Danny want to be married.' It
was a statement, not news. Xanthe, waxen-faced, raised her hands
as if to make a gesture, but they dropped back, strengthless.

'Now,' she said. 'Now.'

'Yes, now. And will you give her away?'

'Give her away? Give Polly to Danny? "Give" her? Me? Now?'

'That's right.'

'It's not. It's bloody not. I'll do no such thing. Not even now.
Especially not now.'

'Xanthe, this is no time for politics,' Ian said, sharply.

'No, it's too late for that too. Did Polly ask?' She turned jerkily to Christopher.

'Yes.'

'Just what you said, Ian, isn't it?' she said rapidly. 'We're all still living. Not really living, not with life in us, you know? But physically, you can hardly say we're dead yet. Luke Lyons is dead and has a coffin to prove it . . .'

'He hasn't, you know,' Ian said to Christopher, underneath Xanthe's voice.

'. . . and we'd put him in the ground if we could unfreeze it to the regulation sanitary depth. But we haven't got any coffins. (What'll they do with us all, Ian? Lime pits?) So we must be what you might call, at another time, alive. You know, lentils and butter-beans in the cupboards as if we might soak them tonight. My God, do you feel like soaking the lentils, Christopher? Do you, Ian? But Polly does, as it were. So if she does, then I can and I'm doing no giving away of woman-flesh as if it were a bag of lentils. If she wants to marry Danny, she can give herself to Danny. Anyway, women can't, can they?'

'If they want it that way, yes.'

'Revolution? Now. I can't believe any of this. None of it.' She stared at the kitchen. At its acute angles, at the atoms knocking each other around like pinballs, at the bright colours dancing around the wine bottle and Mr McAdam and the sink taps. Cerise, lemon, sapphire, quince-green, marguerite, raw-lead, brilliants, heaving and rising and quivering in sharp pulses. 'Oh God,' she said, 'why doesn't it all go away?' She shook Ian's hand off her shoulder. 'No, you have nothing to say to me, Ian love.'

'No,' he said, 'maybe not. Oh, I'm so tired. Danny, of all people . . . what a peculiar thing to do. What an eerie, weird thing to do. Is it funny, d'you think? Comical?'

'No,' Christopher answered him fiercely. He was filling the

kettle. 'Ian, find the coffee powder. Cups, Xanthe – no, mugs. There's a lot to do.'

'There's nothing to do,' Xanthe shouted at him from the table.

'Mugs, mugs, mugs,' he shouted back. 'There's Luke to bury, Freda to comfort, Polly to marry, the bishop to square about a Special Licence over the phone – which he won't do. Why haven't we heard from the bishop? I'd have thought a roneoed "pastoral" would be just the thing for this Sunday – we'll have Sunday won't we? No? No, maybe not. Perhaps that's why he hasn't sent it. But if he did, I'd read it – I would, you know. Candles, we want. The whole store of them. People like candles. Ian, you know that strange fellow who lives in the flat over Stephen's shop? Dee something or other, plays the piano and the organ. How would he be taking this, do you think?'

'Is this coffee powder?'

'No. I think that's a sort of soup or gravy, or both. Xanthe? The coffee jar is red.'

'This?' Ian held up a scarlet cookie tin.

'Yes. Well?'

'I think someone might have to tell him what's going on first. He may not have noticed. Why?'

'I can't see my staid Roley playing the organ into infinity, and certainly not the sort of music I want –'

> *For the Lord our God shall come*
> *And shall take his harvest home*

Xanthe sang to the very coloured, rising table-top.

'Not exactly. Mugs, mugs, mugs. But Dee would, if he could handle it. Could he, Ian?'

'I'd imagine that would be the way he'd want it. You'll have to go to him, though – he'll have the phone off the hook. He only makes out-going calls, apparently. Doesn't like being interrupted. What's in your mind, Christopher?'

'I'm going to hold a requiem for the whole world. For you and Xanthe and Innocent III; for Piltdown Man and Jesus of Nazareth, for Virgil and Luke Lyons – put the coffee powder in, man, the kettle's boiled.'

Ian looked at him for a long moment. 'Who is that going to help?' he asked, softly.

'And who are you going to help?' Christopher answered him.

They watched each other. It had been a long friendship, at times a partnership. It went very deep into both of them. It had love in it, and disappointment, trust, Xanthe, other people's babies and motor accidents, guilts and terrors and a great deal of accustomedness grown out of dreadful nights and false dawns. Once, when Ian had returned from the only holiday he had taken outside Martinminster (where the fishing was so good), they had almost embraced. Ian knew the feel of Christopher's shoulder beside his and he could feel it now, although the man was at the other side of the kitchen from him in one sense. In another sense he was beside him, staring at the same thing but seeing something different. Help – as if there was any help to be given. What had the man said (damn the man): 'It wasn't enough for Salvation, what we did to Him'? Meaning? Meaning, given that the speaker was Christopher? Which way was he facing, this man at his shoulder, whose bones he could feel against his own, although they no longer shared any blood?

Sitting at the table, Christopher pushed a mug towards Xanthe.

'I haven't gone away,' he said softly. 'I'm never going away. Do you believe me?'

'I don't want to be afraid,' she said, not raising her head from the table. 'I don't want to go into this afraid.'

'No.'

'It's everyone sitting afraid at tables with rejected dinners. Where are there people who are doing things, who have the use of their hands and eyes and legs? Why aren't they running away, or rioting, or killing themselves, or screaming? If I went up the bell tower now I ought to be able to hear the whole country screaming, but I wouldn't, would I?'

'No.'

'It's numb in here.' She pressed her hand against her forehead. It was wide and pale and sticky, lined with displaced tresses of hair. 'It's cold-numb and not thinking, and outside it, all around is shot to hell with colours and beats and messages that aren't for me. Christopher, Oh Christopher, I don't want to be so afraid.'

He put his hand on her cheek. 'I'm afraid, too. Everyone is. All over the world there are people sick with being afraid. But it's only a thing – a body-thing –'

'It's my body that's important, Christ! Can't you see that?' She sat up, wrapping her arms around her belly as if her bowels were riven or her stomach opened to the raw air. She hugged and rocked, swaying over her belly, her hips, her breasts, her face distorted with the pain of it. Grunting with the pain of it. 'I'm not afraid of being dead. I'm afraid of dying. Of being not quite dead enough. And of you, in your cloth, saying, "Suicide is the sin against the Holy Ghost," and of being afraid of not believing you. Because you'd be there then; oh then you'd be there enough. And tonight you are stupid enough to ask Ian what he's going to do to help. I'm sorry, my beloved, my beloved Christopher, but you are stupid – stupid.'

He withdrew a little, clasping his hands, looking at the odd pallor of his knuckles. 'Well, Ian?'

Again, there was a pause. It was the silence of profound movement; the shift from one mode of existence to another. Propelled by Xanthe's physicality, they had moved more rapidly through their states of understanding than time allowed for. One of the odours in the tight room was that of her cold-sweat; of fading shampoo and fear and womanness, a smell that hooked into their affection rather than their love. It made her more profoundly one of them than the pungency of sex or the evocations of perfume. Christopher was not aware of it, but it twisted in his mind. Ian was aware of it. He put his hand out behind him and lifted his case, which he had left by the dresser, up on to his knee. He took out a flat, white cardboard packet and a little golden bottle of translucent capsules. He put them on the table, not quite letting go of them. There was no expression on his face. The yellowed electric light made the dark little bottle glow like a luxury Christmas gift.

'Is this what you mean?' he said to Xanthe.

Her mouth twisted. Two gargoyles peered round her shoulders, gripping her by the hair and neck sinews as they leaned forwards across her, blocking out her own face. They reached out, very slowly, panting.

Ian drew the two little containers back a little, closer to him. The gargoyles, watching, swallowed.

'It is, isn't it?'

The gargoyles said nothing; did nothing; sucking at the pills with their eyes only. Ian moved his hands again. The pills moved forwards on the table, towards Xanthe where she cowered behind the two naked expressions.

'One:' he said factually, 'potassium iodate – to build resistance against the effects of radiation. They have been stockpiled by the pharmaceutical firms for a decade or so now. Hence the resistance towards nationalizing such companies. These bottles can now fetch three figures in the Home Counties, where people still like to believe in them and supplies have run out. Two: to kill.'

The eyes switched to the white cardboard package. 'There are not so many of these, because a repeat dose is unnecessary, you understand. None the less, their price on the black market is exceptional. They are not on general sale like the others originally were, but they were issued a few days ago to particular professional departments to dispense in certain strictly defined circumstances and places. Of course, there is the logistical problem that when such circumstances arise, they will have rendered the means of dispersal inoperable. However,' – he tapped the packet with his finger-nail; it made a flat, slightly rattly, noise – 'the demand for them is high. Over the last six months there have been numerous reports of doctors and hospital workers being offered very high sums for these; and gangs that used to deal in speed and crack and so on, have turned over whole networks to the production and marketing of this stuff.' Again he tapped the packet with his nail and edged it further into the centre of the table. Then, very slowly, and raising his hand as if in a mock blessing, he let go of them. Christopher turned away. The things that Xanthe had become were unaware of a slight trickle of saliva from the lips. Ian's hand dropped back over the little box.

The rapping of the Victorian brass knocker on the rectory front door sent the crowded, odorous atoms colliding and knocking, yapping furiously around the kitchen, slapping at the human ears like a nurse at a child deep in fantasy. It maddened them, breaking into the intense, private cabin in which they were travelling, scattering time – past, future and present – around them in jagged chips and split planks. It was Christopher, perhaps because he had travelled further than the other two, who eventually went to answer the knocking. His step was untidy. A moment later he came back, followed by a man in grey fatigues.

'That's it – that's the same uniform,' Ian said loudly.

It was certainly not a police uniform and not quite recognizable as army, with the minimum of insignia and a webbing belt with a number of unoccupied clips. It could almost have been a delivery-boy's uniform, or a security firm's, but was a little too quiet for either; a little too anonymous. The wearer had unreadable, china-blue eyes and carried a white helmet politely by his side. Christopher shrugged, by-passed.

'Dr Ian Hoskins, MD, of 43 Whitegate Street?'

Ian stood up. 'That's me.' He spoke very calmly, but he had gathered up the two little sets of pills in his hands. Xanthe was watching his hands. Christopher was watching his eyes.

The uniformed man held out a plastic-coated card with a photograph on it. Ian moved to read it carefully. 'Martinminster Reserve (North), Special Command,' he said flatly.

'If you would accompany me, sir. You are wanted at headquarters.'

'Whose headquarters?' Christopher snapped.

The uniformed man was looking at Ian. 'Sir? As one of the local general practitioners . . .'

'I see.'

'I have a car, sir.'

'I didn't hear any car,' Christopher snapped again.

Ian tossed the little bottle up in the air. It spun, gleaming like Baltic amber before he caught it and put it in his pocket.

'Cod-liver oil,' he said flatly at, rather than to, Xanthe. 'The others are calcium. I could leave them with you, but you're too healthy to need them. It's a question of finding out if you understand the significance of what you know. Do you understand, my dear?'

Christopher stepped forward. 'Ian, don't –'

But the doctor turned, as if to move to the door, his back to Christopher. The uniformed man held the door for him. Christopher had to step out of their way. The door shut behind them, then the front door. Three sets of footsteps rang on the frozen pavement. Three car doors slammed. A soft engine murmured like satin before the silence shut down.

Christopher leaned across the sink and opened the window on to the dark garden. The silence was out there too. Over the wall, the street-lamp burned sunset red on the low current. Xanthe put her face in her hands and began to cry, very gently, as if she were too tired to stop herself.

'I can't do it again,' she said. 'We've gone further than this. We can't go back and do it again.'

Inverted ogees of snow pressed into the arrow slit which the swallows had used in the summers. The moonlight picked them out among the dense black of the wall. Ivy clutched the stone cross that someone had placed over the door. The ivy had been growing over it for so long that no one knew it was there any more, but ice had collected in the horizontal groove every year and, if anything, constantly deepened it. A torch hung from a beam inside the old granary but none of its light escaped through the black-out ivy. Andrew Medway had placed nineteen brightly coloured, plastic sacks against the wall, under the arrow slit. Into a yellow one, he was shovelling the dry crumbly mixture of aged manure and desiccated soil which covered the floor. The ancient building had not been used as a granary for over a century, but had been fitted out with stalls for milking, although these, in their turn, had fallen into disuse. Hens scratched in there in the winter; hand-tools, spare sheets of corrugated iron, orange rolls of binder-twine, chicken-coops and garden furniture were kept dry there. The floor was dark and powdery on the top, but below the surface it was impacted into hard slabs, very deep and almost odourless.

Andrew had filled six sacks and was half-way through the seventh. A rat scuttled behind an old wooden feeding trough. There was sweat in Andrew's eyes; it trickled, salty, beside his mouth. The radio whined and bubbled beside him, Broadcasting House jammed by one of the exquisite satellites cruising, star-like, overhead. The light of the torch dipped. His shadow leaped gigantically. How many spare batteries had he? One set, two? Would Morag have any, hoarded away? The spade sliced through a large black beetle; its yellow insides spurted out on to his wellington. He stopped digging, unaccountably nauseated. 'No, oh no. No,' he whispered. He picked it up on the spade to throw it away from him; his hand shook; it fell back on to his foot; the pale slime was wet, like all insides, even human's. His, Sam's, Tansy's. He tried to stop himself thinking. What happens to the guts? Do they shrivel like spit on a hob, or implode wetly?

It would not happen. It had just happened to the beetle. It would not happen in a real war – a man's war. Funny how he thought of this thing as not a real war; not a man's war. Not like other wars. Women had been among the protagonists for so long – at Greenham, in Parliament, on the television. The men in the Services had been heard hardly at all. Who knew, who really knew? They would do the bombing, or firing, or whatever – they, as always, were the doers. The protesters, all long-haired wankers and clerics and arty-crafty types like Stephen Ridley with his silly little boxes of spinach seedlings on his sitting-room windowsill – Jesus, no wonder it had been hard to take it all seriously; this war that would not be a man's war. In a man's war Tansy would run the risk of rape. He had never been able to shake that image from his head. There were so many films that used the theme, documented it even, in other parts of the world or other times. Jesus, he would run amok with fighting at the mere thought of it. Oh God, he would run amok. You needed weapons to prevent that, to keep your women.

The half-beetle slipped off his foot. He leaped on it; again screamed out, 'No,' stamped, ground it into the old dung and rat-run soil until it disappeared. His voice had echoed a little; had hummed against the iron tie-rings in the old cow-stalls. He heard it still, vibrating among the rafters. 'No,' to what? The women? The things that women forced out of men? The great anonymous weapons that no hand ever held, no sweat ever clouded? The power that had no parameters, as the millions of women who had marched and marched and would not stay in their homes? Why could they not have stopped this? Why had they brought him to this, dung-shovelling in the night, wanting to shit with fear at the sound of his own echo? He had not cried since his first year at Marlborough. But he remembered the hot, helpless feel of it. He began on the eighth sack. It was blue.

The door creaked. Andrew stood rigid. A runnel of sweat fingered the base of his spine. The latch moved a little, the hinges creaking (such an old door, it had been hung on the day before Borodino). Andrew was exposed, he might as well have been naked, standing there in a suffusion of orange torchlight, with a spade in his hands and a very bright blue sack. He was naked because there were tears on his face. He lunged at the door, spade upraised, howling, 'Get out, get out –'

In the doorway, Morag. White-faced against the night, leaping aside from the flashing spade-edge. 'Christ, Andrew,' screaming.

'Oh God, you bitch.' He dragged her inside, banging the door to keep her noise out of the empty, freezing night. Leaned against it, grunting for breath. 'You silly bitch – you'll wake the dogs, the kids, what'll they think?'

Her eyes, black as scorpions, unutterably old and wicked with stings upraised to kill, crawled along his vision to get at him. He swerved aside, retreated to the wall where the bright sacks stood in line, some still empty.

'What the hell are you doing?' she said angrily.

'Angry? You're angry? What right have you to be angry, coming in on me like this?' (Discovering him naked, relieving himself, uncovered in the torchlight in front of her. That's what crying was – shitting in public with nothing on . . .)

'I heard you,' she said obstinately, watching him; seeing the tears.

He wiped his forehead and his face on his sleeve. 'You couldn't have heard me from the house.'

'I wasn't in the house.'

'Where bloody were you, then? Spying on me –'

'Shut up. It's you that'll wake the dogs. I was in the yard.'

'Doing what in the yard, for God's sake, at this hour?'

She had been going home to Ardcollie, but she could not tell him that. He would think her mad, standing in the snow and ice, shuddering with cold, saying that she was walking through the weedy gateway, hundreds of miles away. She said, 'Breathing,' to turn him off. He looked so odd, livid-faced and sweaty, bundled up in all those old coats and wellingtons at three o'clock in the morning.

'What's that doing?' she asked, touching the radio with her foot. He plunged for it and switched it off, furiously. The shrilling which he had ceased to be aware of, died. A rat was squealing in the manger, surprised by the sudden silence. 'Rats,' Morag said.

'Frightened?'

'You know I hate them.'

'Go back to bed, then. This place is actually seething with rats. Look over there –'

'Don't.'

He laughed at her. 'Where do you imagine they'd be? Scuttling out into the snow to leave the doomed ship? Jumping off Land's End in herds?'

She ignored him, looking pointedly at the bright sacks against the wall. 'Peculiar thing to do,' she said. Her voice was small and dry. It excluded explanation. It exposed him again. It provoked a childish desire to justify himself. He tightened his mouth so that it became a thin white line. She interpreted it as anger and backed

away, frightened of the bright spade gleaming in his hand. Seeing
her fear, he turned dismissively, returning to the sack, shaking the
dry muck firmly down into the bottom of the blue plastic. He
worked directly under the weak torch. She stood almost in the
dark. It was safer there. The skirt of her baby-blue nightdress,
which hung low under her coat, shimmered slightly as she
shivered. She felt weakness opening up in her.

'Help,' she said, but so softly that it scarcely reached him, and he
snapped.

'No thank you. I'll do this on my own.'

Do what? Was he mad? Was he going funny in the head, as she
thought she herself was, thinking she was walking to Ardcollie
when in fact she was just tramping up and down in the snow-
burdened yard? Was Andrew similarly filling Christmas-coloured
plastic bags with old dung in answer to some sudden vacancy in
himself?

'Where are you going to put them?' she asked indirectly.

'Against the cellar door, where do you think? In the attic? If you
and Tansy are going to go over the top, it might shut you up if I
looked as if I took her seriously. I'm only trying to help.' His voice
was thin and cold. She knew the tone. She usually heard it when he
was talking about other women. It was his trick for sounding
sincere. So what was the lie? She stood behind him, useless; in the
dark; doing nothing at all except wondering what he was lying
about while he heaved at the heavy spadefuls which were to stop
the world coming to an end. His breath steamed.

'Shall I bring in the wheelbarrow?' she asked, sarcastically.

'Got it,' he nodded towards a dark corner. It was indeed there.
Ready. She stared hard into the grim stone shadows for another
sign, but found none.

'I'm going to make tea,' she mumbled.

'You can bring me some.'

She decided that she would not. When she was back in bed, sipping in the soft bedside light, she heard him come into the kitchen below. His voice muttered unintelligibly and the kettle banged on the hotplate. Then china smashed. She switched out the light quickly, in case he came upstairs. She was shocked at her fear of him. She had never before had the courage to face that fear, but it had been there – she could see that now – ever since she had been afraid to turn him away when he first decided to marry her. She lay in the dark with the electric blanket on under her, watching the seconds click over on the radio alarm: 3.57, 3.58, 3.59 and so on. When the electricity finally died, it would not stop the time passing. Until . . .

Until? Morag sat up. Put the light on again. Stared at the room around her. It was a tip, a mess of clothes, photographs, light-weight antiques with flawed joints, untidied make-up, brushes with hair felted into them, contraceptives in an unclosed drawer, a hem down on the curtain. Until? Not If, any more? The pale-blue carpet, the worn slippers, the Damart vest. Only a few more days for her skin to touch them? Hands, these hands, slipping wedding-ring and thick cuticles – they were to go, in some way? That was dying? Knowing that you would only touch your lips, your cheeks, a few more times. Like a beloved going away for ever, only magnified beyond comprehension when it was the self parting from the self. It is not possible to say goodbye to one's self; is it therefore not possible to understand the state called dying? Until should still be If, and yet it was not. Somehow one had become the other, and she had been dozing at the time. There was only one person who could tell her how it happened – what had happened.

She half-ran down the passage to Tansy's door and banged on it.
'Tansy, are you awake?'
'No.'
'That's a lie,' Morag said unguardedly.

From inside, Tansy's voice laughed harshly. 'Of course it is,' she said, so that Morag felt the familiar, hot stupidity rush into her, felt thickened and clumsy with it. There was no answer that she would be capable of making.

'Can I come in and talk to you?' she said doggedly, innocent of any concept of self-respect.

'No,' in the same, harsh voice.

'Tansy, I need to talk to you.'

'I've nothing to say to you.'

Next door, Malkie wailed in his sleep. If she had woken him he would call and yell and demand light, attention, Marmite, gluttonous for all-consuming care.

'What are you doing?' Morag hissed. It sounded as if Tansy were dressing or undressing.

'You don't want to know.'

'Oh but I do,' Morag insisted, but it was a distraction. 'I have to talk to you.'

'I'll tell lies,' Tansy warned, laughing again.

Because she had never had any pride in herself, it cost Morag nothing to scrabble at her daughter's door, neither quite knocking nor quite trying the handle.

'Door's locked,' Tansy said imperviously.

'Lovey, please . . .'

All she could hear was the window opening. Then what must be Tansy climbing on to the flat roof over the utility-room.

'Tansy,' she shouted, now beating savagely against the locked door, 'Tansy, come back, darling, please.'

But there was no answer. The silence was absolute. Into it Malkie wailed, 'Mummy, Mummy, I want you.'

She ran down the stairs and out through the back door. There was an extra shadow among the silver and black stripes of the moonlit shrubbery, and then only the stripes.

'Tansy,' she screamed. 'Tansy, come back.' Her voice drifted out among the ribes and kerria and over the railings into the stark branches of the naked ash and beech. Owl-calls, dissipating into stillness among splinters of frost and starlight. The land out there was so vast; in the moonlight even Croke's Wood, hunched up against the skyline and leaking phosphorescent greens, was mountainous and unpredictable. Into all that, Tansy had vanished.

The cold in Morag's veins was nothing to do with the deep frost. Out there was a wilderness of alternatives. Out there, Tansy ceased to be imaginable and therefore to be. Andrew . . . She struggled with her limbs, now as light and formless as the bog-cotton that grew on the heights behind Ardcollie; twisted them round, jerked and dragged them towards the granary door.

'Andrew –' She knew she sounded stupid. Dear Jesus, why did she always sound so stupid?

'What now?' The sacks were coloured like fairy-lights in the fading torch beam. Andrew was heaping them into the wheelbarrow as if it were a sledge, and reindeer waited in the voided stalls.

'Tansy's run away.'

'What do you mean?' He stopped moving; back bent away from her; antipathy holding him rigid.

'She's gone. I heard her climbing out over the utility-room and she disappeared out through the shrubbery.' Her voice rose as she forced words out. 'She was wearing black. Like a – a – one of those models of Malkie's.'

'Don't be stupid.' He sounded breathless. 'You've lost your head. Go and look in her room.'

'Andrew – I saw her go.'

He turned. He straightened slowly. He was huge. He was Gog and Magog, he was Charon, he was one of the kept secrets of another time. The secret split open and burst into the granary. Morag screamed, 'Go, go, go.'

The storm of his passing threw her to the ground, pitching her into the trenches and balks of dirt where he had been digging. The great wooden door screeched on its hinges, hurled back against the iron ivy. His bulk crashed through it and the moonlight plunged in, flooding the stalls and beams and old chains still clinking from rusted rings.

'Oh God,' she whispered into the shit. 'Oh God.' It was totally silent. 'God.'

She went back to the house. Her feet were blue. The cat saw her come in and leaned his back up against her waist when she stood by the table. The floor was littered with pieces of china, the remains of the mug Andrew usually drank out of. She remembered. She had not brought him tea. Well, he was gone now. She dredged up the image – like a devil being cast out he had swept out of the granary. The cat was warm and furry, but she was too weak just now to stroke him. He stroked himself upon her. She put her face down and he bumped her forehead with his own. If she let herself cry, her wet tears would send him away. She wanted to cuddle him, to obliterate herself in his fur, to bury herself in his love. He passed under her arms again, purring profoundly in his throat. She listened to the ignorant purr, filled with pity for him. The broken china must have frightened him.

'Mummy, Mummy, I want you . . .'

Well, so did the cat.

She was sitting by the Aga, the cat on her knee, when Andrew came in. Malkie had fallen asleep in the end. She had not gone upstairs to him. Andrew's in-coming had hurled at her from the door, throwing her seclusion backwards to the far end of her conscious mind, where it bruised and cowered. Physically, she moved her bare feet under the chair. The cold of outside clung like a stink to Andrew's anorak and trousers. There was snow on his boots.

'I can't find her,' he said. He sounded surprised. He came up to the Aga; that brought him very close to Morag. She could not look levelly at him, but had to stare up, like a thrown jail-bird from the floor. 'I followed her footprints to the road, but I can't see anything more there. It's just sheets of ice. What was she doing? Was she really running away? Where to, for Christ's sake?'

'She didn't say,' Morag mumbled. 'She just went. She was very rude.'

'Did she take anything with her? A bag?'

'I couldn't see. I was the other side of a locked door.'

'But how did you get there? Why were you at her door? What did you say to her?'

'Nothing. I didn't say anything.'

'You must have bloody said something, or she wouldn't have known you were there to be rude to,' he said icily. 'Jesus, can you blame her?' He seemed to be speaking to the ceiling. 'So? You said?'

'I just said I wanted to ask her something.'

'What?'

'I didn't get a chance to ask her.'

His face, when he lowered it at her, was covered with pits and pores; with little black hairs, some of them cut blunt, others longer and fine. His skin was slightly greasy, the colours and tones sharply different from eyelids to chin. The nose, the talking lips, the fingers in the eyes, all came straight at her, jabbing at her.

'Ask her what?' the lips drove at her.

But she would not, could not, let him penetrate her fear like this. Not now that she had found it and given it a name. She shut her eyes; flimsy, pale little lids through which even light could seep. 'I didn't get a chance,' she muttered stubbornly. She did not think that he would strike her. That did not come into his canon of the things men did to women. Only this punitive thrusting. She knew

her eyelids were not strong enough to keep him out. Already there
were little red blood spots in them. Her sigh caught her unawares,
it came from so deep in her body. All their conversations had been
like this, unless they were diktats. Suddenly she turned sideways in
the chair, avoiding him (but he was six feet away from her). Her
body mimed what she could not speak. It would not matter, would
it, what she said, now; only what her body said. She opened her
eyes to see what private part he was going to thrust at next. He
was not six feet away; he was leaning right over her.

'What did you do to Tansy?'

'Nothing.' She slipped out of the chair; oh lithe, supple as an
athlete, slithering out of his reach, out of touch. Out of danger?
Good body; it had stayed with her all this time and she had not
known it; just let child-bearing and shopping and slip-shod sex and
hours standing on the cold tiled floor, washing and cooking and
ironing, knock it about and bully it. But it was still with her.

'We did it,' she said, standing away from him, her hands
jammed in her pockets.

'Now what are you trying to put over? What d'you mean, "we"?'

'You and me, Andrew. Not listening to her. She was right, you
know. She's right. There is going to be war. And she's run away
right into it. We made her –'

'You shit of a woman,' he said. The rage uncoiled in him,
visible, streaking out into his muscles and sinews like heavy chains
in a moment of oceanic danger. Watching it, Morag backed right
round the table; he moved, uncoordinated, staring at her. She had
struck him, but did not know how.

'We should have let her talk to us about the war,' she shouted.

'There's no fucking war . . .' He was screaming at somebody –
was it her? 'There can't be a fucking war . . . It can't happen, you
stupid bitch.' He stopped. 'Fucking war,' he whispered, turning
away, gripping the Aga rails. 'It doesn't exist.'

She ran to the window. It had a pale yellow venetian blind over it (it clattered romantically on summer evenings, putting her in mind of Cannes or small Corsican hotels). One side-string broke away from the plastic laterals as she wrenched at it. Outside, over and beyond the barn roof and the skeletal limbs of the shade-tree in the seven-acre, the green aura of Croke's Wood seeped into the sky.

'There it is – there's the war. There.' She was breathless. Andrew did not look up from his own hands, rotating the Aga rail in its sockets, over and over.

'Look at it,' she screamed.

'Pretty bloody stupid if they didn't even pretend to have defences,' he shouted, not looking. Only at the turning rail, over and over.

'Like us? What pretend defence have we? Just saying that it can't happen? What has that done for Tansy? How's that going to protect Sam? Or Malkie? Not a very good pretence, is it?'

He gulped at air; pushed himself away from the Aga. 'All right, all right, damn you. What do you think I've been doing all night, all on my own so as not to scare you, while you've been snivelling and spying and driving Tansy out? I've been out there in the sodding cold, working it all out for you and the kids.' He held his hands out and stared at them; they were filthy and yellowy-white with cold. He sounded sincere, as if he almost believed what he was trying to make her believe. In a moment, she thought sickly, he'll ask me to warm his fingers for him. 'Making sand-bags out there by myself.'

'Shit-bags,' she whispered, acid seething in her gullet.

'Shut your bloody mouth and get on with it. Or would you rather stand there, twittering and whinging and take a nice cup of tea to bed? Or maybe you'd care to take the Land Rover and see if you can find your panic-stricken daughter, before – Jesus – before anyone else does. Or am I to do that at the same time as I'm trying to protect you and the boys in here? Well? Which?' In the white of his face there were two, deep red spots low on his jaws. When he crossed the room his feet fumbled and he had difficulty in opening the door under the stairs. The cellar gawped, black. He clicked the switch but there was no light. 'Fucking bulb.'

She found she had her legs crossed. Deliberately she stood straight. 'You take the Land Rover,' she said. 'You're a better driver than me. I'll do the bags if you tell me what you want.' Her voice was very soft. A little sing-song, as if she were a bit mad, but not dangerously so. He could not see her face; only the old tweed coat sloping off her shoulders and the length of baby-blue nightdress between it and her bare feet. 'What am I to do?' she asked, politely.

And that was when she knew what was coming. When she saw the blanket of ignorance behind his eyes – saw that they were tunnels, blocked off, leading nowhere. They were big eyes, blue and long-sighted, and she had always looked away from the expression in them. But now she looked, because there was no expression at all to be afraid of. He did not know what to do.

For a particle of a second she acknowledged terror. Since Mummy and Daddy it had always been Andrew's will that had been done. ('Whatever are you going to do?' Prue had said in that funny old world the far side of the time that was Now. She had done nothing. There had never been anything of her own inside her that she had had to do. Andrew's will had filled her.) Now there was no Andrew, or the same as no Andrew. How could she do anything?

Extraordinarily, terror passed. She was a good shot now, wasn't she? The memory leaped in her like a quickening child; she had become a good shot. Morag Colquhoun, shooter. She clutched at the front of her coat, twisted the cloth in her hands. She noticed with surprise that her nipples were quite hard.

'I take it you're going to build a bunker in the coal cellar?' she said, still polite, pointing at the chill, dark hole of the cellar door.

'That's what they advise,' he said, coolly. He should have been an actor, she thought, except for the eyes. 'You and the kids can go and sleep in there till you feel better. I can manage on my own – I usually do, anyway.'

'How lucky.' She should not have said that. It brought a pulsing into the dark blotches on his cheeks.

'Set it up while I go after Tansy. I expect she's over at the Dipyard with Stephen Ridley. She's always in and out of that bloody shop of his, drinking tea with all those hippie types and buying anti-nuclear gimmicks.' He was rattling the keys of the Land Rover, shaking and clattering them in his hand, violently, violently.

The Dalmatians burst into barking. Morag started, staring at the window where the broken blind trailed lopsidedly.

'Damn fox – I'll get him one of these nights.'

'Headlights. It's Tansy – something's happened to Tansy.'

She knocked against the wheelbarrow, full of its bright sacks. It scraped on the tiles by the back door. Andrew's hands, useless, dangled at his sides. The coloured patches in his cheeks faded. He said, 'Who?' as if Morag had him by the throat.

'Tansy?' Morag was at the door as the sharp rapping began.

It was Tansy. She looked so little in front of the two, grey-uniformed men. Over the back door Malkie had pinned up a huge circle of cut-out paper holly leaves and ivy and spruce fronds which Sam had once been forced to make at primary school and had hated ever since. Now, in the paled light, it haloed one of the officers. He stood there, natural, of the forest. His eyes shone under the light bulb; the cold had turned his skin thick and dark. Peering out of a forest – what forest? Croke's Wood or somewhere felled when Now was once upon a time and he might have worn a horn or a gold coil around his neck. But all that was in the past now and he was pushing Tansy gently in front of him and fumbling in his top pocket like a policeman.

Morag shouted, 'Tansy,' and grabbed her arm, pulling her properly into the room so that doors could be shut and forests and strangers hurled back into the dark from whence they had slunk, up to the very door of the home.

Tansy's arm felt soft and unnatural. 'Oh bugger,' she whispered. Her eyes slid away from Morag's.

(Tea. Make tea. Retreat to the stove. Fill kettle. Think hard if there are any clean mugs. Think hard about tea-bags, about little spoons. Let the children watch the nasty film over there by the door. Close the gate that keeps Morag Colquhoun safe inside the walled garden at Ardcollie.)

'Got a big cellar, have you, sir?'

Andrew stiffened and brushed his hair back over his head. 'What are you doing with my daughter?' His voice sounded peculiar.

'Just gave her a lift home. It's a bit cold to be walking on a night like this.' He was a big man, solid at the neck and thighs. He sounded as if he came from London. 'You are Mr Andrew Edward Medway, of Crosby Spring Farm, Near Martinminster?'

'Yes. Where did you find her?'

'Very sensible precautions, if I may say so. Got all your tins and lights and essentials down there already I suppose?'

'Who are you? Where are you from?'

Why was Andrew not shouting? She expected him to shout.

'Just the unit in this area, sir. Mind if I have a look?' He took a minimal step towards the cellar door.

'You'll go nowhere in my house.' Still he was not shouting; guttering, rather, as in a nightmare.

'Just as you say, sir. But quite a lot of the wives like a bit of advice on the actual arrangements of the shelter – placing of lights, Elsans and so on, the fresh-air packs, you know?'

The strange noise was Tansy, laughing or something, her head down and one hand to her mouth.

'And you must be Mrs Morag Fiona Medway?' He was reading from a list on a clipboard. The haloed one stood further back, the glittering eyes looking at Andrew's coloured sacks.

Morag stared at them, nodding. 'Colquhoun,' she said, but they did not seem to hear her.

'And Samuel Andrew and Malcolm Kenneth are upstairs in bed? Eleven and nine years old?' But they were not really questions. Still Morag just stared. It must have been Andrew who answered, because the Londoner smiled slightly as if turning away an insult.

'This isn't sand, it's dung,' the forest man said suddenly. He was looking into a yellow fertilizer sack. Tansy made the strange noise again and tore at the cuticle of her thumb with her teeth.

'Didn't get sand in time? Oh dear. Well, I expect manure will do very well. A very thoughtful adjustment to the situation. Now, I expect young Tansy here could do with a nice hot drink, Mrs Medway.'

It was all white and empty. Morag could hear the voices, pinging around the naked walls and flowing past on the cold breeze but because she did not understand the language, she ignored them. She was just pouring the hot water on to the tea-bags when she noticed that the forested one was standing beside her and talking English.

'Fifteen, isn't she?' he was saying in a light, nasal voice.

'Tansy?' Her voice had become blocked up as if there were blood or piss in her throat.

'Nice name, Tansy,' he said, picking up a teaspoon and stirring the floating bags. 'Has she started yet?'

'What? Started what?'

'Her periods. Menstruation.'

Leg-irons, steel doors, a tremendous blind helmet clanged close on her. The walls turning crimson and staggering inwards . . .

'Is she quite regular?'

Through the thick plating and the rubble of the walls she managed to nod turgidly and he was not there any more and boiling water from the kettle wandered slowly over the table edge and scalded her hip and belly.

'And who is your family doctor?' the Londoner was asking Andrew.

'If you –'

'Ian Hoskins,' Tansy said clearly. 'And watch out for my father.'

'We're watching. Thin, sandy-haired gent from Martinminster – tall. A bachelor. That the one?'

'That's Ian. Why do you want to know?'

Andrew had begun to move. The muscles in his arms and calves coiled; there was red in his eyes; the blood in his fists pounded against the rubble that pinned Morag down.

The forested one sat down at the table, pressing Tansy into a chair beside him. 'Have you been helping with all this?' he asked, indicating the cellar door, the shit-sacks. Andrew said something about 'Sitting beside my child' that was thick and gritty, but by the time he had lurched forwards with his hands out, the Londoner was holding his elbow. Andrew spun around; there was a small flutter of movement; there was Andrew stumbling, the cat springing for the windowsill; there was Tansy leaping up with a laugh that was far too old for her; there was Andrew thudding to the floor, his shoulder against the Aga, at Morag's feet. Cautiously she put out a foot to see what it felt like, Andrew being thrown down.

The two men were standing. Morag thought one said, 'There's a place for her in town. She's not on the first list but there is a vacancy. She's a lucky girl. One of the council families moved just before Christmas, and took the daughter out of our area. Tansy is technically a month or so on the young side, but time will put that

right, won't it? You'll get her back in a few days, no doubt. You
understand what all this is about now, don't you, Mrs Medway?'

He said a lot of other things, about Tansy not wanting to wait
till morning and the boys being too young and someone coming to
see them about it all tomorrow. 'She'll be in touch with you, and it
won't be for long, I'm sure.' But with Andrew muttering and
struggling to his feet and being thrust down into the old armchair
and the scald on her belly and the ratlike sounds of Malkie waking
upstairs to wail for her, Morag did not hear much of it. Just Tansy,
who was perhaps crying, suddenly shouting viciously, 'Don't
forget the tinned spaghetti, Ma,' as she went out between the grey
uniforms.

It was absolutely still in the kitchen. Outside, the Dalmatians
barked a little and there was that sensation of headlights sweeping
through the broken blind, but it was nothing. She understood that
Tansy had gone. But she did not know where or with whom. She
understood, too, that she and Andrew had done something terribly
wrong although she did not know what it was. She expected that
Andrew had made her do it, because she had nothing of her own
to do. She was desperately cold. The clock ticked. She forgot about
Andrew crying in the armchair and she forgot that Mummy and
Daddy were dead as she turned to the big range in the kitchen at
Ardcollie and asked Mummy to give her some hot tea. She was
shuddering so much that she was afraid of falling over, and when
Mummy put out her hand to steady her, Morag took it and slipped
to the floor, pulling Mummy with her. 'I'm sorry,' she heard
herself saying. 'Oh Mummy, I'm sorry, I'm sorry.'

The bed was the hurricane's eye. The earth wheeled on
its axis; the moon spun around the wheeling earth, rivers and
oceans swaying and pouring; herds and flocks gathered in invincible
migrations; patterns that gave a name to Time, when Time no

longer was. Stephen felt the billions of men scurrying and working and directing work, spinning in terror of the strange impetus they had loosed as if they were a cyclone of motes spiralling around him. But never quite touching him, for he lay in the bed with Barbara, very still, his face touching the woolly hat pulled over her hair. The wool hat was a reality in a way that the motes were not. There were not very many realities left because most of them existed in Time – a few more mealtimes, a few more times starting the recalcitrant car. Just one or two, perhaps. Then there would be so much noise, so much action, so much running and screaming, suffering. Bleeding and fire; bodies consumed in orchards of burning apple trees; masonry crashing into still lilyponds; bulls running, mutilated, through fallen streets.

Here, in this eye – this I? he wondered – here there was flesh, not black and bubbling, but warm and gentle in his hand. He was blessed. He lay cradled in the motion's nexus, by-passed, ignored by all machinery, left out of the calculations of the civilized world, and this would pass for being blessed, these days. He was not civilized. He was barbarian, as Antethos was, whose ageing profile caught the end of the moonlight through the little windowpanes. The waist of Barbara, that was the waist of Ariadne or Marguerite, or even Europa herself, loved his arm. Soft ewes had worn the wool that lay between his skin and hers, that had brushed primroses and March sun-darts and the footprints of hares. There was a whole world between their skins, and he laid his ear against her shoulder to hear the lapping of the green cretaceous seas in the fibres of the wool that the ewes had borne.

(Between my fingers the planet turns in time, and I touch it all, even the eye-sockets of brontosaurus down among the coal measures, with the whorls of my fingertips, unique to me as my life spirit. Soft breasts, she has, floating as if asleep upon the ages, reflected cupolas of love in the Now of my hand's palm. I hold them, less than boldly, afraid to leave my imprint upon this truth, this first food, this *sine qua non* of us all. To my finger the nipple rises as if in greeting and in the stardust her lips open. What is within? Words? No. Not them. Expressions of the over-convoluted brain, the sick side-turning taken three million years ago – the terminal mistake in evolution – not them. No, the small, sharp teeth of the omnivore; the warm breath of the sleeping mammal; the shining saliva that is still sweet, tastes, now I touch it with my tongue, of cocoa. How dear to taste of cocoa at the world's end . . .)

(Her eyes explore mine, open now. What is there to learn? Too close for learning, only the shine there, and the deep, covered wells that fall directly inward, inward. So full of shapes, her face, planes, textures, leaning up to be touched by my touching with lips that have grown fuller and gentler without words, and, oh, hungrier. Hunger all through the arteries which beat now, thud, as if flailing grain for bread for food for us. By her hipbone it is fireside silk; by her buttocks the cool of riverine boulders; the arches of her feet bridge my calves; her fingers take my neck, drive my spine.)

(A plane, the exact size of my hand, presses into my palm between the covert thighs. Its expanding heat explodes into my belly, my thighs, as power. I spread my hand wide and hear her voice and see her mouth and my shoulders brake the force of the gods, such depth. That the gods feel this. Hear this. Reach this. Reach.)

In the dark unwinding, cradled in the storm's arms, he felt love. It held him in Barbara's arms, warmed and caressed him with Barbara's touch, lapped over and around him, bore him in her gender, but it was not of her. It was not for Barbara. His compelled flesh lay eased, damp and soft, its urgency drained by the deep greed of her vagina. Sated, she lay against him, still soft, full, pungent as a new artifact. The taste of lotus cloyed his tongue.

He saw himself an island where ripe fruit had fallen; inedible fruits never to nourish response. To his lips common words came; he wanted to say, 'I love you,' but, being alone, had no reason to. As if in answer Barbara, who was in so many ways there, moved her arm against his breast. 'That was such a lovely thing to do, on a night like this . . .'

A night like this? He felt his smile in the curled skeins of her hair; felt older, darker faces smiling with his lips at such a night as this. In the wind's rising he thought, Is this not enough? and dozed again.

Snow began to fall, sparsely at first, then in spinning flurries from the north-east. In the thick dark it was invisible, sifting, whispering through stiff twigs; it settled on roofs and boughs, weighed down on Stephen's sleep, pressing out his dreams so that Barbara's hand, moving against his chest, uncovered his heart and he felt all his vital spirit flowing away. The snow settled over the new hair-crack between the house wall and the path, and slid down into it, down past the bulked foundation stones, deeper and deeper into the blackness until it touched Antethos' watching eyes and sealed them with white. Falling faster now, as the tin alarm clock ticked through its hopeless rotations, the snow caught the dog fox out beyond the Medways' farm, spinning low out of the dark into his yellow eyes and his black, elliptical pupils. It caught on the coarse guard hairs outside his fur, clinging to them in lumps and striae which cracked and hardened as he moved. It obliterated all but the spirit of sibilance, blinded all sight, ham-strung his running muscles. There was something – what? – to fear in its pallid scent. He raised his head into it, sniffing. There was only its own smell that was almost no smell, but which strangled. His ears flattened as the fear took him by the throat. He turned, staring; turned, stared again. A flurry caught him on the flank. Head down, he began to lope heavily through the shifting softnesses, one of sweet Polly Anderson's bantams swinging brightly from his jaws.

In No. 2, The Dipyard, the clock on the windowsill stopped. On the snow whirls, swaying between sleep and something other than waking, Stephen felt light steal above him, as a rising lily feels the wings of a dawn swan before day. Empty of dreams, a dead ship, the *Marie Celeste* of men, he swung upon the hour, waiting for discovery. Once he put out his hand and touched the shapes of Barbara's face. Would she discover him? Solve him? Was it that this was truly enough? Was all?

He let his eyes open and watched the pallor creep along the ceiling and the underside of the shelf. It was Barbara who found the tears on his cheeks and wiped them away with her warm fingertips.

She was crying. The snowflakes were streaming around the yard. The tears were streaming down her face. Polly loved the snowflakes passionately, she always had. The mystery of their shape-changing powers had stood in for hopes she never dared acknowledge – that the shape of things could change, that perhaps even she could change. Sex and alcohol, and her fear of the rattle of the postbox – there was to be some spiritual snow that would cover them over and make peaks and curves of a new and very ancient purity that would not smudge and fade away, leaving the empty bottles and the stained sheets sleazy in the mud. Every year she stood before the snow, all her tremendous lovingness laid open, crying to it: Come into me too. Come into me – as if she would shear herself open and expose her cut heart and her betrayed womb to its reshaping. Now it had come again to visit her at the end of time, and it would never penetrate her spirit, never cover her over and recreate the essence of Polly with its cold, clean magic. It had failed her. So hope had failed her, and that dumb, hurtful thing in the dark base of the heart that she named faith – even that was curling up and flaking away. The pain of Polly was giving up. So she wept, twisting the curtain in her hands, and the snow whirled down out of the brown sky, obliterating every shape under its lifeless surface until there was nothing left to know of Polly and Polly's dead and Polly's memories. Uncorrupt; un-quick.

Upstairs Danny was fiddling with the radio, twisting and turning it, clutching it to his quivering stomach as if the heat of his flesh could warm it into speech. His hands shook and his cheeks were studded with blue threads and knots. He, too, was believing – very slowly and in his own way and fighting it like a madman with red veins showing in his eyes. Below him Polly gripped the old curtain, crying for life and corruption. She did not name them, did not perceive them as conditions or states, but felt them in her blood and in the nerves on the surface of her skin. They were in the cloth of the curtain; in her hot tears; in the twisting pain in her bowels. They were herself. She was they. And they were dying. She raised her face from the curtain and, with her eyes shut, cried out aloud, a long, singing cadence that rang in the walls and vibrated in the foundations under the house. It was her music. Her self's music.

Danny heard it and his knees loosened. He sat heavily on the floor by the bed, dropping the cursed radio, slamming his hands over his ears.

The snow swept on, piling up in the corners of the yard, stealing away all the outlines, taking out the walnut tree beyond. There was no life. Not even a bird moved over the surface of the morning.

By the great window, Polly howled and howled and howled. Knew nothing, felt nothing, was only existent in the great sound that poured out of her into the silence that was and was to be, denying it reality with her music; hunting it away down into the future with the music of a still live, carnate being.

Upstairs Danny screamed, threshing his fists on the floor.

As suddenly as it had come, the music left her. Limp, she held on to the faded old curtains, swaying downwards into their folds. Outside, the last echo was muted among the whispering flakes. Only the sifting snow shifted in the drifts. The dull, lightless morning was empty. Polly was empty. Her music had gone out and left her a voided thing, a terrible loneliness around nothing. A hollow shroud. She did not know of herself as a shroud-shape, standing there by the window. She did not know of herself at all. Danny, creeping down the stairs, the radio clutched against his stomach, saw the shroud of her and stared at it. His bottom lip juddered.

And then they came back to her, out of the shadows where the reflected snow-light could not reach; essences of her that were almost familiar, but were changed. Some things never came back – those which had been too tender or too undeveloped to survive the music making – but her essential essence came. Her Pollyness. Not sweet any more, it was less, but very hard and bright and oddly distinct. And her power came. Cold-hammered by the sound which every animal can make only once, which Polly had now made and so never would again, she stretched out her hands to it, as if to take a heavy weapon, and the muscles in her wrists and forearms strained and twisted. She turned from the window, physical, shining; Frankie alight in her eyes and flaring like a diadem in her tangled hair.

When she moved, Danny flung his arm up across his face and shouted, 'Shut up, shut up,' as though she had said something.

She moved slowly towards him, her hands out, brilliant and corrupt and strange. Danny crouched, his teeth bared, his knees drawn up. There was stained white all around his eyeballs.

'No, no . . .'

Within a few inches of him she was unbearable.

'I'm going to die,' he screamed at her. 'I'm going to die, I'm going to die.' His voice ran out. Hot urine steamed on to the tiled floor around his feet. 'I don't want to die.'

'Danny?' But she had Frankie in her eyes and breast and throat.

'Jesus Christ, you scared the shit out of me, screaming. Polly, I'm going to die. Christ, Christ, don't you understand I'm going to die? We're all going to die? You've got to pull yourself together, Polly, screaming like that. Shit – we're going to die, Polly. Christ you and me.'

Could he not see Frankie? Not even, perhaps, see Polly?

'There's nothing on the radio.' He was jabbering now, kneeling in the piss, his left arm twitching. 'All the stations jammed – shrieking and whistling, I've tried and tried. And the electricity's failing. I can't stop it snowing – I can't stop –' Then, 'We've got to get out. We've got to go for help. Help –'

'Danny.'

His eyes rolled up to her at last. He looked at her. At her shining. His mouth stopped making words. A trail of saliva slithered from one corner of it to his chin. His eyes found her eyes. His pupils drove open. Black holes raked at her shining shape. At her self. Unshaven hairs stood out from his shrinking cheeks. 'Help,' he whispered. He looked down. He saw the piss and the blue veins in his ankle. The blackened eyes dragged up again. 'There isn't any help, is there? No.' Then later, when she had not answered, 'No, they aren't going to help us. They won't be any help.'

After a while she said, 'There is only you for you. And me for me,' and left him to moan himself quiet, walking away to the bare window where she stood, staring out at the snow.

       Walford Scott lurched resentfully down the pavement of the Buttermarket. The weight and shape of the coffin he was carrying to Freda Lyons's house made him waddle a little in an undignified manner. This both embarrassed and annoyed him. He was sharing the burden with his wife's nephew, from whom he had already taken a studded neck-collar and a bleached denim jacket with a union jack painted across the shoulders. But despite their unsuitability to the occasion there was nothing he could do about the Dr Marten boots or the skull-shaped ring which glittered every time the youth moved the hand which steadied the drape Scottie had drawn over the raw new coffin. Both of his hearses were practically empty of fuel and the night before Scottie had suffered a vision of himself running out of petrol on the way to the graveyard, and sitting there, impotently turning the starter of the black hearse with Luke Lyons and his flowers at his back, while the world came to an end. Because of this he had decided to carry the coffin to the house instead of risking even the teacupful of precious petrol which it would take to drive it there decently. It had not been worth paying one of his men to come in just to carry the thing along the Buttermarket.

The pavement was cobbled with lumps of rubbish and frozen snow glazed over with stained ice. The centre window of Boots the Chemist had been smashed and an ineffectual attempt made at looting. Now there were four men in grey military dress standing outside it, their backs to the builders who were nailing sheets of weather-board in front of the broken glass. Above them part of the neon sign had been smashed, perhaps by a thrown brick, and the two O's flicked irregularly on and off. 'OO OO O,' in the mucky, snow-laden morning.

'Excuse me, sir.'

Scottie smiled deferentially at the man who had moved into the centre of the pavement. Definitely officer class. So Scottie stopped, raised his eyebrows and looked helpful. He was to give his name, address, occupation and, if he didn't mind, what was he doing carrying coffins around at 11 a.m. in the morning with a young man who was evidently not a mortician? Scottie murmured his explanation about overtime, the petrol shortage and how his wife's nephew was spending Christmas with them because he had a girlfriend in Martinminster. He heard it all himself with a separate sort of ear, and heard how foolish and sick it sounded. Foolishnesses were the last things Scottie would allow around his coffins. He prayed sincerely that he should not become cross, especially with himself.

A few people who had been watching the builders screen the broken window, moved in to watch Scottie. The coffin was set on the ground; there was a little broken glass, some Christmas paper and what looked like spillage from a container of bubble-bath frozen to the pavement, so the coffin sat crookedly.

'OO OO O.' The broken lights struck the gilded plastic nameplate and handles.

Scottie said tightly, 'They can't wait for convenience sake, you know. They just pop off when their time comes and damn the difficulties.'

The grey man smiled slightly. 'I think we'll just have a look,' he said mildly, nodding to one of his men.

OO OO.

This one had pink palms and fingertips to his black hands. They slipped delicately along the perfect ruching of the white lining inside the long box, as tender and sensitive as a pinafored virgin's. OO OO. Into the pearly, satin-sweet privacy of the box the hot, inquisitive eyes of the bystanders poked and probed. The black hands with their own pink lining finished their search, caressed the exquisite folds and withdrew gently. Scottie sighed. Onlookers turned away, uncertain of their sin.

'I'm sorry,' the grey officer said gently and Scottie knelt among the frozen bits and pieces and replaced the lid. Lifting the coffin awkwardly, Scottie and his wife's nephew set off again across the uneven, smirched paving-stones.

'What were they looking for, mate? Acid?' the youth asked resignedly.

But Scottie was wondering how to charge Freda for the second-hand coffin which this one had somehow become under the greedy eyes glinting OO OO into its most discreet privacies.

Stephen had come into the shop to hear the books, but they were silent. He stood among them in an aisle near the back of the shop, his hands spread out, resting on their spines.

It was so odd, the quietness . . .

He had left Barbara at home with Tinker. She had said she would make a cake for tea. He had never, in his adult life, left behind in his home a woman who would make a cake for his return. He had even cried about it a little on his way into Martinminster. None of the intricately compounded words that he knew expressed the making of that cake; could make the name of that cake.

He had been so surprised to find that he had all the items required for cake-making in his larder. He had laughed about it – how he had never known that cakes could be made out of ordinary things like that. Barbara, in her woollen clothes and her striped woolly hat, had padded about in his thickest socks and his summer espadrilles, since she said that her wellingtons made her feet tired. She seemed different now that he knew the roundels of her breasts and the primitive slope of her belly; she rolled peculiar little cigarettes and peered distrustfully at the mouse droppings behind his cooker. He had moments of panic that he did not know who she was or where she came from, but as she knew all those things and they did not seem to trouble her, he let the panic subside unanswered. He thought that she must just go away, but he did not know how that might make him feel, and he knew very certainly that he did not want to know because right now he wanted to buy her a bar of soap. As he had never wanted to buy anyone anything so feminine and obvious before, he wanted time in which to understand where that desire came from, before anything else happened.

Boots was closed. It stood, malevolently saying 'OO OO O' over its smashed window, flaring OO OO whitely over the metal buttons and flashes on the grey uniforms of the men outside it. Stephen decided to go to the chemist's down Cooper's Hill. He went to the back of the shop and opened the till. There was £37 in it and he took it all out and put it in his pocket. As an afterthought he scribbled £37 on an order form and clipped it into the notes compartment of the till and stood looking at it. It was an act of hope. Some part of him must believe that one day he might have to think about his accounts again, but he could not contact that part. Not in his head or in his heart. It must live in his viscera, he thought. Unreachable. He looked more closely at the form. The small black writing was quite noticeably uneven. So his hands were afraid . . . Stephen-body was shaking. Very slightly, but manifestly.

There was no one in the shop to see his body. There had been no one all morning. The *Complete Works of Browning* and *The Art of Bonsai* did not sell well at the end of the world. None the less, he kept his back to the books. He was afraid of them. He had always been frightened of them. He had once been quite close to a girl who had written, and published, a novel during the time he had known her. That act of creation had terrified him far more than any of the odd things she had demanded of his shy body on the bright scatter-cushions in front of the gasfire. That other love, and the burning possessiveness for the people she had made, had scorched his very sense of himself and when, some months later, he had been in a bookshop and seen the book picked up and idly flicked through he had felt at once sick and humiliated by the shoddy rudeness of those gloved hands which had passed over the intimacies of people with whose privacies he had eaten, slept and lived for months. Not only were they there, out on their own and naked before all comers in a way he did not understand, but months of his own life were tossed into the trash when the book was dropped back on to the stand and another taken up.

That every created thing in some way depleted the creator and took into itself a nucleus of pure pain which might somehow, sometime, be released into the mind of the beholder, became a fixed point in his mind. The potency of the artifact terrified him. He turned around between books, carved walking-sticks, great paintings in galleries and wholesome pottery on country stalls, as if he were the needle of a compass that could not point away from a pole of agonies. It was with this sensibility that he heard the books in his shop cry out – sometimes in glory, sometimes in intolerable grief. When, rarely, he thought of Christopher's God – Pancreator – it was with horror that so terrible an idol should be thrown up by the cruel minds of good men. He never, of course, shared these thoughts with anyone, suspecting them to be a trifle daft for a bachelor bookseller in Martinminster . . . Only Mary, next door in the Dipyard, suffering among her Tracies and Buddies, had seen a most passionate tenderness in his eyes when she found him watching her over the wall.

But now the books were silent. Creation, it must be, had passed over into destruction. The great pages of Phaidon photographs were pressed darkly together, God's hand and Adam's, separate in the last night; the exhausted words that had once spiralled so beautifully out of bygone minds were folded upon each other, unlit and at ultimate rest.

He wondered at the silence.

Had he, perhaps, expected sirens? Running footsteps, old people howling like AWAKs, motorbikes, children in fear? Gunshots, even?

The street was nearly empty. Upstairs windows were lit, as on a dark Sunday. It was as if all the families had retreated and were waiting, since it was not yet time to go down screaming. How very private, he thought, this dying has become. The public trauma, the mass scream, were not there. Only little collections of lives, separate from each other, distanced, doing their dying in isolation.

So very lonely, this day. This Now.

Beneath his fingertips the spines of all his books were not quite cold yet.

So very lonely, dying, not yet dead.

This Now, that can go no further, because there is no longer a future tense. That, at least, has already achieved corruption.

Entirely Stephen-mind, he pulled away. The abstraction, the beloved abstraction of eternity, wheeled away from him, left him only with words which no longer had any meanings that he could contain, because the meaning had become the word and the familiar duality of thought no longer applied. Thoughts and flesh were different in kind. Stephen-body reached, lurched at Stephen-mind, clutched at the eyeballs, panic at sight.

(This is fear. This is real. I'm falling apart. Loosing. Maddening. Oh real fear. The books' spines are not quite cold. My hands, which are not quite cold either, know this. How else can we tell we are still living?)

Panic at seeing, in real ways, what was giving him such fear. Only the wind in the street. Only OO OO reflecting on blind windows from Boots around the corner. And the old man who had been lurking outside the shop for the last how long. Stephen had glimpsed him several times, once quite close, his burned-out face turned towards the dun sky, his eyes milky with age. Something about him made Stephen think of his own father. But the old man was not in any way like him. None the less, Stephen had a clear memory of the old man holding his hand, even of the feel of it, once. He let go of the books to step forward, but as he moved along the aisle the old man was not there – only the empty street and Stephen alone in his shop with the unspeaking books.

It was so very quiet, this Now. As if Time, too tired and disenchanted to go on, had come to a standstill on the sixth day of this cold Christmas. Outside Stephen's shop.

He took his hand from the shelf and looked at it. The fingers were stretched out – quivering very slightly. Why did it so desperately yearn to hold the old man's hand? Again.

He felt tears. He was growing used to them now and he did not know if they were for himself or for the old man who had started to move on again. He moved, and so the tears moved, slowly, obeying omnipotent laws, down Stephen's cheeks and on to his coat.

There was no shame in crying. Shame was other people's affair and there was no one here.

So the moment, the standstill, was over. An oddly shaped white car nosed down the street, a green light flashing on its roof. EE EE, like Boots. A scattering of snowflakes twisted in the broken air behind it. A second battery of lights came on – at half-strength – in the Co-op, as if it were going to open. To whom? Dimly Stephen could see the manager in his rather bright blue suit coming towards the front of the shop. He stopped at various points among the goods and did something, then wandered forwards and did whatever it was again. After a while he reached the front window opposite the book shop. A stretched, coughing noise broke in Stephen's throat as he watched the manager prop a large orange sign in front of a pyramid of salad-cream jars. 'This Week's Bargain,' it said, '23p Each!!' Then he unlocked the doors and stood there, clasping his hands and looking out furtively into the snow-lined street. Stephen, who was now retching violently, retreated to the mail-order table where it was quite dark, and beat on it until his hands hurt.

'Screwing, bloody screwing the last stupid coin out of the last stupid handbag in the world,' he screamed, hot now, confused, sweat trickling over his ribcage and no tears left.

'Maybe I stole it,' he said later, handing the bar of soap to Barbara. 'There was no one in the shop, just a note that said "Gone to church – please leave money for goods." I left fifty pence. Would that be about right?'

Barbara smiled. It was the sort of smile that is often painted on the faces of children, but which real children seldom have. It was real on her. 'No,' she said, 'it wouldn't be all right. You have stolen nearly all of it.' She held it up to her nose, sniffing through the delicate green and cream wrapper. 'Cucumber and oatmeal,' she murmured.

'Do you like it?' he asked anxiously.

'It's bliss. A boy gave me some once, for a present.'

'You can bath with it,' he said, brushing aside the boy. 'The water's very hot, it'll boil in the pipes soon if we don't run some off.' Anyway, he wanted to see her in the bath.

'After tea,' she said dreamily. 'We're having tuna pancakes and cake. But I can't find any parsley.'

'For tea? Tuna pancakes for tea?' He was not used to 'tea' in her sense. He could see that he had gone wrong and that there was no question of Barbara having made a mistake. He said hurriedly, 'There's parsley hanging up in the larder.'

'Hanging up? Why?'

He showed her the intricate little bunches of heads, hanging like a forest cover repeated in a smaller dimension.

'Where did you get them?'

'I grew them.'

'In your garden? You?'

He laughed. 'Do I look so helpless?

She looked at him. 'Yes,' she said dispassionately.

'I needn't be,' he said violently. 'Helpless, maybe, but not – not a non-maker.'

She was not listening to him. To the words, maybe, but not to the sense in them. He leaned on his table where she was now snipping at a parsley head. 'I've found something to make.' Once he had said it he was afraid again so he threw the word 'tea' in to make nothing of what he meant. He meant the wiggles in her hair and tea at half-five and her high-arched, narrow feet as he had seen them, cold on his bare bedroom floor. These things would not cry out. Whatever he 'made' of them, it would not go out from him, screaming and alone. It would be in him – would be him. If anything screamed, it would be he.

'What's going on in town?' She said it so quietly that he realized at once that this was what she had been wanting to know, and all the time he had been talking nonsense to her, so he told her about the white car and Scottie carrying the coffin around the streets and OO OO Boots and the Co-op manager screwing sales at the end of time. Even how that had made him sick over the mail orders.

'Bastard,' she said, softly. 'Poor, ignorant bastard.'

But Stephen did not see why he was 'poor'. The man did not understand, did not believe; not as he and Barbara and the newless radio and the grey men in white cars believed. So he did not have diarrhoea at three in the morning or feel his hand shaking on his own cheek when he shaved. Or see Time come to a stop in his doorway. But he said nothing of that, only, 'He's one of millions. He'll be all right. Right up to' – he did not know what to call it, out loud – 'to the time, he'll be all right.'

She was looking at him again, out of eyes like shallow ice. 'I won't be.'

'No.' It was true.

'And you, Stephen?'

'No. Nor me.'

The quietness again, and the privateness. Then he said gently, 'Had you thought what you would do?'

'Do? There won't be anything to do.'

So, she had not thought. He looked at her hands, at the pretty little silver thing around her narrow wrist and the little turquoise ring on her finger. Her fingertips were stained green from the parsley. Little hollows rippled between the hand bones. Her hand bones. What was he to make of it?

'I shan't hold you to anything,' she said suddenly, turning away to wash the colour off her fingers. She sounded abrasive, accusatory.

'That has nothing to do with me,' he said.

And then he held out his arms and she turned from the sink and came to him, running the few steps. Barbara running? And the hot water hawked and spat in the pipes and Tinker turned around in her box and stared at the wall where death should be, if only it would come in time.

THE THIRD MODE

'ARE YOU THE vicar, sir?'

Christopher was attempting to light the church furnace in the crypt and was not open to discussing the distinction between rector and vicar.

'It looks like something off the Darjeeling railway,' the man said, edging closer to stare at the massive ironwork.

'She's marvellous when she's got a good body in her,' Christopher said obligingly, wiping coke black across his face. 'Yes, I'm the rector.'

'The Rev. Christopher Geraint Fletcher? Of The Rectory, Holywell Passage, Martinminster?'

'I'm not going anywhere,' Christopher said flatly, thrusting a long taper into the pyramid of shavings and chips which he had built at the front of the furnace.

'Sorry, sir?'

'One of your – gang? – came and took away the doctor from my house last night and he hasn't been home since. He started off with name and address, exactly the same way.'

'Which doctor would that be, sir?'

'Why, my doctor,' Christopher said pleasantly. The firelighter in the centre of the pyramid exploded into flame. Then he looked up. This was not the man who had taken Ian away last night, but he had the same quiet, careful look. How dangerous these quiet men are, he thought.

'If I could have a word with you, sir?'

It was unlikely, Christopher thought, that he had come for spiritual counsel, not with that clipboard, that gun and those eyes. 'I shall be here for some time,' he said unemotionally, indicating the draught handles and pressure-gauges on the furnace. 'She's called Bessie, if you're interested in her, and this has been her address for ninety years. Conceived in Nottingham. A one-off job, I'm told. There are none like her.'

'Custom built?'

'Far from it. She used to heat the Gaiety Playhouse in Hereford before she got religion.'

'"Conversion" would be too coarse a joke. I'm sticking with sheer admiration.'

Christopher appreciated this for a minute, then he said, 'What do you want with me?'

'A number of things, sir. Can I give you a hand with Bessie while we talk?'

'Thank you, but only loving familiarity is effective at this stage. And prayer.'

The stranger seated himself quietly on an upturned bucket in the corner. Christopher knew that when he stood up he would have a black ring on the back of his trousers, but it seemed too late to say anything.

'We are concerned about the old people. It seems that the home, Woodview, is wanting to close until things return to normal. You know, not the sick, just the very old, without families, some of them.'

'I know them well.'

'Yes, I know. It's the ones without homes to go to, or too far away for the communications system as it is at the moment.'

'No, I don't imagine many of them can still bicycle easily.' Christopher kept his back turned.

'Well. It's a matter of place, you see. Of where. Old people need a place that has a meaning for them.'

Christopher felt his stomach turn over, but he did not know why. There was no time to think out why. Dangerous, these quiet men. He felt the danger but could not locate it. 'How many of them have you on your little list?'

'Not so little, I'm afraid, sir. Fifty-four.'

'There aren't fifty-four rooms in the rectory.'

'No sir. We were thinking of the church itself.'

Christopher sat back on his heels and said wanly, 'I'm not a very practical man, I'm afraid.'

'You would be provided with everything necessary – food, bedding, sanitary arrangements, fuel. And help, of course.'

'Of course. Do I want soldiers in my church? I have a wedding and a funeral. I think I don't want soldiers, but I do want the old people.'

'Not soldiers, sir. Of course not soldiers.'

The vehemence of the man's voice took Christopher by surprise. 'Why of course?' he said slowly. 'It's a war. It's always soldiers in a war.'

'No, sir,'

'You mean, not in this sort of war.'

'No, sir. We don't have a war yet.'

Christopher shook his head. 'That isn't what you meant.' Then he said, 'How long for?' sounding quite innocent.

'Only as long as necessary.'

Bessie was going well now. They both watched the flames curling over the kindling sticks and listened to the crackling wind in the body of the furnace.

Later Christopher said, 'What else did you want of me?'

The stranger, who was smoking a cigarette quietly on his bucket, said carefully, 'We are uncertain how well the usual social constraints are going to stand up to this sort of stress.'

Christopher kept his face blank. 'Rape and pillage?' he offered.
'We still have prayers for such occasions, thank you.'

'Well, pillage anyway. There have been attempts at looting in
the town.'

'You can scarcely expect me to rush out to Woollies in my
cassock, commanding instant morality, can you? Not these days,
and certainly not me. This isn't the Third World, you know. Their
"thing" about priests doesn't extend to Martinminster, though I
suppose you could try Father Cronin from the Catholic church –
he can be quite alarming I'm afraid. Anyway, I thought you had
C S gas and guns for that sort of thing?'

The man on the bucket ignored him. Bessie gave a sharp bang in
the belly of her boiler and Christopher hastily began placing lumps
of coke around and between the pieces of wood. The bright orange
flames died down and black smoke eddied out of the open fire-
door.

'It's the question of preservation that I'm interested in,' the man
said.

'And what is it – or who – that you want to preserve?
Especially, as it were.'

'Relics.'

'Relics?' Christopher turned and stared at him. The man had his
clipboard on his knee and he was smiling a little at Christopher's
tone.

'Relics of what? Of who? Whom . . .'

'There are spaces allocated to the churches as well as to museums
and art galleries and so on, where precious items can be stored in
times of – well, emergency. In case of law and order breaking
down. "Pillage", in fact.'

'Good God,' Christopher said softly.

'All Souls have a very nice Communion Cup – Jacobean. They
have given us that to put away for them, and –'

' – the Bible from St Bartholomew's, I suppose,' Christopher interrupted.

'I'm going there next. I understand you have something known as the Montgomery Paten here in St Martin's and –'

'I suggest you hurry on to St Bartholomew's,' Christopher said. 'You will have a lot to do if Woodview is closing. Or will someone else take over from you, a logistics pundit, perhaps? Will he carry a gun too?'

'If you would let me explain, sir.'

'You don't need to, officer. I understand very well what you want. It's like sending the song of the whales out into space, isn't it? My wife told me about that. It's a very beautiful idea that afterwards, if there is ever such a time, "they", whoever "they" may be, will have at their disposal little caches of our interior grace . . . outward and visible signs of what we failed to be, don't you think? I suggest you go, now. I have a funeral and, God help me, a wedding to prepare for.'

'None the less, sir, there is always a possibility of looting and sacrilege.'

'Not the slightest. There's not going to be anyone to do it. And in any case, looting and sacrilege wear different faces at different times. Who knows what extreme need the Montgomery Paten may sometime answer? And in the mean time my parishioners, in their extremity, will be served from that paten as they always have been, and their church will not be looted in the name of contemporary chauvinism, nor their altar despoiled in the cause of historicity.' And he shovelled coke into the belly of the furnace, scraping, noisy with the shovel, slamming the fire-door shut, his left arm suddenly shaking. He tried to hide it, wrapping it around his chest to keep it still. 'You're so quiet,' he shouted at the mild man in the corner who was concerned for old people and sacred things, 'so dreadfully, frighteningly quiet. Even the streets are empty – when does the shouting start? Is there a schedule for that too?'

(He hadn't looked for storage space, had he? Hadn't asked about drains or water supplies or anything that implied a long time. Ask about the storage space, damn you. Give me a form to fill in asking for a month's worth of coke and I'll hand over the Montgomery Paten. Please. Please?)

'We're not planning on much shouting, sir,' the quiet man said from his bucket. Then he left, a black stain on his uniform.

Christopher hauled himself up the stone steps from the crypt, dragging on the iron handrail. His knees were very heavy and stiff. Moving was difficult, an intolerable effort. At the door into the north transept he stopped, holding on to the frame with his shaking left hand. He could hear the rustle of Alice King's overalls as she wiped the frozen condensation off the brass rail of the Lady Chapel opposite him. He ought to call out cheerfully to her that Bessie was roaring away and the radiators would warm up any minute now, but his throat was silent.

(Do you know what they're going to do to you, Alice? They're going to shoot you. If you don't lie down peacefully in the church to die with the rest of us, they will shoot you. There is going to be no looting, no hysteria, no screaming. It's all going to be very decent and quiet. Like these quiet, quiet men. Just some shots, dull because of the silencers – more like thumps, really. Or perhaps the soft hiss of gas. You see, Alice, they're not planning for much shouting. He's just told me so. He's just told me everything.)

Over St Polten the cold had formed a thick, frozen vapour that kept the morning dingy – almost dark. Here and there light from greenish arc-lamps fizzed out like sherbet into the fog. From all around came the tapping and clangour of invisible chisels and axes chipping ice from frozen locomotive brakes; chipping and tapping as if the ice-elves from the high Karakoram had broken out and re-emerged here in the bitter yards; unseen, cold, not of us in the same way as the huge engines were not or the frozen rail-roads. The tall carriage stood alone in the siding, without context. It could not be seen, nor could anything be seen from it, and the ice-chippers scraped and sharpened their irons out and away from the in-turned, orange-lit box with its centralized bier and its four deep-Asian watchers. They had not spoken for some time. They had made tea in the mountain fashion, leaves, milk and sugar all brewed together, and from it steam had condensed and formed a glaze of ice over the boots and trouser legs of the cadaver in their midst and on the glass inside their shuttered windows. Their breath, tainted by wurst and nicotine, laboured in the stiff air.

It was only some time after the chipping, chipping had ceased that they were aware of silence. They looked at each other out of their deep, roof-of-Asia eyes, pin-point, jet exchanges, direct from one fear to the depths of another. Only the closed eyes of the dead Minister for Defence were protected from the answer. After a long while the eldest of the four climbed stiffly down on to the snow outside. The rail-yard was pale with opaque daylight, but the green sherbet moons had gone out. There was no form, no shape, no mankind in the whiteness. He held his hand out behind him, touching the solidity of the carriage as if it, too, might cease. A thin film iced over the sharp shine on his metal buttons, beginning to fade him.

Being deep-Asian, he had little body hair and the sudden *frisson* that took him shrilled around the edge of his scalp and the root of his penis. When his skin was still again and the near-pain of it eased, he turned and pulled himself slowly back into the carriage. The linoleum floor was stained and spattered; the tea steam congealed against the roof; the corpse was stiff and protuberant; the methane lamp was insufficient; his fellows were bleached out like things a flood had passed over and despoiled a long time ago.

'They are all gone,' he told them. Then again, so that the fact should come to them from reality and not from his uncertain self, he half-opened the door to the silence and the white outside. 'All. They are all gone.'

One by one they stood up, settled the machine-guns on their shoulders and filed out, down the high steps on to the blank ground. Then, four together and without looking at each other, they moved away into the frozen fog.

They were some way off when the rigor began to loosen around the Minister's head, which was not far from the stewing tea, and the mouth suddenly fell open. Otherwise nothing changed.

Around Martinminster everything was changing. It happened personally, inside each individual as they became more aware of the calm-faced men in grey uniforms. The Town Hall was shut. Danny stood outside it, pushing at the side door where the Births, Marriages and Deaths offices were. There was even a padlocked chain across the main door. The banks were shut too, and there was a thin-looking guard dog tethered in the porch in front of the Abbey National. By late morning the shops had all closed and only a market stall selling oilskins was still hoping to trade. There were grey men outside the garages and chemists. The carpark was empty and there were two white jeeps and an oddly shaped white car near the place where the papers had always said there was no bunker.

The telephone was not dead, it just made a sound like a cheap chime doorbell. In the end Xanthe managed to reach Polly by dialling her as if she were telephoning from London and not through the local exchange. For some reason the connection was made, although the line was bad. Polly's voice sounded scratched, whistling as if she had a hole in her throat.

'Of course I have to marry Danny now,' she said scrappily. 'There isn't any other time.'

'But do you want to, Polly, really-really?'

'No. But I have to. It's what I have to do. I have to do it now. Make Christopher do it now, Xanthe, for God's sake, before I have to –'

'What? Before you have to what? I didn't hear . . .'

'– anything else. Other things to do, you see. Make Christopher hurry, make him.'

'I can't "make" Christopher do anything, you know that. Polly, I can't hear you. Wouldn't you like him to just – well, bless you, or whatever he does to divorced people? Wouldn't you rather do that, Poll?'

'– do all the other things, then. And I have to. Have to. Xanthe, help me –'

Polly was so far away. Almost out of earshot, inner earshot, so that Xanthe could not understand whether Polly was talking to her, actually, or whether she was not eavesdropping on something which was happening inside Polly and which the mysterious telephone connection was relaying to her on some authority other than Polly's.

'Polly, are you there?'

'Oh yes, I'm here. It's just that I'm – something – very busy, I think. With all this to do. Do you see?'

'Polly, are you sure about the blessing?'

She could not go on. She had no inspiration to say If. 'If it doesn't happen . . .' was not there to be said any more. And Polly did not say it either. They did not betray each other into what would have been the subversion of hope. It was, in Xanthe, as if hope were the newest of treasons, a Young King as it were, waiting to be crowned when the Old King fell, as he had to fall, in the forest, in the wood (Croke's Wood?) of his own volition, too full of knowing for redemption. One of the men who had come to take Tansy had come out of that forest. Or perhaps the forest, in its death-spasm, was shooting out extreme, gripping growths as it had done through the windows of houses in the town when it had flung young Tansy bodily through the door of Danny's shop and as it had done when it enthralled Xanthe in its roots and saplings, clutched at her and named to her its name. And in the same sense they were all members of the Old King, and if they would not go willingly into the forest then certainly it would reach out and grow around them. Only, this time, the forest would fall too, so that there could be no Young King suckled in its arborous breasts.

'– afraid,' Polly was ending something. 'I've buggered everything else up that I've ever done – but not this, Xanthe. I promise you. I know. It's only, you see, for a few days . . . I'll be able –'

'Able,' Xanthe repeated as if she had reached the end of a long, long walk. Then suddenly, 'Polly, Polly, don't get lost – Poll?' But the line was dead.

'Marriage is a celebration, my love. Surely you, of all people, know that?' Christopher said when she went to him in the church.

'Not this one. This is something horrible – I can feel it. You mustn't let it happen, Christopher; it'll kill her – kill our Polly.' She stopped and looked away from him, downwards at the dead brown tiles on the church floor. 'Not that sort of death – I know, I know. But Polly's a different sort of person. She's not like us – she's like we ought to be in some way, inside. Don't you see? She belongs to people, not just to one Danny.' And then remembering how Polly had said, 'Everyone has a Christopher of their own,' she added, 'Especially not to Danny.'

'That is not for us to say,' Christopher said severely.

'It might be. If she can't see it, and he certainly couldn't, then oughtn't we to say it? She's going to fail in some way – at the end, when it's going to matter so – so – she'll fail, she'll turn back into Polly and leave him.'

'And would that have to be called failure? Or might not

marrying him at all, when he needs her to, might that not be failure?'

'Not in the absolute.' Xanthe was so sure she was right. She, who understood so little about people and great ideas, had an idea of Polly turning away, a goddess in an elemental catastrophe, and turning to ash, while she, Xanthe, still burned. The burning caught hold in her, turned this way and that into flames of love; love for the luxuriant coils of Polly's hair, for the wide, free remarking of Polly's eyes for the exuberance and wickedness and wholeness of Polly who was everything earth grew towards harvest. To be laid, as a freak storm lays unfilled grain-heads, and for there to be no hope of harvest – how they would all starve to carnal death without the harvesting of Polly. That she was beautiful, the image came, with vine leaves in her hair, of that vine from which Communion wine was made no less than Dionysian.

'She's home,' was all Xanthe managed of her idea, 'she's home and idol. Lares and Penates to all our poor bread-ovens, mine and Stephen's and Morag's. Don't lay her waste, Christopher, don't –'

As he always did, he put his arms around her, to put out the flames that hurt her so much. But this time she did not want to be put out, and thrashed in his arms. She had been living in truth for twelve hours now, and it was too long.

Watching them struggle by the altar steps, Alice King wiped the beads of moisture off the big coarse radiator, which had now begun to click as it warmed up. She looked up at the Annunciation window above her and thought how dreary it was that you had to wait nine months for the good news to materialize, and how the worst news had no Gabriel of its own to prepare you. Like Luke Lyons dying. Poor Freda. If this was going to be a long war, like the last one, she would not see it out. Not without Luke. Why bother, without Luke? You had to have someone to care for in hard times, or you let yourself go. She herself had been a widow for nearly nineteen years now, but, even so, she could have done with her old man at a time like this – in spite of everything. Mrs Fletcher, freeing herself up there from the rector's arms, she had no idea. No idea at all, when a man looked at you like the rector was doing now. So much of it was sad, really. It made you low to think about it. Or cross. She gave the radiator a sniping little kick to stop it clicking and moved her brassing-rags over to the sidesman's staff. From there she would be able to hear more clearly who was to be married so dubiously. Before or after they buried Luke? The rector had given no sign either way.

'She's my mother, Christopher,' Xanthe was saying.

Alice whistled through her teeth in surprise. No wonder.

'She's all our mothers – it's what she's for – what she is.' She was clawing at his sleeve now, as if she would bleed understanding out of him. 'She's a source of something for us, nourishment for a self a lot of us don't have and we keep going back to her and drawing on her and coming away less – famished, if you like. She isn't bad, or stained or lost; she's lovely because she is complete. If you marry her to Danny it would be like tainting a food-store. We can't find another now, Christopher, it's too late –'

'My love, you are talking in symbols and this is no time for symbols. Polly is a very real woman. You cannot turn her into a tool against your own need. Her requirements are not yours.'

She turned from him. Above the altar the stained glass Crucifixion was dull in front of the dull sky. Christopher's cry last night, 'It was not enough, what we did to Him,' rang in her ears as if he had spoken from a mouth of cold brass. What she had inside her was the answer to his cry, but she could not find words for it, no music for it, as if Christopher's angels (in which he had so beautifully partly believed) had taken all the music and the trumpets when they fled, howling, back to Heaven. When? At the end of the Middle Ages? Last night? Fled from Man and Woman,

as the warhead makers and Polly were Man and Woman. So
immediate, the eternal verities, so little, after all that talk about
them; little and intimate and here in a church beside her, Xanthe.
That was the answer. She placed her hands over her belly, where
her womb would be if it were big with child, and held something
against herself or in herself which she felt like an ache and which
was called 'Real life'. Death did not make life untrue. First there
was life and then there was death and then there was no more
death because life was over. So simple, after all the talk. She looked
up and there, of course, was Polly, up there on the crude Rood,
Polly with her hair crowned with blackthorn blossoms and her
garlanded arms stretched out among the flowering branches. Polly
now – that was what Christopher must have meant about it not
being enough what they did to Jesus. Because now they had Polly.

'Polly,' she called to her.

'You're losing your grip a bit, my beloved. Here, sit down here.
Alice, get some water from the vestry, quick.'

'Oh no I'm not. I've just understood something,' she said softly.
'Christopher, when is the marriage?'

Christopher had not astonished himself by the authority with
which he had dismissed the quiet man in grey that morning. As a
man, indeed as a clergyman, he had seldom given anyone any
trouble, and only Xanthe really knew that he could afford to be
swayed on the surface because he was as strong as a tap-root
underneath. Once he found himself knowing, as he had known
over the matter of the Montgomery Paten, that he was alone and
that he had been granted, or cursed with (and he did not know
which) a new and very terrible duty, he had gone back to his
bedroom and put on his black frontage and clerical collar, which,
in the modern way, he did not normally wear on weekdays, rather
as a ship's captain might dress in his best uniform to take up his
stand on his dying bridge. A romantic, rather useless gesture these

days, he thought, but it satisfied him. The uniform enclosed him, took him away inside itself, had a significance which he, Christopher, had not. When he returned to the church, it was as the master of a ship. The thoughts developed quite logically in his head; captains could marry, and commit for burial, and he was about to do both. A master lived by an iron rule, he thought. He had a ship to take over the rim of the world as medieval masters had done, a full complement of passengers – his congregation, his friends, the old folk from Woodview, even his own wife – and he must sail them out of this world. No harbour, though they did not know that; no landfall. Straight out over the edge.

He spared a little of his secretive, half-born smile for the images of the barque of life and the safe haven of the everlasting arms, all of which he now knew to be images, and, ridiculously, suffered a spasm of the sort of nervousness that he used to feel as a schoolboy before reading the lesson in chapel, or appearing in the school play. Very mundane and physical and not at all equal to the exalted circumstances of the time. His smiles came and went irregularly and he had to return twice to visit the bathroom. Then, when he was as nearly ready as he would ever be, he scribbled a note on the sermon pad in the vestry, set his verger on the creaking bicycle and sent him round to Polly's place. Not at all at ease in the snow-clogged, horse-reeking yard, the reluctant verger found Polly in the big barn where her ponies were sheltering, tearing twine off bales of hay with her bare hands. She was far from clean, had obviously been crying and had spikes of hay sticking to her fair hair and anorak. She opened Christopher's note, kissed the embarrassed verger and plunged, rather like a lifeboat in heavy seas, through the drifts to Danny, who had just returned from the locked and useless Town Hall.

'Danny –' she said. She wanted to go on, but the thing she was going to do, and the thing Danny thought she was going to do were so different that she could not bring them together in words. Instead she held up the note. Christopher would marry them at two o'clock that afternoon, regardless of law or licence. The circumstances, said the note, merited it.

The verger pedalled ostentatiously back to Christopher. Polly shouted at Danny until he gave in and walked, in his fur bootees, two miles down the road to the Dipyard. Pushing open the back door too quickly in his anxiety to find warmth and shelter and possibly a whisky, he stumbled through the kitchen and found Stephen soaping a naked girl with long, fluffily permed hair, in an old tin tub in front of the living-room fire. Danny groped around for a few not-too-sexy jokes, delivered them clumsily and asked Stephen to come to his wedding. The curious girl, holding a frayed towel against her front, rose from the tin tub and disappeared into the kitchen, leaving a trail of wet footprints on the carpet and an indelible image in Danny's mind of wet, heavy buttocks below a thin, slightly curving spine, and a drifting walk as if she were only partially awake. Stephen, who was managing to look both pale and feverish, had had the good luck to have filled his car with petrol the evening before the pumps were locked. When the girl was dry and dressed he drove his dog and his girl and Danny back to Polly where they set about creating a wedding for her.

Without any laws or licences it was all very simple. There was a moment, when Stephen had brought Morag and Polly to the church, when Barbara had lifted a vase of white chrysanthemums from the font and placed them on the chancel steps. Christopher said gently, 'That is where they will stand,' and she had nodded at him and said shyly, 'Can we take those candles?' gesturing at the altar.

When he brought them to her she set them one above the other on the steps and began to smile. Stephen, watching her, felt his shaking hands interlocking, each needing a hand to hold, but finding no other there. Barbara was turning slowly round, only her eyes fully awake, like a dancer rising into a new sequence, and then moving out around the windowsills and the Lady Chapel and the Roll of Honour, each time circling back to the steps with ivy and fish-paste jars of hellebore and winter-flowering jasmine. Slowly the brown tiled steps grew into a gateway, incipient, half-realized. Xanthe came back from the rectory with two pink and white cyclamens in pots, a huge, scarlet starred poinsettia and high, intricate fern. Stephen drove back to the Dipyard, swallowed his timorousness and begged from Lucy, who could be relied on to have the correct things in bloom, six pots of forced hyacinths, curled and waxy and heady with perfume, and a bowl of jonquils, pale with the strain of blooming in this terrible season. From his own house he brought a pepper plant, globular with fruit, fecund and unlikely, and then, with a smile, he put on the seat beside him a pot of rosemary from the kitchen window, its lavender flowers as delicate as a sea mist in autumn. All these he brought to Barbara and the smile she turned on him was the first greeting of Eve to Adam in the garden that morning. She knelt there, Barbara, in her wellington boots and her long woollen skirt, her Botticelli hair capped by the woolly hat she wore even in bed, even making love, and grew, up from the earth-brown tiles, up the side of the pulpit on the one hand and the brazen eagle-wings of the lectern on the other, an arbour of flowers and leaves, lit by the six greater altar candles and perfumed with old incense and the spring that was not to be, and Christopher sat in the choir stalls and watched her with tears in his eyes and blood on his hands where his nails were digging into his palms; and Alice King rested from her polishing and put out a hand to Xanthe, which was a thing she would never do, and said slowly, 'If old Luke could just rest there a while, after . . .', and Xanthe nodded, because Luke and the garden he had grown around Freda were there on the chancel steps too, with

Paradise and Croke's Wood and the Rood-tree, their sweet-scented flowers entwined among the branches of the Ardcollie firs and rhododendrons and stepped with the daisies that Christopher had once picked while Eden played.

They gathered together around their arbour, Barbara and Morag and Andrew and Stephen and Xanthe. Sam, embarrassed by the nakedness of the adults' faces, sat sulkily in the front pew pretending to fondle Tinker; tickling her tea-stained moustaches and whispering 'At 'em, boy,' into her ear as he swished hymnbooks along the seat. At the back of the church Malkie was stretched out on his stomach in the last pew, watching the young men in carefully pressed grey trousers and highly polished black leather shoes who were carrying in blocks of precisely folded grey blankets and piling them against the Sunday School table. Every now and again he mouthed, 'Pow!' at them, but they took no notice. In the centre of the sweet arbour Christopher was marrying Polly and Danny, and once or twice he looked between their shoulders and stared without curiosity at the young men. It was Barbara who thought of a ring, and passed to Danny one of the little blue and silver ones she wore on her finger. When it was over, Christopher looked suddenly at Stephen. You? his eyes asked.

'We can't do that to Primavera,' Stephen said aloud, having just discovered who Barbara was.

'Primavera? What an unusual name –' Morag said hoarsely. She had not spoken since they had arrived in the church. Xanthe stared down at Lucy's pink hyacinths in case the low moan of winter in Morag's voice had turned the frail petals brown. But nothing had happened. In the arbour Polly stood rapt, her hands on her big breasts, her lips shining, her coiled hair shining, her shining eyes watching Frankie who was far off, out and through, beyond all the flowers, but he was watching her too, even from that distance.

Sweet Polly Anderson, he called to her, laughing at her there with her new, ageing husband. You've had your face turned to me all this time, haven't you, girl? His beautiful, golden voice showered laughter down the high, stone pillars, along the cold, brass rails and around the swung, high mouths of the bronze bells way up in the tower. You've been turned to me all this fucking time!

Suddenly, out of the back of the church, one of the young men said shyly, 'Congratulations . . .' and when Christopher caught his eye and smiled slightly, they all said it, 'Congratulations,' and 'Great thing to do,' and 'Be happy, man,' and laughed a little and a few of them clapped – such an odd thing to do in a church but Christopher did not seem to mind, standing on the bridge of his old ship, dressed overall in flowers. So everyone clapped, even Sam and Xanthe (but not Malkie), and laughed, and Christopher suddenly snapped out a hymn number and they became flustered until they found it in the dull little green books at the pew-ends.

'And you,' Christopher called to the young men, so peremptorily that they shuffled forwards, picking up books as they came up the aisle. They all stood together, the flowers and the young men and the bright candleflames and the old white dog and Primavera in wellington boots and everyone, everyone who was in any way whatsoever there, and they sang:

> *Morning hath broken, like the first morning,*
> *Blackbird hath spoken, like the first bird,*

very fast and high so that their voices should not choke up in their weeping throats.

Night returned to Martinminster and Croke's Wood as if it belonged there. The crisis broke overtly when the first dusk was thickening among the houses of the town and the hedges of the deep country roads, as if there were some tenebrous link between the doings of men and the pattern of the skies. Silent crows clenched bare branches and ivy-gripped buildings, unmoving, as the shadows crept through the lanes from the east on the slight, bitter wind. In the conduit under the road from Dybart Hill the hedge-pig's blood slowed imponderably. In the blackthorns, twigs cracked. The first road-block was thrown across the long hill leading up towards the Dipyard and Croke's Wood. Already the green lights were fingering the private undersides of the spruce plantation. Near the bank where, by a glowing furnace, Antethos of the Dobunni had watched his sword sharpened by his last iron-smith, the hare's flattened belly pressed against clover-stems blackened by frost and only the east wind still sighed. The town of Martinminster threw a faint blur into the sky, its dimmed street-lamps yellow and sulphurous. Here and there among the streets the bright flash of headlamps wavered like Christmas streamers fallen from favour, and beyond the town Croke's Wood was dressing in a necklace of gold and scarlet where the lanterns of the road-blocks were lighting up on every road, lane and track that led up towards the green, stealthy light. Above the clouds the moon must have been rising and the stars brightening and from their blue and silver spaces the faint whine and mumble of the distant Blackbirds and the AWACs patrolling their grids, stealing, echoless, around the brilliant skies. It was ten to five and still wonderful with sundown and luminous ether where they flew. In the creeping dark below, the emergency generators in the big milking parlours began to putt and mutter as the herds of Friesians and dairy shorthorns stood waiting for the relief of evening milking, their great bags and pendulous udders urgent to give.

In the homes of the better-equipped people, like Lucy in No. 3, The Dipyard, the deep-freezers began to clatter as the power supply weakened. In their harsh depths, deep in the sirloins, in the pork legs and lamb shoulders, slow bacteria emerged towards revivification. The gas supply along Freda Lyons's terrace popped and died. By five to five the dog fox was on his way out of Croke's Wood, heading downhill, and Walford Scott was bringing tall wax candles out of the Chapel of Rest and into his living-room. He had plenty – not many people kept their dead in their own homes these days, like dear old Freda was doing. Freda, for whom so much light had gone out anyway, did not notice that it was night now, and sat on in the flickering glow of her lounge fire, not even really seeing Luke's empty chair or listening to Alice King's fumbling account of whatever it was that had disturbed her so greatly in the church when she had gone to clean the brasses before lunch.

'Not dressed for it all, not one of them. He had a tie on, granted, but the colour of it! And the girl what put all the flowers round, she was still wearing her wellington boots when they started marrying. And them boys, and a dog – honest, Freda, it was a funny set-up, it was really. You'd think they could have waited till tomorrow, just to press a few clothes up, wouldn't you? Not easy for the rector. Not at all easy.'

'No,' said Freda, thinking of Luke, 'it's not easy. Not at all easy.'

At one minute to five all the radio programmes came to an end. Whether they had been listening to Alice Cooper or Webern, Duke Ellington or part eleven of *The Mill on the Floss*, everyone heard, for exactly a minute, the tranquil theme of Vaughan Williams, *Fantasia on a Theme by Tallis*. So English, so green and irrelevant and sweet and a little sad. They listened. After it came the familiar pips and the unfamiliar announcement that the news broadcast to follow, and all subsequent editions until further notice, would be issued by the National Government's Centre for Response. There would be no unauthorized commentary or debate. Everyone was requested to have a battery operated radio available and to listen in to all bulletins. By five past five anyone who was going to believe it, did. By ten past the first pharmacies had been seriously looted and the first Armoured Personnel Carriers were cruising outside the banks, the supermarkets, the garages and post offices. The main post office had armed grey men around it already and a lorry parked among the little red vans in its car-park. The five-o-nine from Paddington clicked quietly into the marshalling yard behind the station platforms and when the engine died its lights went out too. The slam of the driver's door echoed for a very long time among the rails and the dark, forsaken sheds. It was twelve minutes past five, night-time, and there were no stars.

Christopher wound his scarf over his white collar and pulled on the black shoes he always wore for Holy Communion (he hated the squeak or ring of shoes on the church tiles during the administration of the Sacrament and Xanthe had given him this pair for – as she put it – a 'birthday' present. They were far above his means.) He was aware of feeling insecure and a trifle ridiculous, and both the feelings were too trivial for the occasion. He was frightened too, on a purely physical level. Afraid, perhaps, simply of hurting himself. Outside he moved quickly up the narrow, flagged lane that ran from the side gate of the church past the rectory garden, and emerged into the lower end of the Buttermarket. Even from the house he had been able to hear the curious growling sound made by a moving crowd of people, and the anonymous grating of many feet on the icy pavement. It had been threatening not only his sense of purpose, his infantile, as he now felt it to be, conception of himself as a leader, a ship's captain responsible for the deaths of those in his care, but also even his will to act on a very simple level. He wanted, he knew, to think it all away, to come to terms with the movements of the town in his head; analyse, theorize, understand them, so that he need not, in fact, go out among them. But he knew, too, that the choice not to act had been taken from him by events. By time. This Now that had come had negated the purposes of thought; had left no option other than action open to him. That which had been set in motion was pure action – one of the three pure acts of Creation, Crucifixion, and destruction – and during the activity nothing else could exist. Part of it, contained by it, only his function remained valid; there was no more being, only doing.

He stepped from the lane on to the corner of the Buttermarket. The street was like an Italian city at summer sundown; it was filled with a faint yellow light from the faded electric bulbs in houses and shops and, in the soft glow, boys and young men in small groups and girls in twos and threes swung up and down the trafficless road, up and down the pavement as if it were a courtship promenade. In the doorway of the Abbey National the guard dog barked incessantly. Land Rovers with dipped headlamps covered by heavy wire mesh, patrolled each side of the road, up and down, and turned and returned. In the frost-thin air the promenaders were murmuring. It was a deep sound, throaty and indistinct, over which the few bursts of laughter carried high, jackal peals. Instead of swinging skirts and swaggering denims, the young people were muffled in dark, bulky jackets, their hands heavily gloved, their hair hidden under caps. Their eyes were bright, but as with fever.

Yes, he was afraid of them. In his mind's eye he saw the quiet eyes of the grey man who had come to him that morning. Of what would he be afraid?

Christopher paused at the end of the lane, hunched against the corner window of the Home Decorating Centre. The mood of the street, tense, watchful, wicked but without any sense of wickedness, slithered around him, took him by the arm, drew him further into the Buttermarket. A pair of young men stumbled against him. One of them, his lips shiny pale, held Christopher in his arms for a fraction of time. When he was freed, their eyes met. Christopher felt himself shudder back against the shop window with a suddenness that pierced him with guilt. Mirror boy, mirror eyes, pass on (lest I fall on your breast in my need). Watching, Christopher saw the youth raise a bottle to his lips. What must he raise to his own? Prayer? Give us this day . . . Rage surged up in his arms and neck. He said out loud, 'Give us this day. Give us this day,' and his voice was the same as the surging crowd. He heard it and could not hear it, so in tune was it with the street's voice. 'Give us this day.'

   Glass smashed, not far from him. The siren from one of the vehicles howled in response. The shifting crowd halted, turned, moved towards the sound. Over the moving heads a spotlight flared out from a roof, searching the shop windows. There was a scream as the vehicles circled, fast now, blaring at the slow crowd in their way. A girl tripped sideways, fell, brushed by the hard, white armour above the wheels. Shouting, the thumps of fists on the sides of the vehicle, random and then rhythmical, pound, pound, pound . . . Cold, coming from inside Christopher, crept out, cramping and crippling him. He pushed out of his corner, head down, shoving his way up the Buttermarket against the crowd. The noise swelled behind him and he turned up his collar as if to stop it from taking him by the throat.

   When he reached the doorway of Stephen's shop he found the second door up to the flat above unlocked. He pushed through and stood for a moment in the dark at the foot of the stairs. The eccentric organist had not answered any of the telephone calls Christopher had tried to make, but it might have been the telephone that was not working, or it might be that the fellow really did unplug it, as Ian had said (Ian, come back. Give Ian back). He was obliged to shout. There was no answer. He went up. The door into the flat was open, the rooms were empty. There was no coat on the hook, no food in the kitchen, no soap in the bathroom, no blanket on the bed. On the living-room floor records, sheet music, cassettes were stacked in austere piles. The umbrous glow of the street outside turned the frost-ferns on the window panes into spires of coral grown in blood. To Christopher there had never been so empty a room; so lonely a man to stand within it. Searching, he found that he had no pain and no prayer. Alone, he picked up a number of cassettes from the floor and thrust them into his coat pocket. Alone, he wrote a note on a record sleeve and alone he left the deserted flat and returned to the street. Down at the far end there was now shouting, and more spotlights.

He did not know how to break a shop window. Not without sirens and lights converging on him. It could be done, but not by him. He did not know how to pick a lock or even the best way of breaking down a door. In any case, the Electrical Goods shop was protected by a fitted steel mesh grille. He had not thought of such a thing. He stood alone on the pavement, staring in at the washing-machines and toasters and video-recorders all washed in the stammering mauve of a dying strip-light. He swallowed harshly and turned away. He was alone when he joined the fringe of the crowd outside Woolworths.

Here he could smell alchohol and a new, sour smell which he knew was fear, although he had never met it before. A group of girls were clustered around the entrance to the store, their jackets bundled up around their necks as his was, their feet in tall, fur-lined boots. A grey-uniformed man stood between them and the broken centre door which hung tilt-wise and futile, half open, twisted on its hinges. The body of the crowd, swaying and rhythmic still, beat noise out of the far end of the street: OO OO, OO OO. He wanted to say to the girls, as he inched up beside them, 'Take care,

he'll have a gun,' but the calm logical eyes of the man told him
that there was no gun. The men with guns did not use logic; they
had something better. Jostling, the girls moved in. One of them
had a long cigarette. She puffed smoke lightly into the grey man's
face. He did not move. The skin of Christopher's face stretched
with concentration. The girls were against the grey man now, tall,
lovely girls with perfumed bodies and smooth, coloured cheeks
which they pressed right up against the grey uniform, panting
short white breaths into the bloody, staining light. One thrust her
hips forwards and then her leg. Above her head the grey man's
eyes found Christopher, staring, and he opened his mouth to – and
the girl pressed her own mouth against it, sudden as a lover.
Christopher saw her teeth clamp on the man's bottom lip. There
was the sound, shocking in its minuteness, of a giggle and a
raucous, muffled cry. A cigarette lighter flared. Two of the girls,
lighter and smaller than those pressed around the grey man, slipped
past him into the shop. Christopher went with them.

Only the front counters and the tills appeared to have been
wrecked. Christopher, at the side counter, broke the bronze chain
that held the big cassette-players to the shelves. The alarm bell gave
a low buzz. In the dark aisles the girls were taking clothes and
jewellery. He could hear them. He peered at the label on the
machine he held and turned to the batteries rack. It was empty. In a
little store-room behind the table lamps and hair dryers, peering at
labels in the deep orange light, he found a carton of them and
pulled it out on to the floor.

'HP2's,' a voice said. 'Share 'em out, mate.'

Watching his own arm reaching out, he took half of them and
thrust them into his trouser pockets. Black, cosmeticked eyes
grinned at him. 'Not very handy, are you?' she said huskily
through the dim glow. 'Take a poly-bag – there are hundreds of
them on the floor by the birthday cards.'

Such bright eyes, so quick, like little match flames showing up a myriad of responses he had not known existed. Dangerous, unknown, there in the dark so close to him. Still he felt no pain and no prayer. The girls were gathered at the counter, now wrenching, as he had done, radios, cassette players and Walkmans out of the muted chain-alarms; piling cassettes into bags, any cassettes, all the cassettes.

'Want some rock, beginner?' Again the matches flared down the lines, bright and sparkling, almost Roman candles showering a glitter of exotic instancy across his cold solitude.

Light. Any light but that blood-stained opacity in the street. He stared at the pointed little chin, at the warm, honey-down hair line under the hood of the jacket, at the lit-up eyes in the bare, soiled gloom. His throat spoke. He said, 'God bless you,' as he turned and ran for the door. Behind him someone laughed, merrily, it seemed to him. He swerved between the broken tills, the floor slippery with polythene bags. He tried not to look at the grey man, caught against the glass door, who was on his knees now, his cheeks streaming with tears. Christopher had to see the fat, dark blood where it had splashed on the pavement, on the grey uniform, and filled the hollows where the man's chin was still crushed against the girl's. Christopher's eyes saw it and the girl's hands on the man's head and between his legs, and his throat had no words, even for himself, as he looked away and started out into the crowd, across the street and down, stumbling and half running like a thief, into the dark lane that ran along the rectory wall where the bloody light did not reach.

In his own kitchen he stood alone. The fire shifted in the Aga. The slow kettle puffed a little steam up under the calendar. He was panting and his heart was uncomfortable in his chest. His face was stiff with cold. He put the big, shiny cassette-player on the table and turned his back on it. His pockets, weighted with cassettes and batteries, clogged his movements. He piled them on the table beside the machine. His knees felt unstrung. He had to sit down. His hair dropped over his forehead, his scarf sprawled between his elbows. He put his head in his hands, but still he did not pray.

Stephen watched the needle of the fuel gauge hiccough from the nearly full mark to the half empty. It was the only gauge still working on the old car, and he would have preferred it if it had given up like the others. It was not important what the gauge was measuring; it was the activity itself which was displaced; the visible indication of an approaching void. He and Barbara had already taken all the Medways home to Crosby Spring and Polly and Danny back to Polly's place, and all the time the needle had been measuring, measuring. He wondered if, when he reached the Dipyard, he would be able to smash a spanner through the little dial.

The road had been unsalted for days and since he was neither a good driver like Xanthe or Andrew, nor a dashing one like Danny, he crept and slithered over the glassy white, impacted surface, feeling incompetent and a little frightened. It was the pinnacle, he thought, of irony or stupidity, to be afraid of bumping into a hedge at twenty miles an hour when the government had just suggested that you retreat to your bunker and hide in it in case warheads were travelling purposefully towards you from six thousand miles away, with an aim accuracy of thirty feet. He wondered if the movement of his lips was a smile or a grimace. And if there were any difference, now. The headlamps swayed and glided over the baulks of snow on the verges, little crystals of frost flashing blue and diamond-prismed on their surfaces. The sky was very black above; the fields very black on either side. Hostile, black, suspended in non-life, thorn, hazel, holly, bittersharp and angular, clenched themselves rigid, brushed neither by fear nor ignorance but bound in an intense isolation, which was neither dying nor living and was enemy to both. The sun-spawned lemons of Crete turned wrinkled and dark in his head, their musty, juiceless pith became gall.

The dog fox was in the middle of the road, napalm-eyed.

'Christ!' Stephen cried out. 'He's so thin!' The steering wheel turned loose and slick in his hands, his foot stayed flat on the boards – no brakes held the hard black tyres from sliding across the glassy snow like wilful mercury. Barbara's sounds, high and broken, hit his hearing and her hands grabbed and clutched at the loose metal handles of the door.

'My fox, my fox, he's still here. I'm alive – help him, help me. The fox –'

Dog fox, all curved spine and balancing brush, black as a twist of blown bracken, was gone. 'Go back, go back,' she was crying, wrenching at the door, kicking at it, the car sliding sideways across the trapped road in an arc of crazed lights that did not shine on danger coming but on the welts the fox had scored in the snow.

'He's all right, he's all right. We didn't hit him,' Stephen was shouting as the old car slewed into the hedge and stopped. 'He's all right.'

But she was gone, the door swinging open, the throat-stopping cold surging in. Slipping and slithering in the arrested headlamps, Barbara had scrambled across the road and scrabbled at the hedge-bank on the far side. He could hear her calling, 'Wait for me, wait for me. For God's sake don't leave me here,' into the black everywhere beyond the pale, whiplash lights.

'Oh Jesus,' he whispered, leaning his head against the steering wheel. 'Oh Jesus, why that?' His knees like water, his hands jabbed between them. He would have to go across the road and fetch her. He could see the way she was tumbled, like a broken thing flung out of a passing window, crumpled against the bank where the fox had leaped up and thrust his way through the roots of the hedge above. Abused, as she had looked abused when she pushed her way into his home the first night. She had seen the fox then.

'He's all right,' he shouted again, leaning across the passenger seat. There was a warm sort of hurt on the side of his head. He must have banged it against the clamp of the seat-belt when the car skidded. He would have to scramble out and fetch her. He could hear her, still making that choking, high cry as if she did not know how to weep ordinarily. Yet he knew that she did. There were no tears on her face when he knelt clumsily in the snow beside her, pulling at her shoulders to lift her up against him.

'He's not hurt,' he said shakily. 'We missed him.'

'He's gone.'

'Well, you wouldn't expect him to want to stay, would you?'

'He's gone.'

'Come on, Barbara. He'll be all right now –' Her teeth in his hand were harder and sharper than anything he had ever felt. He cried out, horror kicking up inside him.

'All right?' she screamed, letting go suddenly. He snatched his hand to his mouth and sucked at it. Salt, wet and warm, cloyed his tongue. 'He'll be all right? And me? All right? We're not all right – I'm going to die, and he's going to die and it's not his fault. It's not his business. Not his sin. He's perfect and beautiful and no god-damned politician ever taught him which was called right and what was called wrong. He's right and he's going to die for it just the same.'

There was no answer. It was such a long time since there had been any answers to anything. He put his arms around her, for his own sake rather than for hers; to put his hurt head against her woolly hat, his hurt hand against her body where it would find soothing. After a minute she softened against him; she would not go for him again just now.

'What do you want him for, so badly?' he asked, tenderness coming up in him from the leaning weight of her against his chest. His cheek found the striped woolly cap and leaned on it.

'I don't know,' she said, blankly. 'I want to say sorry, really. It's just, if I could say sorry, when it happened.'

'To him? To that particular fox?'

'Yes. He's that fox and all foxes. He's trees, too, and sunsets and windflowers in the dew and little yellow babies on the Yangtze-Kiang – and you and me. I met him on the road the other night. When I knew, and nobody else did because you weren't there yet. So it was him that I met. He didn't know, but I did. Don't you see? He's one of the things I knew, but he wouldn't stop to listen. Or now. He wouldn't know if I said sorry. He hasn't got any "sorry" – but I'd know I'd said it. Even if it couldn't be heard or the sound understood. It'd be something, wouldn't it, Stephen? Wouldn't it be something to have said it?'

He said, 'Yes,' because there was nothing else to say, and because the lie it was would not be heard, nor the sound understood anymore. So he helped her to her feet and patted the snow off her and they helped each other to balance on the glassy road as they went back to the car.

The little white dog had curled up in the warm patch on the driving seat. Her whole, hairy body was shaking with cold and fright. Stephen picked her up and, when Barbara was settled beside him, put the shivering creature in her lap.

'Keep Tinker warm,' he said, and turned his attention to the car so that she should have a little privacy to weep in. Then, when she was sobbing quietly, he said, 'I've never seen such a beautiful garden as the one you grew in the church this afternoon.'

In less than a quarter of a mile they came to the road-block. It was a simple pole, red and white, and at either end it carried a scarlet and a green lantern. In the centre a white reflector had the letters MD stencilled across it. Three grey men stood at one side by a canvas shelter and a brazier burning in a metal container, and on the other the grim density of an Armoured Personnel Carrier bulked black under its spinning, flashing light. On either side of the painted pole, salt and grit had been thrown down on the ice to make it easy to stop. Above, the thorns and holly held the coloured lights tight down on the narrow, twisty road. As Stephen braked cautiously, the grey men stepped up to the car. Each of them carried an automatic rifle, a 7.62mm FAL.

'My God,' Stephen said, and he started laughing, and then could not stop laughing, his shaking hands pounding the steering wheel. 'My God, it's really real.'

    Morag stood in the middle of Tansy's bedroom. Through the uncurtained window that looked out over the flat roof of the utility-room, she could see the rhythmic flaring of the light on the roof of the APC deep in the frozen road, and the confused progress of a car's lamps twisting and turning among the hedges. She thought it was probably Stephen on his way home to the Dipyard with the girl with the strange name. The bright, distant lights were absolutely clear through the frost, sparkling a little as if they wished to be stars and fly up through the coarse, thick-bellied clouds that pressed them down on to the earth. She wondered, briefly, what the regularly flashing, bluish light was, for Crosby Spring was outside the protective circle that had been thrown up around the hill where Croke's Wood glowed green, and so Morag was unaware of the road-blocks. From here she could not see Croke's Wood, only the dark that was a peculiar dark, drawn, as it was, over all that invisible white. The window was slightly opened. The air that came in through it was sharp, pure and chaste, uninterrupted by anything between Morag and outside. It touched her skin, her hands and hair and face, telling her very surely that

Tansy was not there. Tansy was no longer anywhere that had anything to do with Morag. She had gone. She was over, in a way that had to mean something, but was beautifully empty of meaning. Morag had been having difficulty with words ever since the grey men had visited the kitchen last night. It was as if she, who had been so full of sick matter, had been broken into and in some way drained, leaving only this emptiness, this lacuna around which words and images drifted aimlessly with no firm surface on which to settle and be understood. It was very quiet, the bits and pieces of her being around in the emptiness, with nothing bumping against her or oozing out of her or thrusting its way into her. She supposed they were only bits and pieces, because some of her had definitely gone. She could not, for instance, think.

When Stephen had brought them all back from the church because Andrew would not use up what little petrol he had on an affair like Danny marrying Polly, she had been a little sad. She had been quite happy in the church, sniffing at the flowers and watching the candle flames glow and uprise, but then Sam and Malkie had been hungry and she had been unable to imagine food. Instead, leaving Andrew and Sam to open tins and cut bread, she had gone and sat on the upstairs lavatory, squeezing the last soiled, solid item from her body. She would never, she was sure, eat again. Equally, she could not think about Tansy. Andrew (and Malkie) had talked incessantly about why, to where and by whom Tansy had been taken away – Andrew shouting, suffused with some terrible urge that made him dark-coloured, stiff in his movements, thick of tongue, as if some forbidden tumescence had filled his whole being, making of him only this hard, angry seeking which was without law and without relief. Tansy was gone. Tansy was over. There was no Tansy left in Morag. Only what her eyes could see; a dark poster on a pale blue cupboard door, its slogan, Gilroy's 'Life's a Bitch and then You Die.'

She was smiling at the cold, chaste air in and out of her when the door opened and Sam crept in behind her.

'Mummy?'

Oh, now, here was something. It all came in pictures at her, what she had to do. Little bright isolated visions coming in, perhaps, through the open window or through one of the gaps in her mind. Of Sam in his green anorak, and Christopher going to the back of the church, after he had married Polly and Danny, to direct the young men who had sung so earnestly and had carried cardboard boxes into the bell ringers' chamber at the end of the dim aisle; Christopher, almost as tall as Andrew. Of Malkie spitting cabbage on to a wistfully clean tablecloth. Of Andrew in the yard with the shotgun.

'Mummy, are you all right?'

How significant Sam was. And how warm and solid, but sweetly so, with his still-treble voice and his still-silky cheeks.

'Go,' she said, 'and put on your warmest outdoor clothes – boots, gloves, green coat, scarf that Auntie Jan gave you for Christmas.' Her voice sounded peculiar, quite firm and close-to. Not mad at all. It was a long time since she had heard it sound like that, but she remembered it. 'You and I are going for a secret trip, so don't let Daddy and Malkie see you. I'll be here.'

'Daddy – well, I think you ought to be downstairs. Daddy's in a bit of a bate and –'

'Later. I'll go and help Daddy later. First you and I have something very important to do. Quick sticks, now.'

She heard him go out behind her. She was not thinking, no, but she was doing. Something was happening. More pictures. Hiroshima clips and nauseous mock-ups of lowering Neanderthals and millions of insects with hard, clackety-clackety scales and naughty eyes and a sun – was it a sun? – so descant white, riding higher than any sun rode and lighter, with feet of fire and wings of lace-locked spray, and Sam with a rhododendron garland around his neck, laughing inside Ardcollie gates. She rubbed her hands together with delight and then bent down to massage the calves of her legs to bring the blood powerfully, full of iron and oxygen, swinging through the muscles. How easily she bent – how supple her spine was. When she stood up she held her left arm out in front of her, finger pointing straight at the bluish flashes down there in the road, in the outside beautiful air. The fingertip and the light came together. Stayed together. Not even the little wind rustled them. Not even the breath, easing in and out of her deep lungs, wavered between them. Her hand was as steady as a rock.

'Where are we going?' he said, creeping in behind her again. Then, when she turned round, 'Hey, Mummy, you look pretty!'

'I'm taking you to spend the night with Uncle Christopher in the church. For fun and because he needs a bit of help. You know what a scatter-brain Auntie Xanthe is. Then, when everything is ready, here and there, I'll come for you. Come on, we have to walk. What do you say we climb out of the window like Tansy did? Oh Sam, don't be an ass. She's done it since we built the utility-room. I've always known she did!'

'Mum, about Tansy –'

'Tansy's fine, lovey. I know all about where Tansy is. Tansy will be fine.'

'I mean, she is my sister, even if we do fight.'

'I know, I know. All brothers and sisters fight. Tansy's O K. Don't listen to Daddy – all fathers go peculiar when their daughters start going away from home and having boyfriends and all that sort of thing. Come on, open the window wide.'

'Daddy says it's you that's gone peculiar.'

'Yes? Well, he always says that, doesn't he, when we don't agree about something? That's not new! Out you go.'

She could even have been captain of the lacrosse team with this strong, incisive will to win . . . and so fast. She was on the ground among the spiny clematis trailers before Sam had dropped down from the flat roof on to the water-butt.

'Wow,' he said, his teeth gleaming. 'I didn't know you could do things like that!'

'There are a lot of things I can do that you don't know about. Come on, down through the shrubbery.'

It was ten past seven and very dark. Too dark to see the dog fox behind the muck-spreader at the side of the back lane. But he saw them and smelt them, and his ruff rose in horror at the smell of the woman. But he was not her prey and she hurried on, her child by the hand, away from him into the trees.

'I can't,' Danny said. ' I won't. If they're going to kill me, they can do it to my face sitting up. I won't go and hide in the coal-hole with an old tin jerry and a can of baked beans under the spare-room mattress. Not knowing what – or when. I couldn't, Poll. Fucking hell, old sweet, I'd shake the shelter to bits myself, never mind the bomb.'

She laughed. Her belly was churning and her laugh was big and a bit jagged, as if it might trip over into some other sound, but it was a full, noisy laugh; a tribute to Danny's obstinate wish to be brave. 'Open that brandy,' she said. 'That's what I want – good, heady stuff with some fire in it. Hey, and put it in a brandy glass so's I can cuddle it.'

'That's my girl. If we drink enough, when it hits us we'll just go bang and know nothing about it – like a petrol bomb. Poof.' He unscrewed the new bottle and held it up. 'Boof!' he said, grinning. Then, 'Could it? I say, Poll, could we – can people just – you know?'

'Boof? Yes, why not? I've got to go and shut the horses up properly.' She heard his vomit splash on the floor behind her. 'You clean that up and I'll be back in ten minutes.'

'Don't leave me, Poll.'

'The horses, Danny, the horses.'

The storm lantern swayed on its hook. They came up to her under its light, nuzzling and nosing and nipping each other jealously aside. Their winter beards and whiskers and their long black eyelashes glinted in the little paraffin flame-light; their breath steamed about her, breast high, sweet, musky. Love hurt. Love, hard like a foreign stone inside, hurt. Derry and Tammy and Cider, they were old now, sway-backed with the weight of her memories and broken hopes and all her unkept promises. And flashy little Charlie, pushing his nose in at waist height, greedy at her pockets, too young and ridiculous for this, all brown-and-white patches and rolling, wicked eyes peering up at her for fun and bread. For fun. Billy and Cinders and Mr Champs, so sweet and small and obstinate, so oddly beloved by Danny, those three. Dalton and Carna, favoured for their pure white coats; Tramp with his massive puller's shoulders, and Hopkins, her own last love, her last partner, her caring. She took his long brown cheeks between her hands and stared at his dark, unperceiving eyes. Because he could not tell when she lied, she said, 'There'll be dandelions and ash leaves and Mars bars. I'll get you hunting horns and long forest tracks and clean winds and sweet turf. You'll see. Where we're going, it'll be there. We're all going, together. You'll see.'

She pushed among them, tightening the tarpaulin that kept the wind out of the far end of the long shed; pushing down the ball-cock in the water-trough to see if the pipes had frozen up again yet; spreading hay along the rack in more equal distribution; plucking a strand of straw out of Derry's rope-heavy tail; telling them lies and lies about fields and sunshine and corn and sloping, breast-shaped hillsides bright with thrush song and coltsfoot and honey'd clovers. In the sound of her voice and the yellow lamp light they felt safe and stopped pestering her for comfits. She stayed with them for a few minutes, just standing there, doing nothing in her cut-down boots and holey gloves, looking at their long, thin, sinuous necks up which no vomit could rise, but which could scream.

'There'll be clover,' she shouted at them. 'D'you hear me, you buggers, there'll be bloody clover – there will – there will,' and knew that there would be no more clover ever again.

Too fat and heavy, now, Polly. Too raddled. Too old for this. Too thick in the thighs and weak in the breast, her body obtruded between her and her Pollyness and her laughing, profane Frankie. Too late. Too like Danny, 'Don't leave me, Poll.' Who was there for her to hold on to? Tell her that, County-bloody-Council, National-bloody-Government, NATO. Who was she to hold on to when the bells were tolling? Though, of course, they wouldn't toll, would they? The best thing, the safest thing for everyone was not to know. Like they didn't tell you about cancer or the anonymous AIDS tests, in case you couldn't take it and caused trouble. Oh no, they wouldn't ring any bells, blare any sirens so what would they do? Sweet fucking all. They'd just not be there any more, having gone deep underground, somewhere constructed years ago and long prepared, taking their little breeding herds of pubescent kids like Tansy, just in case . . . in case . . . and the rest would be silence. Until the vomiting began . . .

It would take weeks. If you didn't hear it or see it and if you mistook the wind for a January storm, then, no, they wouldn't tell you any different. Even Danny had understood that before she had (how that east wind moaned in the barn rafters, wailing among the iron girders, whistling in the corrugated iron. So lonely, the wind; touching and touching and never embracing). She thought she had been embraced; that there had been, once, nameless people who cared about her, Polly. Given her a DHSS number and tax forms and sent her reminders about cervical smear and car licences and brochures about holidays in Majorca or a chance to win a food processor or vote out the Government. They had seemed to care. She had believed in them, in a way. Even this afternoon, when she had signed her name in Christopher's great big Parish Register, she must have been believing in them, or else why sign?

How high the barn roof was, rattling in the wind, up there in the empty dark. No birds, no moss even, no lichen. Just dark iron girders in a dark void space where the wind passed. She had heard, sometime, how there would be darkness then too. Dark and cold. For ever and without sunrise. How afraid she was. At last, how afraid. The thick flesh, with its creases and smells and involuntary movements, it wouldn't take it. Perhaps they did know best, after all. Why else this cold, leaking sweat in her armpits, this pain in her stomach, this chill in her ovaries? The lantern was so small, so unsteady. Her heart was unsteady. The rail she was leaning against was unsteady. The wind moaned, blind, loveless in the dark. She called out suddenly, 'Who's there?' because no one was there. Not even Frankie. Her cold thighs, clamped close, knew that Frankie was not there. She was alone.

'I've kept my face turned to you all this time – be here now. Be here.' But she was alone. Whose prey was she? 'Oh God, give me back Frankie. Oh God, give me back Frankie. Oh God, give me back Frankie. Not save me, just Frankie. I can't do it alone.'

Cannot. A wall, sheet-iron and clammy-cold, immediately against the eyes, so close. No way through it, or round it, or back from it. Can and Not. Fear, like guilt, like loose water spraying the cavities inside, drenching and streaming down inside the frame – it ached bitterly and would not cease. Pouring Polly out of Polly, washing her away almost. Almost gone. Black temples and crimson eyes and blue-green, drained arteries washed out and wrinkled and all the muscles rinsed off the bone – dear God, it hurts and there is no running from it. I Can Not. Make it other or over. Oh no, no praying, Poll, no God. World without end has come to an end; the Second Coming cancelled. Miracles are off, Polly. There is no one up there to make it other or over. Just you, and what is happening. That's all there is. Like you said to Danny, 'You for you and me for me.' Even Can Not won't work now. There is nothing left but facts. You Are and It Is. Thè Great Declension of the great I A M. What else?

She thought she could not stand, but she could. Or breathe, but her lungs were doing it. There might be some who could will death, but not in her community. It was a forgotten skill. Could not live; cannot die. But being alive was not a choice for Polly, only a fact. She held on to the fact of the rail she had been leaning against – put her weight on the fact of the hard ground under the trampled straw. Felt the fact of herself being. The horses had moved; so time had passed – was still a fact. Time had always been out of control. She understood that now. You could not mess with it or delude it or ignore it. It was in there in the dying and recycling cells of the flesh, as it was out there among the turning stars beyond the clouds. It was the final God – the one that was dying now.

She turned her head and the horses came into closer view. Most of them had their backs to her, munching the hay in the long rack, now that there was a little light in the barn. For ten thousand years they had walked together, her species and theirs. That was a long time; as long, almost as it took her to look at them and see them as real and alive and in some way standing at her shoulder, to be known. To judge. Her head felt light when she moved it and her hands wayward, the wrists and forearms aching. It was with difficulty that she took the lantern off the bracket and turned her huge, distracted flesh to face the door. It was laborious, consuming, to say, 'I'll be back,' and foolish, since the words meant nothing to them.

But to her? Again her stomach shivered and shrank. How much time? How would it happen? What would happen? She did not know. No one had ever told her. There would be a terrible explosion – Polly Anderson had never seen or heard any explosion in her life. What was a 'terrible' explosion? There would be a great cloud, a fireball, a hurricane. She had never experienced any of these things; they were words and photographs in colour or in the films. If they took out Croke's Wood because of whatever it was that was secreted in there among the spruce trees, she would know. She would just go and there would be nothing and no action that ought to have been taken, because time would stop on Croke's Wood – a mile and a half away. But if they took out R A F Brawdy or the power stations along the Severn or Sizewell – she might not know. Would she? She did not even know that. Then there would be things she should have done and had not done because she had not known when to do them. What to do was clear; but not when. 'I'll be back,' was so important; it scored her, turned her cold wateriness to heat, burning in her head and firing her body. She would come straight back – after.

Time, how much time? Time had a function; it was a setting in which to do things, commit actions. Actions in time and space. Now she must run, banging the big door, jabbing at the bolts with fingers swollen with hot, pumping blood; not seeing properly, but peering only at one thing at a time; first the bolt, then the jumping lantern-light on the snow and on her own deep tracks in it. The yard was odd shaped in the drifts, un-angled, tilting, blurred around and smudged; an artifact left outside to spoil in the weather. The snow dragged at her feet, pulled against her stride, slowing her, sucking the strength that had poured away so rapidly in the shed and then come sweeping back with this pounding, hectic urgency.

The back door was heavy on its hinges. Why? Usually she flung it open, crashing, light. Now clumsy, she banged her shoulder against the jamb, pushing herself through. At the sight of Danny her stomach tightened again. He was standing by the cupboard, staring at the shelves. The reality of him ached in her; of his big shoulders and the cloth of his khaki, para-military jersey, cue for masculinity; of the texture of his softening, balding hair. On the floor an untidy heap of tins and packets with dented sides and torn labels, cluttered around his feet. He turned, and she saw that the pupils of his eyes were wide and glaring in the dim light. She stared into them, pulling herself across the floor with her mind, her legs stiff and incapable. His voice was high and brisk and capable.

'There's nothing here worth taking anywhere. I've been looking. It seemed a bit weak not to look. Seemed a bit silly looking, though. Didn't know what to do, Poll. Horses OK? Little 'uns warm enough?'

She nodded, her head huge and light, not easy to wield with just a couple of vertebrae holding it on to the big, clumsy body.

'I got your brandy glass,' he went on, 'on the table. Why don't we sit by the fire and, and –'

'We're married now,' she said.

'Yes. Yes, that's why I thought sitting by the fire . . .' He opened the stove door and the heat surged out, savage, compulsive, whispering to itself. She reached the old cane chair and sat heavily in it, thrusting her hands into the blast of the heat. Millions of women, sitting just so; how many of them were like her? When Danny brought her glass and came to join her, his steps were quick and small, pattering almost as if the uneven running of her heart were manipulating his body. He sat beside her, jerking his chair very close to hers, wanting, she knew, to hold her or be held by her. But he did not touch her, lighting a cigarette with rapid, puffy gestures, drawing deeply and blowing out the smoke as if to inhale it were too slow, too profound an action for his muscles to make.

His hands were shivering, a much faster trembling than the ill-formed shakiness of her own. In his neck a nerve twitched.

'Thought we might just sit here and, you know, work it out later. I cleared up – that. Sorry about it, you know?'

She shook her head. It had been a small matter. She had not minded.

'There'll be instructions on the TV every hour on the hour, and more on the radio at 8.30 and 9.45,' he said. 'Suppose we should look, really. Shouldn't we? Or not, perhaps. Seems a bit silly either way.' Then, 'We haven't got any of those iodine tablets people have been talking about, have we?'

She shook her head. 'They were sold out months ago. I did ask, last week, after we'd seen that programme – remember? But they just laughed at me. It seems that all the Greens and hippies and peace-people and that lot, have been stocking up on them for most of the year.'

'Wonder how they knew when none of us did.'

'We didn't want to know. They did. That's all. Xanthe was in on it – she knows a lot of those sort of people through the bird rescue thing. She often said it was going to happen, but in a sort of way she didn't seem to mind, really. So I didn't listen. Not that pills will make the slightest odds.'

'No, no, no. Nothing for it, really. All the food in all those deep-freezes will be going off already too. People like Joanie and all – never thought ahead about the electricity going. First thing, of course, when you come to think of it. How's the cognac?'

She held the glass in both hands, turning it in the heat from the stove. The fumes were heady and delusive. She should have had gin. Gin had no memory; it belonged only to the last few years with Danny and growing older. It did not crush her under old flowers, press-dried nostalgias. Her unsteady body leaned around the bulbous glass, drawing on the liquid for its thin, pushing blood's sake.

'I want to say something, Poll. Don't laugh at me, will you? No, don't look. I like the side of your head. Used to it, I suppose –'

No, he had never demanded much. Just bed and acceptance. He had never asked for love, now that she thought of it. Never asked for her, for Polly. Or for her to turn her face to him in the night. Nothing like that; just hoping she would let him stay. Nor was he asking now. He knew how she was. Perhaps he really loved her, after all? Perhaps, now that she came to think of it, that was why he was here, now. Because he loved her? She wondered.

'Danny –'

'No, Poll. Let me say.' He put his hand on the arm of her chair – he who had so often rolled those hands among her breasts and thighs, so enthusiastic and wilful, hot; and this cold, shivering hand on the arm of her chair was also Danny's and he did not touch her. 'Thought I'd like to tell you that I think it's very – well, kindly. Nice of you, Poll, to let me marry you. Appreciate it, really.'

'I owe you, Danny,' she said, out loud, too, so that he could hear her thinking. 'There are some things about people that you know a lot more about than I do. Here, hold my hand. Old Poll's got the scares.'

He did better than that. He took her hand into his lap and put his other arm around her shoulder, and she could feel it there and had somewhere to rest her wild, bumping head. And right through him she could feel the little shivering coming from the innermost nucleus of his being, outwards until it made his skin tremble.

'You're a brave man, Danny, after all. Who would ever have thought it?'

'Don't put any hope in me, Poll. I'll crack.'

'No, you won't.'

'Polly, Oh Polly, don't. I'm near through already. I won't last, you know that –'

'You will. I promise you. Look at me, Danny. It's a promise.

because I know what is going to happen. Trust me. You are going to be all right.'

Drive the words along the pattern. The template is all set up. Get the words going in the head, smoothly, the way they ought to, and ride them down the course; just don't let the nerves or the idiot mind hold them back. The run is clear and fair. Get on to it now and ride straight on down it – never look to the side. Her breath came short; panting, bratchet-breath on a low scent, hunting. Her hand twisted in Danny's, caught his wrist, pulse and artery running away in there, away from her if she could not hunt them down in time. Predator now, not prey, hunting Danny to death. (No, never look sideways, but there is something there, all the same, also hunting, out to the side.)

A very old man, whose name might be Death, hunting in the woods, with a long, wolfish stride; with long, aged thighs and a sharp, high-ridged nose. Alone and barefoot, he was running in the forest that lay the other side of Croke's Wood. The untrue side, the side they were all afraid to walk in, even at high noon, which had been hacked and burned down centuries ago, millennia ago, and into which they were all creeping back with wide, haunted eyes, deeper and further into the forest where the old man was hunting. The forest that was gnarled before the first shoots of Brocéliande were flushed green.

Other men out tonight, too. Not hunters, these, but woodsmen, gardeners, stockmen; old men who had forgotten the names of their moon-thrown sweethearts, but remembered their eyes; men who knew what prison was and some who had mended starlings' broken wings. They were out among the bitter lanes and fields, in small gardens where roses slept deep and under sweet blue cedars; not hunting, not saying goodbye even. Just being there, in their place, among other things in their own place. From time to time one or another of them was noticed by the grey men around the perimeter fence of Croke's Wood, or by the road-blocks in the valleys below. Short signals ran along the newly laid GWEN systems – a solitary man at such and such coordinates, moving east; a stationary man among trees at ten to five from the APC behind the Dipyard, at about six hundred yards; Morag staggering, apparently drunk, across the fields towards Crosby Spring. Watch that one . . . The young men watched carefully. The older men did not spend their attention. They had seen this before. At six minutes to nine the dog fox slipped under the loose corner of the shed in Polly's place and his vixen appeared on the patch of trampled snow outside the brushwood pile, fifty yards outside the fence in Croke's Wood.

The snow was green; citrus green, butcher's shop green, under the lights inside the wire fence. The vixen stood, head up, sniffing. In his steel tower between the regular spruces, the sentry looked down on her. She was thin, her flanks drawn in, her belly ragged where she had lain quiet for too long. Her coat was patchy. The green light flicked her whiskers and the black hair on her hocks. The sentry was down-wind of her, high up among the scented spruce, and she did not catch his odour, only the smell of snow and dark and her own hungry breath. She stood, one pad raised, immobile. Very slowly the sentry lifted his rifle. It was one of the light, new Lee Enfields and she came true in the sights, true just behind the shoulder, where a shot should go. He smiled a little and the vixen slipped out of the green light, away to his left. He had never seen a wild fox close-to before and had had the impression that they were bigger than that . . . He wondered if, had he been free to shoot, he would have done so. In the dark the vixen, belly-low and tense, crawled the plough. She had a different routine from her dog's, different ways. The dark wind clasped her tight.

It cried in the keyhole and under the door of the vestry, a small sound and alien. Elemental, *distrait*, at odds with the books and surplices and the thick, tasselled cloth on the wooden table. Slip-paper book markers quivered as they felt the cold on the wind. Christopher did not see them. He sat on a hard, upright chair, his back against the cupboard where the hymn sheets were stored. Its handle dug into his shoulder but he did not feel that either. He was holding the cassette-recorder on his lap, gazing at it.

'Whose is it, love?' Xanthe said, coming in from the choir of the church, carrying a cardboard box full of smaller cardboard boxes. 'What do I do with the rubbish?'

'Keep it. Keep everything that will burn.'

'It's huge, isn't it? What is it for? Who gave it to you?'

'Woolworths. It belongs to Woolworths.'

'You never bought it! Aren't they closed?'

'I stole it.'

'I would have too. Is it Ian's?'

'I told you, I stole it. Looted it.' His soft voice howled through the room as if he had shouted. His cheeks looked so thin, hollowed and shadowed by the wind-swung bulb hanging from the ceiling. She thought, He won't live to be as old as this, and said, 'Oh Christopher.'

'Out there,' he said, 'things have changed. Probably it happened when the radio announced that we must prepare for a nuclear strike. Such unfamiliar words, you know, not like "war" or "call-up". Actually told us to prepare for it. Well, out there –' he gestured minimally towards the outside door, 'they are preparing.'

'And us?' she said, coming up close to him. He reached out and took her hand, carried it to his dark cheek. Felt his wedding ring upon it. 'We are preparing to be killed,' he said. 'It's different. They are preparing to die. It doesn't feel the same.'

She whispered, 'It is the same to me.'

He said, 'We are all selfish about our own deaths.'

There was not enough left in her to hate him, as love does hate;

only enough to gather together, like a cronish tribeswoman, hugged against her breast for herself alone. Selfishly, as he had just said. Compared to her, he would have it easy, this garnering of selfishness. In the dowsed light his lank hair draped like a hanging-judge's cap and she did not want it to touch her.

'Are they – violent?' How practical she was, how secular. He had his face against her skirt. It had never taken up the musty, incense and damp smell of church as his own clothes had. It smelled only of Xanthe.

'Not very,' he said carefully, girls with cosmeticked eyes nuzzling his mind. 'Not yet. And there are guards about in the streets.' He thought her natural mind was judging the strength of the doors, the leaded, stained-glass windows, the cellar shute.

'Enough guards?'

'Well . . .' Well, they bled, the same as anyone else. 'There was some trouble and Woolworths was opened. I didn't see why not – why not me too. The musical fellow above Stephen's shop has gone. I'd just been there and it's all tidy and empty. He's got out.'

'Where to?'

'Who knows? Perhaps he's found an empty church somewhere with a pump organ to play, or a music shop with five virgin pianos. Perhaps he's on the road, singing. I left a note and took these.' He tapped the cassettes in his pockets. 'I haven't looked to see what they are –'

'Go on. Why did you stop so suddenly? What did you do, Christopher?'

'I told you.'

'No, I want to know what you did.'

He released himself from her, rose suddenly and stepped away, his back turned. 'I don't know what I did. I don't know how it qualifies – what it means.'

'What did you do?' Because she would know what it meant.

What it signified to her, selfish as she was about her own death. Had he not just said so? What he did was her property now, not his. It was a part of her dying, how he would be, and she was claiming it. 'Tell me –' viciously at his back. She would fight him for her right to him; even that, if he would not give it willingly.

'All right. I covered my dog-collar and went to the electrical store on the corner, but I didn't know how to break in.'

'What did you want?'

'I wanted music! I can't play and you can't even sing and we're going over that edge to music, no other way.'

'What "edge"?'

He had not told her about the ship of souls sailing over the end-of-the-world-no-landfall. She thought he meant his own mind cracking. Let her; it would be easier for her that way.

'Then when they broke into Woollies, I went with them, bust a chain and stole that thing. It was the biggest one in the shop. Then I stole batteries to make it go – the right size batteries, I even saw to that. What does that make it?'

'Oh Christopher.'

'Oh Christopher, dear Christopher,' he shouted. 'Damn Christopher. I'm a priest, aren't I? And Ian's a doctor. So where is Ian? Do you know?' His eyes were wonderful again, full of fired coals and jet lights, burning his face away. 'I know. But I'm here, in my church –' He stopped, and then added, '– and so is the Montgomery Paten. Do you understand, Xanthe? Do you know what I'm talking about?' He reached out and took her hand again, but this time fiercely, blanching the knuckles, not giving her time to answer, not even time to be in, wheeling her away with him in the direction he must not be stopped from taking. 'Where's Sam?' He thrust his head round the door into the body of the church, his gripping hand fastening Xanthe to him. 'Sam? What are you doing down there?'

'Putting tea-bags in tins so's they won't go musty.' The boy's voice carried lightly among the stone pillars and marble tablets and the hard, cold altar rails.

'Come up here, I want you.'

Footsteps almost running in the dim wilderness of stone, the height of which went high above the dark and had no known finity. Sam, young and cold and homesick, running at the lit vestry and the bodies of Christopher and Xanthe like a young beast separated from the herd. Pushing in close between them for warmth, or something similar to warmth.

'See that thing, Sam? I don't know anything about them. Make it work for me. Be in charge of the thing. You kids have all these gadgets. Set it up so that it plays full blast right through the church. Find the best place for it – the loudest – and if it lifts the halos off the angels' heads, well and good. There are the tapes or cassettes or whatever – I've no idea what they are, but I want music. Big, big sounds. Now, make it go. Xanthe, a candle in every window, lit. Every single window, and the lamps in the porch too. And then I'll teach you both a marvellous trick.'

'What?' Xanthe said, dully.

'How to ring church bells,' he answered. In his hand, hers was stiff and heavy.

'Wow, Uncle Christopher! Me, too?'

'Of course. She'll take you right up off your feet.'

'While the tapes are on? Groo–vy!' Sam's eyes wider now, not so screwed up; not so invulnerable. Then, fidgeting through the cassettes, 'What are these, anyway? Never heard of any of them. Oh Uncle Christopher, honestly! They're awful. Beethoveny stuff and Oh, for goodness sakes – "BBC Sound Effects: Summer Out of Doors".'

. . . and the sun burst out above the soft pigeons and shone, June bright, and bird sung along the chains of daisies that shackled

Xanthe's hands to Christopher's and she smiled at him in the blinding sunlight of twenty past nine on this sixth night of Christmas.

At about ten o'clock the wind rose and a break appeared in the clouds to the east. The unlit night slipped into sudden, azure moonshine. All around Barbara the great stars of Earth's spiralled galaxy pulsed and glowed, notating with bright forms a harmony across receptive space. Millions upon millions of descant notes intervalled upon each other, reflecting and visible, register upon register, chorded round with singing winds and planets about whose poles auroras rang (worlds without end, without beginning, without centre or organization; multiplicities of exquisite chance). It was her moon, riding close and blue-white, that clipped the planet closest; pouring down on her so much pure light that her least intimacy, her smallest detail, became a beloved's eyes sparkling in response; each minute frost particle a mirage of imagined stars shining, to Barbara, in mutual love: earth and sky-space.

Barbara was suffering very terribly now. It seemed to her that the time of fear was over and the time of pain begun; that she had moved from an active state into a passive one in which knowing and waiting and fearing had no existence, and in which only suffering was; that in this consummation of the present, Time, like the eyes of the dead, was already closed. She put the tips of her fingers against the space she had scraped free of frost in the windowpane and let her eyes take in the shining outdoors. All the months past in which the great elms and limes had swayed green-tall and wonderful into their burning autumn, she had not had the courage to love them. When winter stripped them and showed her their discreet limbs and most particular structures, she had turned away, unable to say 'I love you' to that which was to be lost, lest the losing be unbearable and the knowledge of the loss too protracted for her little braveries. Only the dog fox had forced her with love; coming in out of an unseen parallel in the night to watch her, judge and smash her cowardice. A visitant, paraclete or supplicant or observer, she did not know in which form he visited, out of existences for which she was not great enough to suffer.

But now the suffering had begun, electing her through which to project itself; streaming into her on the moonlight, piercing her brow and her hands with starpoints, unravelling its profound anguish before her feet in hectares of untrodden snow. The fingertips, which were so small, pressed against the glass, and so strong was the moonlight and so weak the dimmed bulbs in the room behind her that the brilliant night made of them pale, translucent ovals through which the earth shone unhindered as if it and her flesh were but concomitant states of revelation in a chaos so majestic that neither could endure with it nor acknowledge it. No mourning for the death of life itself; it will pass without rite or hope of requiem.

She said, 'Calcium, the base stuff of sea-shells and the stuff of my ankle bones, is the same stuff. And there are chalk cliffs of it rising from the green sea and it flows in breast milk. Ammonites and idols and your knuckle bones – it ought to be happiness to be of such a company. It ought to be comfort. Will there be ammonites again? Will the cliffs stand or will they crumble like a vole's bones? Stephen, do you know?'

But he did not know. Only that with white chalks mystical signs had been made on laboratory blackboards and by the signs, Death had been called up. He had been right to be afraid of things written. He said, 'It isn't that it is not enough to be human; it is too much. We accept that this is to be the end – in our great egocentricity we claim that it will all come to nothing; voles, me, you, the white petals of next week's snowdrops. Other things, other beings may come – yes, like ammonites again and trilobites and things which will never confess to a name, because, for God's sake, no more humankind. Even so, they say, who knows what may not happen in Tierra del Fuego or Sumatra? After all, the computers in Canberra will still be working; they don't get radiation sickness and they've found a way of protecting them now – immunizing them, didn't you know? – against changes in the magnetic field, the sort of thing that killed off all the dinosaurs. But it won't kill the computers. They invented it in North London. Think of it – the hoof-print of mankind in North London.'

So she thought of the dark, snow-cowled Afterworld spinning through the skies, and the little green screens that went on and on relating and re-telling and re-forming. Projecting, she thought suddenly, the undiscovered, the ultimate mysteries that there would be no one there to implement and so the screen would clear and relate another set of data and the beginning of life would go back into the darkness again. There was such beauty in that, she thought. But she could not comprehend it, only was vaguely aware of a beautiful thing passing by. She said, thinking of the lie that time now was, 'The sea-shells are my mother and my sister, and I am killing them.'

'You are killing me, too,' he said, 'and I you, and each one everyone. We are all sentenced for murder and matricide. Only the long-dead and the mad, perhaps, are innocent. But I doubt it. There is no more innocence. We killed her at Nagasaki, or Olduvai, I forget now which it was, and began the death-agony of our sister sea-shell.'

'You do understand,' she said in wonder.

'No. I know, but I do not understand.'

Her flesh no longer felt old to Polly. It had come firm and taut around her, tuned in to the hot arteries, the light musculature resilient on the bone. She sensed it, felt along it, sought out its health in the flexing spine, in the steadied hands, the skin supple and tough now, in the vulva, cool and small, and in the hard muscles over the stomach. The heart, which she had feared for its intemperance, beat light and fast and regular, and the ligaments of the neck were vibrant with strength. It was well with her, in her. Centrally, threading through the eyes of the vertebrae, the nerve and its mind linked and meshed powers. Surprisingly it caused Danny to say to her, as Sam had said to Morag in her madness, 'I say, you are pretty.'

If there had been a God left she would have thanked Him then for the merciful blindness He had thrown over Danny (don't look to the side). Deceptive, laying spring-traps with the steady voice and the conker-velvet eyes that caressed his eyes and deluded him into thinking that he could see in the dark, she said, 'It must be this sitting together. It has restored me. Danny, is this your wedding present to me? This sureness you give me?'

'I?' He laughed a little; a pleasant sound in the soft clinking of the stove-side. 'I would like to think that I could give you anything at all. No, Poll, it's not my present to you – it's yours to me that you can think it is. Makes quite a man of me, in a manner of speaking.'

Meaning it, she said softly, 'Then it is something we can share . . .' putting her hand on his cheek and almost, oh very nearly, loving him (don't look out to the side now). Then, 'Danny, it's night. I want to sleep through the dark like an animal, until the day comes back and I can see again. Will you come to bed with me? Just to see me to sleep?'

'Just that? On our wedding night?' He was not looking at her, but at his own knees where the taut cloth betrayed his trembling.

'Just that. Some things are best begun in chastity.'

'Oh God – Oh thank God. Thank God, Poll –'

The cellar door gaped wide, evil-smiling, evil-smelling. It was a dark hole, damp from beaded condensation and steam which dripped like viscous fluid down the red painted jambs. Leading downwards, the yellow and orange and harsh blue shit-bags were stacked against the steps, and deep inside, a hot candle flame leaped and jumped, twitching the walls tight in spasms of shadow. In and out Andrew hurried, ever heavier bundles and cartons scoring the sides, scarring the red paintwork. Morag stood apart from him, out in the big room; quarry-tiles unmatted, table unclothed, shelves disburdened. Andrew had not stoked the Aga and the cold crept from each corner of the room towards the centre, fingering the chair-backs and dresser with stealthy, disruptive questions; lifting wrappers, shifting aside the paper-thin wafers of dried honesty on the sideboard. Moonlight struck bright through the broken yellow blind, clashing on the blade of the bread-knife, striking the zinc draining-board, jangling in the metallic insets in the hanging Christmas cards. The long, pale strip-light flickered mauves and gun-metal blues along the length of the ceiling, adding nothing to the white moonlight, taking nothing from it. Moonshine emptied the room of colour, washed, striped, hatched it in blue and black and silver. Only on the wall where the cellar door flared open was there no white light, just the hot little flame throbbing beyond the red door.

In the new emptiness created by the moon, Morag stood by herself in the profound blue space between the dresser and the table. The strange colourlessness suited her. It made highlights in her quiet brown hair and lit up the bone structure in her thin, pointed face. Her grey eyes shone with its reflections, merged softly and imperceptibly into its sheen; where it made vacant desolation in the untidy room, it made beautiful designs out of her scattered elements. She was staring at it, into it, regardless of Andrew's form surging around her and pushing in and out of the red door. From the depths of the cellar she could just hear Malkie singing, his child's voice oddly out of sorts with the words he had been repeating for days now, learned from a record of Tansy's.

> *Generals gather in their masses,*
> *Just like witches at Black Sabbaths,*

so that she knew she must not look at the black and red stew where her child-son caroused among the tins and blankets and camping stoves, uniformed and flashed and braided, his beardless face old with intention. Just one more of the generals – she was not surprised to find him among his peers. She had half-seen him that way for some time. The singing did not greatly disturb her, it was too far away. Growing further all the time. From the room's corners the cold reached her. It stroked her forehead and kissed her lips, seeking out all the naively open pores of her skin and creeping in through them into her head. The cold inside her head was important because it was a cold born of space and thin, northern air. It made her feel a little afraid again, as she had before she had taken Sam to Christopher and Xanthe in the church, making the disintegrated parts of her drift around and sway and collide in a confusion that was sometimes noisy and sometimes desolately silent.

'For God's sake, woman, if you can't help, stand out of the way.'

She was not in the way. She was too small and light to be in anything's way, all disparate like this. Andrew could walk through her, displacing parts of her as if she were a broken ice-floe on a restless sea. His voice was discordant, out of element, not belonging to the cold waste which she had become. It intruded and then faded, echoless, away, without cause or effect. She turned round slowly, round and round, seeking the way to Ardcollie. Could she collect enough of her pieces together to make that journey? Andrew was collecting things.

'Malcolm, get your arse up here and do some of the running round – you're going to have plenty of time down there.'

Morag saw he was taller than Andrew now; like a seraph with his satin cheeks and unsexed voice; only not one of Christ's seraphim who, she knew, were rainbow-white and sandalled. This one was booted and had blood on his tongue when he sang,

> *In the fields the bodies burning,*
> *And the war-machine keeps turning.*

'Shut up, for God's sake! That's a disgusting song.'

'Well, it's true, isn't it? Tansy says it's a prophecy. She has an album with it on in her room. It's by Ozzie Osbourne. He eats live bats in front of millions – you can watch it on the telly. Shall I go and get it for her for when she gets back?'

'You'll go into the sitting-room and get the poker cards and Monopoly and Scrabble –'

'Ugh. I won't get Trivial Pursuit, Dad. I hate that and you always win anyway. It's not fair.'

'Tansy always wins Monopoly. I suppose you hate that too? I suppose you think you'll win one day? Some game or other – I suppose you might.'

Malkie stared at Morag. 'Does she want anything? She's useless at games isn't she. She never wins anything, so it doesn't matter what she plays, does it, Dad?' He could not, Morag knew, see much of her. Not many of her fragments were in his view.

'She has her own games. Go and do what I said. Morag? Mor– ag!' Andrew put his coloured, great face close to her and shouted. She moved away, bumped by the sound of him.

'What?' she said aggressively.

'Oh, you can still hear? Malcolm – out. Do what you're bloody told.' He turned back to her, towering, the moonlight catching out the coarse bristle on his cheeks. There was a blackhead near his nose.

'Go away,' she said, directly to his body; to the too-adjacent face. 'Get it away.'

'Me, is it, now?' he asked. 'Tansy gone, then Sam, and it's me now?'

From the sitting-room Malkie's 'Mary was that mother mild' voice pierced the dark and in the kitchen a light shaft struck the cellar doorstep. The moon was winging on her ordained course in the depths of the blue, blue heavens.

> *Death and hatred to mankind,*
> *Poisoning their brain-washed mind –*
> *Oh Lord. Yeah!*

The pieces of her crashed against each other, inside her, rocking her on her feet and jerking her round again so that she was left, panting, staring at the greedy cellar doorway where the moonlight hesitated but did not enter.

'Me, is it?' He was behind her now. He had done that before – once, very long ago in some terrible place whose frontiers had been closed ever since. She had submitted, then, pink and naked, squealing and grunting miserably.

But not now. Oh no. 'You'll turn into bacon down there!' she shouted, and her laugh rang silvery around the exquisite moonshine as the apposition struck her. 'When the heat gets to you, in there – crackling and all! Your turn, Andrew, your turn!'

'And where do you think you'll be, you crass idiot?' He tried to catch hold of her but she slipped away, little petite dance steps pattering on the moon-struck floor.

'Out in the cool, cool snow, of course. Out there –' She made a dart at the back door. It opened for her (had she actually touched it?) and there, beyond the cut-out holly and Christmas ivy, was the forest, thick and dark green and whispering. The first pungent foliage pressed against her face, the nearest rough trunk was almost secure between her outstretched palms when his giant hand gripped her arm and hurled her back and the door slammed in front of her eyes and the kitchen was there, walls and walls of kitchen and killed wood turned and broken and sawn and pierced to make tables to eat off. Flesh meals – with thin, bloody water offered in a wide dish –

'Jesus Christ.' The nausea in his voice stank. She was not surprised.

'Morag – you've – you've messed yourself. Go and clean up before the kid sees you. Go on – I'm not going to fucking touch you. Christ, I won't touch you –'

'It's not me,' she said, his ignorance and stupidity affecting her like sea-fog, so that she had to put out her hands again to feel her way back to the forest which lay between her and Ardcollie. She had the lie of it now; first this sea, floes and fogs and the clutching cold and the fetid stench of rotting ice. Then, along the strait tracks through the snow-pure forest where the tall trees on either side guarded and protected the traveller against straying or becoming lost or falling among the gnarled root grips and so weathering away, down, down into the busy soil to feed the infant trees, for each one was made of a traveller's elementals. She had always known that. But not her; she would not become a tree because the trees themselves would direct her, and at the end of the virgin ride the rhododendrons and unhinged gates of Ardcollie would be open for her to come home.

Andrew could see where she was going. He could hear Malcolm dropping the Scrabble box and all the little plastic squares clattering on the passage floor. That would give him time to deal with Morag. If he could see how to do it. Christ – if only he could feel

sorry for her, he might know what to do. But, shit, he had to go
and fetch Sam back and that meant leaving Morag with Malkie
and God knows what she might do. He would have to tie her up –
that was the best thing. Shut Malcolm in the cellar, tie Morag to a
chair or something – that would mean touching her, Jesus! – take
the Land Rover over to the church to pick up Sam – damn fool,
Christopher, couldn't he see that Morag had flipped and there was
no telephone? He put his hands over his face. Did it matter what he
did? It would all come to the same in the end – 'bacon; crackling
and all' – except for Tansy. She would be all right in the bunker –
God, if only he knew where it was – with the military. They knew
what to do, with that calm, quiet efficiency. That's where he
should be himself, not – he couldn't evade the word – panicking
around here with a mad, incontinent woman and two kids. In
uniform. Oh God Almighty, help me. It's not fair, dear God, it
isn't fair – we have no orders – nobody's telling us what to do,
what to expect. 'In the fields the bodies burning' – he would kill
the store cattle one by one, for meat. That meant cartridges – dry,
in a biscuit tin near his mattress, with the .22 and the shotgun. And
its cartridges. He did know what to do. When it came to logistics,
he did know. Keep vandals off and roaming bands – there would
be violent gangs coming for his meat and his women, always were.
Take both guns down, and the saw, hatchet, cleaver, everything he
would need for butchering. Oh yes, he knew what to do. He saw
that while he had been seeing himself in action, his fingers had
shredded, into minute triangles, the list he had made for himself,
dictation-wise, from the radio announcements. The fucking tears
came back under his hot eyelids.

      She felt his feet against her calves. 'Danny, you've got
your socks on!'
   His whole body was cold. She felt it, solid and chill, shivering

against her. Her heart pounded – he, who had his manicured, now shrinking hand on her peace-soft breast, felt it leap inside her. He moved so that his hand, now turned sideways, lay between her breasts and the palm, filled with the sweet, dolorous warmth, could no longer feel the beat within.

'Not sleepy,' he murmured against the black coil of her hay-scented hair.

'Going to be awake for a long time, feeling the feet cold.' He moved them back, away from her. 'Thought the socks would do the trick. Sorry, old pet.'

Running true. Luck was with you, or inspiration, or maybe something incalculably greater than those, when the going was fast and the quarry, the Great Quarry, in full view. Even in the oldest stories, Love was the Great Quarry. Her heart struck, faster and faster, great hooves in her secret body, pounding, pounding.

'This is not a good night to lie awake, Danny,' she said in her clear, carrying voice.

'The worst. I'd rather be asleep when – bit childish, that, but, d'you know, I don't really want to know. What Stephen said this afternoon, about never knowing who pressed the button first, I mean, what the hell, really? Isn't it? Funny chap, that, having a woman at the very last minute, after all. Sweet, really, don't you think?'

'You have a woman, too, Danny,' the way these lies are told; tenderly.

'Oh God, I know, Poll, I know.' Then, very softly, as if he did not quite want her to hear, 'Trying awfully hard so that you'll have a man – don't think I'll make it though, will I.' It was not a question.

'I promised you. Trust me.' (No matter what you hear, never look out to the side.) 'All the same, I'm going to get us a hot drink. You're colder than me, you stay here and keep the bed warm. The damned electric blanket's hardly working at all.'

On her way she pulled back the curtains.

Twenty minutes past eleven. The moon free-wheeling down the sky now, on her way to tomorrow already.

She did not see his hand coming, not until it smashed into her space, crashing her fragments against each other, dragging their unseeable undersides screaming into the exposing storm.

'Don't touch me – don't – dirty, dirty –'

Malkie's feet running to the noise, jattering like a stranded salmon on a gravelly moraine –

'Wicked, wicked! Filthy wicked –' Morag screamed, grabbing at the big, claw-coloured hands; the huge round head that loomed up at her eyes. The moon was in her, straight through, low down, coming quick, quick-silver quick through the other window, darting to her across the congealed tangle of screaming and blows. It was in her now, flicking up and down like mercury, fighting her battle with its winged feet flashing in the moonlight in her limbs. Andrew had her by the mouse-brown hair, throat back, wrenching her, arc-down, into a chair. Her boot caught him on the knee-cap and he cried out, 'Mad! You crazy cunt –' and so she knew everything all at once. Where the loaded gun was; how long a stride that lovely, trim body could take, fluid and easy and full of grace; the gun in her hands now, its wooden stock warm and fatherly in her shoulder and its long, hard barrel sticking out in front of her.

'I have one, too,' she said, calmly, Andrew's sick face lined up neatly in the sights. 'I have one now. It's big, isn't it? How do you stop it shooting, Andrew?'

Whispering, he said, 'You put it down on the table. It's loaded. When it's on the table it can't shoot.'

'Not on its own? You always said it had to shoot when it was loaded.'

'I never said that, Morag. Put it down and I will unload it. I won't let it go off.'

'But you always did, didn't you? When you had it, Andrew, you never, never put it down. Why should I?'

'Because it's dangerous.'

'Oh I know, I know.' She was smiling at him along the stock of the shotgun. Her face, so thin now, flushed a delicate pink over the cheek-bones, her straight, winner's shoulders as still as a steel cradle for the gun (in the doorway Malkie stood still. He might have been only four foot eight). Her finger found the safety catch and clicked it through. Andrew swayed, took hold of the back of the chair he had been pulling Morag into. His knuckles were as white and glassy as iced snow.

'Cunt,' she said, her top lip lifting. 'Why did you call me that?'

He could not answer. His throat worked terribly, but there was no sound. Just a rasping breath or two. Not that there was an answer. His stomach was gone, retracted into a small, cold lead knot below the creaking of his lungs.

'Put the gun down, Morag,' he whispered again. It came out wrong; pitiful, not commanding. Not how he had willed it.

'Stand in the cellar door, Andrew.'

'Why?' Stalling.

'Because I want you to.'

'Why?' Could he jump her? Not from here. Anyway, his legs . . .

'Go!' Screaming again. The sound like a whistle blast, so direct, so functional. Would his legs? Would they?

What had made him think she was daft? The fog, maybe; but that had swirled away when the quick-silver moon cut through it. This was bright and simple, straight on from here, the snow so bright and white and no fear of straying. The gates were nearly in sight, on along there – just now, they'll be there. Just this bit, here, and then –

He shuffled on the way to the door.

'Stop there – don't touch it.'

He had lost his chance. He had his back to her. But she wouldn't do it. They never did. Not the women. Don't let him piss himself in front of Malkie. Like she had. She wouldn't do it. They never did. To be able to hold on to the door frame – oh please . . . He was at the entrance to the cellar. Very exactly in front of it. Within, the hot little candle jerked his shadow across the rigid frame. He put his enormous, coloured hands on to the wet, red labia of the jambs, bracing himself in them. And she fired.

Because he fell backwards, out of the doorway, she laughed.

Then. There was nothing else to do with Malkie, really, because she wasn't going to be here and she shouldn't leave him alone. That wasn't right. He was only nine and would never be able to cope with Andrew's list of things the radio had said to do. It was rather nasty, doing it, and she did not do it terribly accurately, but afterwards she moved on, up the forest ride in the snow and the gates of Ardcollie were standing ready for her when she reached them. The rhododendrons glittered in the frost, every leaf node and branch fork a nest of shimmering crystals in blues and pinks and greens and fire-white, and from the stone gate-pillars the trailing icicles rang chimes of silver and cut glass, and because she couldn't wait to tell, she called, as she started to dance up the long, silent drive, still carrying her lacrosse stick, 'Mummy, guess what I've learned to do! I scored a goal! Mummy! Mummy, where are you? Mummy?'

It was Polly's feet that were cold when she came back. She pressed the soles of them gratefully down on to Danny's socks, deep under the duvet.

'You were a long time. Nearly came down to see if I could help you. Didn't like it without you.' He was smiling a bit and, to her hurt, blushing. 'They say it's just a piece of paper, this marrying thing – but it's a damned odd paper. Magical, in a way, if you know what I mean. Has a powerful effect. Saying all sorts of things to you tonight. Only said, "Roll over, Poll," last night. It's the bit of paper that's done that.'

She did not look at him, but moved sideways so that her sumptuous black head rested against his chest. 'You're not saying anything I didn't know. So I could have said "No," couldn't I?'

'Thought you would. Expected you to. Would have bought rings and so forth, if I'd ever thought you'd say "Yes". Didn't actually mean to ask, if it comes to that. It just sort of popped out.'

'Like our talking now,' she said. But she was lying. 'Just popping out. Like mouse-holes. You know the mice are there and then one day, suddenly, when you're thinking about the price of bran and oats, there they all are in front of you, running about.'

'Not sure I wanted you to see my mice, old sweetheart.'

'I like mice. It's the dark holes that frighten me.'

The moonlight spread over and up the bed and flowed across the walls, all the little flowers on the faded wallpaper opening to receive it. She put out the flickering bedside bulb. They did not need it.

'Like having an extra day,' he said, staring at the brilliant starry sky beyond the uncurtained window. 'It's been so gloomy lately, since Christmas. All that snow and fog and clouds. Dark at lunchtime. Quite got me down. This is beautiful.'

When the shooting started each felt the other leap, as if electricity jumped them. Once. Then two more. Then silence.

'Oh God,' he whispered. Later, 'Someone after a fox, could it be?'

'Andrew, perhaps. It came from over there. It came from over that way.' Her voice was thin. Tinny, almost. But foxes do not warrant investigation and the low rumble of the Saracen and the far-off whines of cars on ice carried far on the frost-bitten air. In her head Polly saw the displacement in Morag's eyes that afternoon in the church; the way she had wrapped her faded coat around her, tight as mummy-bands. 'Run –' she cried aloud. 'Run –'

'What, pet?'

'The fox – if they didn't get him – to run. The moon's so bright –'

'Ah.' He did not believe her.

She felt sorrow in him, tremendous, languorous grief, weighting his body so that he seemed to sink heavier into the mattress. She cried out to him, 'I have to say that. It has to be a fox, because if it isn't – Danny, if it's too late I'm sorry,' and turned away, forceful, driving.

He spoke very slowly, then, taking her hand and sitting up, settling both their pillows behind them. 'Let's have those hot drinks, Poll. It's going to be a hellish cold night.'

He was a brave man. In his way, he was brave.

The heart, intemperate in Polly, was roaring now, she could even hear it inside her ears, muffling outside sounds. It beat in a line across her shoulders so that her arms ached, and rose, pounding, in her throat. Danny must feel it too, their pillows so close together. Because of the blood in her ears she could not tell how her voice sounded when she tried to say, or said, 'I'm a coward, Danny.'

(They said the Great Quarry could turn, at bay. Turn and kill. Which the predator; who the prey?) Fear of that was the greatest of her fears. She spoke again.

'Drink it, Danny, please. All of it.'

He stared into the mug, steam rose in his eyes. 'What is it? It's horrible looking.'

'I have to tell you. There's sleeping stuff in it. Some of those powders that Ian gave me when I had trouble with the Inland

Revenue last summer. But I didn't use them all – and I remembered them just now. That's what took so long – looking for them.'

Hanging on to the table, screaming silently at the kettle, Don't boil yet – give me a few more minutes. Don't boil yet. That, and putting milk and baking powder in her own mug to create the same, smoky effect. That was what had taken the time.

'Look, mine's all cloudy. I have to sleep tonight, Danny. I have to stop for a little.' (Go for it now, go for it. Before he turns his great head to you and you look into his eyes.) 'I couldn't face you in the morning if I was the only one to have slept. If you'd been awake all through – the night. Please sleep, Danny. Please –'

He clutched the mug in his hand. 'Another mouse, Polly. Want to see it?'

'Go on, then.'

'Won't we – I mean, suppose we kept it. Mightn't it –?'

'I'm sorry. I'm so, so sorry. You see, there wouldn't be enough . . . he only gave me enough for a few nights –'

(Now. The mort is prepared.)

'Ah. Sorry I said –'

'Damn it, Danny, I'd bloody counted them. Don't think I hadn't. One for you and one for me and two for you and two for me and there weren't enough. I'm not sorry I said it. I'm not as brave as you are. Sleep with me tonight. Sleep for me. Sleep for old Poll –' It did not matter that her voice was bleeding openly. It only made him drink the thick, gritty lemon and whiskey and all the little heaps of white powder, to soothe her. In her own throat her lemon and milk met green bile, curdled and burned her gorge as if it were bane. When he became drowsy she turned and, holding his hand in hers, lay on her side, facing him.

'Oh Poll. You needn't –' he murmured.

'I have to.'

(The mort is set.)

It took about an hour. She had expected only minutes. She lay in the bed beside him the whole time, his chilling, quieting hand in hers. The moon was slipping in the sky, down outside the window. Near the end, the shadow of the central sash-frame darkened across Danny's face and for a moment she thought terribly that his eyes were open.

'I said you wouldn't break,' she said clearly. 'I promised you you'd be all right. Do you see?'

But it was only a shadow cast by the moon.

When she was certain, she pulled the sheet up over his face, and dressed in the moonlight. Once, tying a scarf round her throat, she thought, 'and If –?' But when she crossed to the window she could see the flashing lights and spotlamps over in Andrew's yard and knew that there would be no after-If.

The dog fox heard Morag coming. He had been drinking from the horses' water-trough which was largely clear of ice, there in the steamy barn. At his smell the brown horse, Hopkins, who knew things about foxes of which the quieter, riding-school ponies were unaware, snorted and stamped in a corner, his ears back, his big head moving restlessly up and down. The dog fox watched him warily whilst he drank. He did not trust horses when they had that meady, sour smell on them. Since he had been unable to force his way past the mended netting of the hen-run, he had filled the prime looseness of his belly with the crushed oats Polly had spilled on the snow that morning when the verger had brought Christopher's note. Now he slipped off the edge of the trough and slunk under the loose corner of the barn, out on to the white snow. The night was loud and dangerous and too bright. From Crosby Spring the whirr of machines, the cries of men hunting, the thrust of lights came clearly across the fields. Then there was a single shot – not the deep explosive crashes of a shotgun as before, but the high, sharp, echoless crack of a rifle. The dog fox, who had fed a little, turned towards Croke's Wood again, running scared along the hedge beyond the barn. At least the fields behind the Dipyard were silent.

The wicked moon searched for him and found him as he passed behind the sycamore at the lane's end.

The church doors stood wide open, even into the deep frost. The candles in all the windows flared and streamed in the draught. Balanced on the tall pulpit, the stolen cassette-player sang with the voices of angels, sang about angels, sang to the angels. From the capitals of the four supporters of the transept crossing, stone Michael, stone Gabriel, stone Azrael and stone Raphael sent the sound about and about the vaults and ribs and groins and traceries, singing, ringing, shalom.

He could not compromise. The old people from Woodview came in a coach, driven and attended by grey men. They came into the church in clusters, pausing, at first in awe and then in something that many of them felt as love. At the door Christopher watched them, each head passing under his gaze until his full complement was reached. He did not speak or hold out his hand or give any word of greeting.

They had cardigans and woollen scarves and bright, Christmas-gift gloves and their feet were soft in lined boots. Old Mr Palmer had real galoshes on against the snow. Some of them had brought photographs in frames, some magazines, some knitting in bulging polythene bags; some had brought spare batteries for hearing-aids, and Norah Robertson had a blue budgerigar in a cage. All this Christopher, expressionless, saw. Discomfited by his ungiving eyes they were for once relieved to find Xanthe who, in her usual state of alarmed inefficiency, was begging a young boy to tick off their names on a list. 'I can't ask them,' she was muttering. 'I ought to know them all and I don't. Please, Sam, please do it for me.'

Institutionalized, the older inhabitants of Woodview took over the list and dealt with the matter among themselves. They apportioned blankets and mugs fairly, the oldest, thinnest and sickest receiving the most, and then sat, politely and patiently in the back pews to listen to the angels whose voices came from a sweet arbour of blossoming flowers, redolent and antiphonal on the chancel steps.

From the south door Christopher watched. He would make no compromise. 'Come,' he said to the grey man who had visited him that morning and who had also been in charge of the transfer of the old people from Woodview. 'I have something to show you.'

He led him up the centre aisle, under stone Gabriel, stone Michael, stone Azrael and stone Raphael and through Barbara's garden into the choir. There, just at the nave end of the north stalls, beside the ferns and rosemary, the cyclamens and pampas, Luke Lyons lay on his bier in the closed, satin-lined box that Scottie had nailed him into.

'I believe I have to ask your permission to bury him tomorrow,' Christopher said.

'You don't do it gently, Rector.'

'Why should I? It is not gentle.'

'King Jesus, it is said, has a garden.' And then again, when Christopher had made no reply, 'I will be here tomorrow for the burial. And there will be three more. I must ask you to perform the offices.'

'How curious, three. Has there been an accident? Drop your eyes if you must answer me. That is the Montgomery Paten up there and the Sacrament is reserved upon that altar.'

'There was no accident. A woman – a Mrs Morag Medway – turned a gun on her husband and her child. She was herself shot when she was preparing to fire on the patrol who had gone to the scene. My men.'

'Are you guilty of this?'

The stone archangels did not even pause for the grey man's answer, 'We are all guilty of this and I will not lower my eyes.'

'Then be afraid, for you may see God.'

'Oh my friend, I am afraid.'

When the grey man turned and moved slowly up the chancel, Christopher went beside him and then, at the rails, in front of him where he turned, as if to bar the way through. The calm eyes stared at Christopher as if he were of only incidental significance. They were not hungry, those eyes, or frightened or angry, but were filled with tenderness and a strange innocence. They were staring at the paten whose pale silver shone in the candlelight, and in whose embrace already the blessed wafers lay, thin and white as dried honesty. They were filled with tears and the tears, streaming unchecked, also reflected the candlelight.

'I'm sorry,' Christopher said. 'I'm so very sorry –'

'Will you serve me?'

'If you will forgive me.'

And he did serve him, and in the back of the church Alice King showed Xanthe how to ladle out soup properly from the field-kitchen and even persuaded Freda Lyons to help with the mugs, giving her little things to do to keep her from staring up there to where her Luke lay in the garden.

When the two men came back through the arbour of glowing flowers they came, each one, alone. Whatever had happened up there had not passed between them, but to each one individually. When they reached the old people, sitting in their pews, drinking tomato soup and listening to the angels, chatting a little (and some of the men furtively looking for something to use as an ashtray), the grey man indicated Sam as he collected up the empty soup packets.

'Not yours – you have no children, Rector.'

'No, not ours in that way. Yours? You have his sister in one of your breeding factory farms and you have just asked me to commit his mother, his father and his brother for burial.'

The grey man's step was clear and firm on the aisle floor. 'And will you?'

'If you want me to bury them, you must bring them here. Otherwise let the dead bury their dead. I am not leaving my church.'

'And you will not be gentle.'

'There will be no compromise,' and then, suddenly, for the first time showing something of his heart, 'Ian! Oh Ian. They've let you come back.'

The doctor was sitting on the outside of one of the pews. Next, in fact, to the caged budgerigar. He had a mug of soup balanced on a Book of Common Prayer in front of him. He rose, very tall, his coat sleeve torn half out of the seams, his trousers dark up to the knees where snow had melted into them. There were open grazes on his face and hands. He held these out to Christopher as if in greeting.

'They shoot people,' he said softly, indicating the grey man beside them. 'Did you know that, Christopher? They shoot people.'

'Yes. I know it.'

'They didn't shoot me because doctors are valuable commodities. But they wanted to – Oh Christ, how they did want to.'

'Why,' said the grey man calmly, 'should we need to shoot you?'

'Because I ran away.' Ian was talking to Christopher only, his judging, watching eyes still glittering with night air. The running and, yes, the fear, were still in him; in his breath and the pulses in his cold-whitened temples. 'I'm not a radiation expert or a gynaecologist or a geneticist – I'm a GP. These are GPs too; general public – geriatric patients – good people. I came out to where I belong. And I've things I could tell, if it were wise to tell them. That's why he might think he needs to shoot me.'

'And do I?'

Ian laughed. A few heads turned to look up at him. They knew his laugh from Woodview. It was not always at anything funny, but it always offered another aspect to anxiety. They liked to hear him laugh, especially now. He said, 'I'm a doctor. I don't tell. And Christopher's a priest and he doesn't tell, either. Would you believe, we don't even tell each other? So you may not need to shoot either of us.'

'No,' said the grey man, looking away over Ian's shoulder. 'I probably won't.'

The great south door had opened. Cold, surging up the body of the church, whipped the candle flames into frenzies of bending brilliance. 'Excuse me –' and he slipped away from them before they turned and, together, shoulder to shoulder, hurried after him.

'Sweet Jesus – in a church?' Ian said.

'Oh God.' Christopher had stopped. He put his hand out to the font and gripped it, leaning on it. 'Oh dear God.' Then suddenly, 'No. No. Never. Not in my church –' and he lunged forwards, his hands high up, open, forbidding this thing to come into his church. From the Sunday School corner Xanthe heard him. It was every sound in the world. It was her sound, her music, and she moved to it, running, even in his church, running again because, after all, she had not been destroyed that evening in the kitchen, but only lost and was now found as the innocent always should be. He felt her, when she reached him, but did not lower his arms. His eyes blazed like pit fires.

The gas cylinders were on wheels, special-purpose, dark, iron carriages. Each one of the six was attended by two grey men, one pulling the noiseless, simple carriage; the other walking beside it with an FAL automatic rifle.

'No,' Christopher was calling still. 'No – not in here,' holding his arms up; standing, now, directly in their way. 'Never.'

'And there shall be no more crying and no more pain, is it?' Ian said softly.

The grey man had turned and was looking at him out of his quiet, loving eyes. 'And how much crying and how much pain are you asking me to load upon your altar – to crush it?'

'All of it,' Christopher cried out. 'It is mine.'

Xanthe knew the words, they were her own. They were the words she had howled out of her own forest at Christopher and Ian, and they came to her out of his as something so familiar that they belonged rather to her than to him. Owning them, she owned him and his sudden move forwards. One of the grey men with a rifle moved in answer. There was a tiny click. She stepped in front of Christopher. The whiplash light streaked across her shining hair. She stood tall, claiming her own; utterly selfish, just as he had said.

Behind her the grey man was holding Ian in his arms. There was thick saliva between Ian's parted lips.

Christopher, his arms soaring above Xanthe's bright head, palms out, cried again, 'Never,' and she felt his body pressing forwards against her.

'No, Christopher. This is mine. I have to do it for you.'

But the feel of him faded away. His arms dropped. He was no longer pressing forwards behind her back. The emptiness against her spine was stark. Very slowly she turned to look at him. His eyes were searching for something, oddly, up there among the inside-out colours of the stained glass. He had to move before he could see it clearly. The rifleman lowered the gun a little. Christopher took Xanthe by the arm and made her look where he was looking. At the Christ in the Crucifixion window.

He said, gently, 'Someone already has.'

When the six cylinders were parked discreetly behind the font, from where they could be moved to the vestry when the old people from Woodview were asleep, Christopher, who was standing alone by the font, said to the grey man, 'And in the fullness of time, will you ask me to serve these men, too?'

But the grey man shook his head. He was watching Xanthe where she sat, broken at last, leaning her forehead against the cold stone of one of the great aisle pillars. He only said, 'Some do it with a kiss,' before he left the church and walked out into the blue, star-sweet night.

It was nearly three o'clock in the morning and Polly did not care about the Afterworld. The moon was still there, but slipping, her shadow-making long drawn out and unrelieved. There was so much love in Polly, her breast was still full of it and her heart overflowing, so that from time to time she moaned, almost as she did in the slow, ecstatic rhythms of Frankie's love-making. They were not sounds that Danny would have known, but in a way it was Danny as well as Frankie who was drawing them out of her. He had given her her chance of redemption – quite unexpectedly and without really intending to; 'You wouldn't ever marry me, Poll, would you?' He would never have known, as Polly had always known, that it was more blessed to kill than to be killed for. So he died, with all his small braveries wrapped around him by her, and she had given him that in return for her ultimate corruptibility. Or was it incorruptibility? In the extreme they were the same, after all.

The road in front of her was white, eerie as it had not been before when the moon was high. She sat deep on old Hoppy, loving him – loving them all, trotting obediently up the road in front of her, their coloured backs all washed dim and dappled in the shadow and the night. There were no street-lamps lit on the outskirts of Martinminster and few lights still burning orange behind the drawn curtains in the houses. The lovingness that had hunted Danny down so implacably, was still gripping her. She was no longer deluded by the chimera of choice or will; had become just love-machinery, grinding on and on until its course was run. She had no tears and no fear. The horses' hooves clopped solemnly on the glazed surface of the road. She drove them from behind, riding on Hoppy, right up the Buttermarket into the flashing lights and arc lamps around the Saracens and Land Rovers clustered in the centre of the wide street. As she passed the entrance to St Martin's Lane she could just hear the angels singing in Christopher's church and see the warm glow of his many candles resting on the snow of the walls and railings of the dark lane. Christopher would know if she were ultimately corrupt or redeemed, and that it made no difference in the end. Dear Christopher . . .

Sweet Polly Anderson had no doubt that the grey men were soldiers. The sort of love that she had for men found out who was able to kill and who was not, by standing at their shoulders. The vehicles were parked apparently at random, but in fact blocking the street. The horses and ponies circled, stopped, puzzled by the lights and the slow-moving men who emerged out of dark doorways and presently surrounded them.

Love-machinery, her rich coiled hair, her little double chin and her big, glorious eyes, Polly Anderson dismounted among the soldiers in the blaze of lights which put out the lovely moon that had shone all night on her loving. She waited until one of the soldiers approached her cautiously, feeling his way among the restless animals. Little Charlie nipped at his pocket, looking for bread and the soldier ruffled his mane.

'Yes?' he said, politely.

'Shoot my horses.'

The soldier put out his hand to Hoppy's neck. Unexpectedly he said, 'My daughter has a pony. A little one.'

'Shoot my horses.' It was the sound of love, inexorable, on its way.

The soldier stepped back. He would not stand beside Polly. Only Hoppy could stand at her shoulder now.

'Madam, I can't do that,' he said, quietly.

'You are a soldier. Only you can do it.'

Behind him, one murmured, 'The abattoir –'

'Closed down,' said Polly Anderson in her clear, carrying voice. The horses moved restlessly around. The smell of them overlaid the smell of diesel and warm-running oil and their hooves were louder than the gently ticking engines.

'Why are you asking me to do that? I have no power to shoot animals. I can't do that –'

'Can't?' she said. 'Haven't you the courage, or the humanity? Or does it frighten you to kill so many ignorant beasts? Here, put your hand here on Hoppy's neck like you did before. That's why you must shoot him. Have you ever heard a horse scream? No? I have.'

Again someone, shamed, in the circling lights, muttered, 'Shut up, for God's sake –'

'No,' she said loudly. 'When you get radiation sickness you vomit. Yes? Don't be frightened, we all know that much. You vomit and vomit. Until you die. Cats will do it, the dogs and pigs and foxes, oh, and people of course. But horses can't. They're different. They scream in agony because they can't vomit. Won't you be more embarrassed when you hear my horses screaming, than when you pull the trigger? There are eleven of them here – to scream.'

But not one of the soldiers looked at her. She said, 'I'm a big woman and I shall drive these horses up and down and up and down this street; stampede them among your trucks and your men until you are forced to take either them or me. And if you take me first, you will think of me when the screaming starts.

'They have lived as a herd and they'll stay and die together – all eleven of them. Screaming.'

'Oh shit,' one said.

Smiling at him, Polly, in the flash-flash light, her eyes in sequence shining and pitch, called to him, 'Look, this one is Hopkins. He loves open fields and eating dandelions. That's Billy, the tiny one – he kicks his heels up if you tickle his tummy. That's Derry – he's twenty-two and his teeth hurt him a bit these days. The two chestnuts are both mares, Cider and Tammy –'

'I'm going. I can't listen to this.' A young soldier, that one, his mouth curling in hate as she gave the animals' names, identities, warm, blood-pulsing lives.

'You'll stand where you are. What do you think this is, Pet's Corner?' the soldier by Polly snapped. Someone else made an artificial retching sound in the shadow by the APC. Instantly Polly began again. 'Sorry about Charlie, he's only a baby and very greedy. That's Cinders beside him; I got him from a circus. He'll lie down and pretend to sleep if you tell him the right way – Cinders –'

'Sergeant, what's going on?' He had come up St Martin's Lane after he had left the church, Xanthe, broken by Christopher, still in his eyes, and his own dried tears still streaking his face.

'Sir, the lady wants us to shoot all these horses, sir. Seems they can't vomit, sir, and the lady thinks they are in danger of undue suffering if they were to be exposed to any radiation problem. Sir.'

'I see.' He looked at Polly and into Polly, sweet Polly Anderson, his eyes so loving; like Frankie's in the dawn. 'I did know that about horses. Are they all yours?'

(This, after all, and not the other, was the mort.)

Now that it had come, she could only whisper, 'Yes. They are all mine.'

'Have you papers at home to show it?'

'Sweet God, perhaps. For lack of papers? For that?'

Lover's eyes. Like her own. They stood, shoulder to shoulder. Beyond them, hutched up against the vehicles, the soldiers fidgeted, distressed. There was nothing graceless or awkward about Polly and the grey man, looking into each other's eyes under the hard bright lights on the snow.

'Please?' she whispered. It was all she had left.

'Shoot the horses,' he said.

He sent for a humane killer. He had Cooper's Lane blocked off. He radioed for one of the refrigerated trucks. It hissed in the still, still air. He ordered four of the soldiers to help him. The rest retreated sickly behind the Saracens and did not watch. One by one he himself brought the horses to the head of the lane. The scant blood flowed freely downhill. The dull thuds brought no one to any window.

Polly sat huddled on the step of a doorway. He would not allow her to hold them. She put her head down and the tears came as they roped Hoppy's body into the meat truck. The tears were vast. They flowed out between her fingers and the overburdening of her heart drained away, ran out and emptied on to the stained snow. He stood above her, then, and said, 'Loss doesn't hurt as much as love,' and touched her hair with his bloody hand. 'Come, there is somewhere I am going to take you.'

To her he felt like Frankie, being small and light and having his arm around her because she was too old and weak now to walk as sweet Polly Anderson had done. Half-way down the lane she could hear the angels again, singing, and murmured, 'Christopher.'

'No. His wife. She, too, has just lost everything.'

'I didn't fail, Frankie – I didn't. Honestly.'

'How did you know my name?'

The moon's night was nearly over. It had been a wicked

night, but dawn was not far off. Because Hiroshima had happened in high daytime Stephen had never imagined the world coming to an end in the dark. Therefore each day, whichever day it was to be, had lost its identity and become a universal day in which time and place had no part. A day whose inwardness was to be expressed in a matter of seconds. So Stephen's movements were very slow, because it was, in fact, still night. Only five past six on the seventh day of this Christmas. He had thought that there was nothing left of her in his house, and then he came across the coloured cloth bag with the bright lemons still untouched inside it. He picked it up and held it against him and crossed to the window where the space she had cleared in the frost-ferns had sealed over with a new, more intricate pattern, quite distinct from the ferns. More like interlocked sunbursts, he thought, wiping them away with his sleeve. Now that the moon had sunk so low over the hill, Barbara's footprints were lost in the deep dark around the house, and away over the fields between the Dipyard and Croke's Wood where the moonlight still lit the snow with a dim, fading luminescence; it was too far off to pick out her tracks in all that gentle white. He hoped that she would have found the fox as he had found the lemons. He would take them with him. At eight o'clock the grey man would come and lock up his house, and Lucy's next door, making certain that they moved into Martinminster. Or wherever they chose, so long as it was outside the magic circle cast around the installations in Croke's Wood.

Barbara would be there by now, with her boots and her striped woolly hat, picked out clear and sharp by the seeping green light that leaked out over the snow. He was not sorry. At the road-block they had been told what would happen to unauthorized persons found in the vicinity of what used to be, so very long ago, a great forest where hart roamed beautiful, and which stretched back, out of place, into the reaches behind the mind. She had fully, exactly understood, and he had made no effort to stop her going. He had stood here, at this window, watching her, Barbara running, running up the field where the wicked moon had not then been low enough to conceal the dog fox from her.

For himself, he and Tinker would go to the shop where the books would not yet be completely cold. He had the old coin with Antethos' head on it, in his pocket, but he did not think that the town was the right place for Antethos to be forgotten in. He brought it out in the palm of his hand and flicked it up, tossing it. It came down with Antethos' head still there in the end of the moonlight. He opened the back door and stood for a moment in the bitter night. Then he pushed the coin into the snow against the wall of the house, down as far as he could thrust it. The warmth his hand had imparted to it made the coin greasy in the snow and after he had gone back indoors to wait for the grey man to come and seal his house, it began to move downwards, through the snow, to the deep crack that had opened between the house wall and the path. There it slipped down into the broken heart of the earth.

Only the green gleam in Croke's Wood was left shining when, at twenty minutes past seven, the last lights went out.

THE FOURTH MODE

FOR THE BEST IN PAPERBACKS, LOOK FOR THE

In every corner of the world, on every subject under the sun, Penguin represents quality and variety – the very best in publishing today.

For complete information about books available from Penguin – including Pelicans, Puffins, Peregrines and Penguin Classics – and how to order them, write to us at the appropriate address below. Please note that for copyright reasons the selection of books varies from country to country.

In the United Kingdom: Please write to *Dept E.P., Penguin Books Ltd, Harmondsworth, Middlesex, UB7 0DA*

If you have any difficulty in obtaining a title, please send your order with the correct money, plus ten per cent for postage and packaging, to *PO Box No 11, West Drayton, Middlesex*

In the United States: Please write to *Dept BA, Penguin, 299 Murray Hill Parkway, East Rutherford, New Jersey 07073*

In Canada: Please write to *Penguin Books Canada Ltd, 2801 John Street, Markham, Ontario L3R 1B4*

In Australia: Please write to the *Marketing Department, Penguin Books Australia Ltd, P.O. Box 257, Ringwood, Victoria 3134*

In New Zealand: Please write to the *Marketing Department, Penguin Books (NZ) Ltd, Private Bag, Takapuna, Auckland 9*

In India: Please write to *Penguin Overseas Ltd, 706 Eros Apartments, 56 Nehru Place, New Delhi, 110019*

In Holland: Please write to *Penguin Books Nederland B.V., Postbus 195, NL–1380AD Weesp, Netherlands*

In Germany: Please write to *Penguin Books Ltd, Friedrichstrasse 10–12, D–6000 Frankfurt Main 1, Federal Republic of Germany*

In Spain: Please write to *Longman Penguin España, Calle San Nicolas 15, E–28013 Madrid, Spain*

In France: Please write to *Penguin Books Ltd, 39 Rue de Montmorency, F-75003, Paris, France*

In Japan: Please write to *Longman Penguin Japan Co Ltd, Yamaguchi Building, 2–12–9 Kanda Jimbocho, Chiyoda-Ku, Tokyo 101, Japan*

Barefoot Gen: A Cartoon Story of Hiroshima
Barefoot Gen: The Day After   Keiji Nakazawa

'Some of the best comics ever done . . . Nakazawa, I'm sure, will be considered one of the great comic artists of this century, because he tells the truth in a plain, straightforward way, filled with real human feelings' – R. Crumb, cartoonist

On Extended Wings   Diane Ackerman

On Extended Wings is a rhapsody in blue that stretches from Leonardo to the Wright Brothers – and gives us some amazing aerial views of New York State. It is a book about learning to fly and learning to learn, mingling philosophy with flying lore, juxtaposing joy and grace against the tragic pull of gravity.

Blood and Water and Other Tales   Patrick McGrath

'Touched with subtle humour and irony, rich with erudite atmospheric prose, *Blood and Water and Other Tales* is the extraordinary debut of a writer who stretches the limits of gothic horror, creating unforgettable literature' – Graham Swift

Men Behaving Badly   Simon Nye

Deborah has moved into the flat upstairs. For Gary, a keen philatelist and fan of *Gardeners' Question Time*, the only drawback is that he hasn't yet got around to buying a double bed. Dermot, meanwhile, is wondering if it might be possible to tone down his chaotic, sex-maniac image. But what of Deborah, wooed with a black cashmere jumper from Gary and with tickets for a disaster movie from Dermot?

Man's Work   John Connelly

'*Man's Work* is the announcement that a major new writer is on the American scene' – John Lahr, author of *Prick Up Your Ears*

'Everybody goes to college now in America, and plenty of kids expecting to graduate into the Yuppie life get disappointed. There's not enough room for my characters.' Post-teenage waitresses, salesmen, unemployed cable-TV installers: John Connelly writes about America's not-quite-no-hopers with a deadpan brilliance that is compellingly his own.

Cambodia: A Book for People Who Find Television Too Slow   Brian Fawcett

'Four hundred years from now, you will find yourself staring into a television set with a canned soft drink in your hand, wondering what you should buy with your next pay cheque.'

'An essay, a short story, a novella, a harangue, a poem, a rant': *Cambodia* attacks the whole of contemporary culture. Brian Fawcett eats 'universal chicken' in a franchise off the freeway, hatches plans for a Mission for Destitute Professionals, and warns of the annihilation of individual memory and imagination. Like Cambodia (now called Kampuchea), we are being mentally wiped out.

The Heart of Rock and Roll: The 1001 Best Singles Ever Made   Dave Marsh

'There are about fifty rock acts, from Elton John to the Eagles, who made great singles but lousy albums. There is not *one* who made great albums but lousy singles ... Singles are the real historical imprint of rock. It is individual singles that most often leave their mark ... writing about albums means *not* writing about everything from "Blue Suede Shoes" to "96 Tears" to "My Toot Toot".'

Jaguars Ripped My Flesh   Tim Cahill

'It's jaunty, irreverent, full of arduous adventures and loaded with the sort of one-liners Mike Hammer would have enjoyed ... there are wild adventures told in a colourful, colloquial, saloon-yarn style, which now and then rises to a fine description of the landscape in which Mr Cahill is hanging, falling, drowning, climbing, being bitten, dealing with his hangover or discovering natural beauty' – *New York Times*

In the Eyes of Mr Fury   Philip Ridley

A stunning first novel about first love and failed love, finding out and growing up on a mean but magical street in inner-city Thatcherland. It is a book full of marvels, wizardy and poetry by one of Britain's most fertile new talents.

Joe Bob Goes to the Drive-In   Joe Bob Briggs

Joe Bob Briggs, the foremost expert on drive-in movies, has seen 14,500 movies out under the stars like God intended. in the privacy of his personal automobile. I said there aren't enough hours in the night-time to see 12 movies in Chillicothe, Okla, in one night and Joe Bob said, 'You hant seen these movies'.

Caris Davis' Stealth: The Black Edition
Caris Davis' Stealth: The White Edition   Caris Davis

Night life, low life, high life, fast life and sometimes very very slow life – this is Caris Davis's vision of life in London now. Featuring a collection of varyingly attractive misfits who criss-cross into each other's lives, these two novels are enormously energetic and oddly tender.